NOT YOUR CHILD

SHEILA NORTON

Boldwood

First published in Great Britain in 2024 by Boldwood Books Ltd.

Copyright © Sheila Norton, 2024

Cover Design by Colin Thomas

Cover Photography: Colin Thomas

Every effort has been made to obtain the necessary permissions with reference to copyright material, both illustrative and quoted. We apologise for any omissions in this respect and will be pleased to make the appropriate acknowledgements in any future edition.

A CIP catalogue record for this book is available from the British Library.

Paperback ISBN 978-1-78513-669-6

Large Print ISBN 978-1-78513-670-2

Hardback ISBN 978-1-78513-668-9

Ebook ISBN 978-1-78513-671-9

Kindle ISBN 978-1-78513-672-6

Audio CD ISBN 978-1-78513-663-4

MP3 CD ISBN 978-1-78513-664-1

Digital audio download ISBN 978-1-78513-667-2

Boldwood Books Ltd
23 Bowerdean Street
London SW6 3TN
www.boldwoodbooks.com

1

GEMMA

Sometimes, now, I think about how differently everything would have turned out if I hadn't been at work that day – the day I got the message from the stranger on Instagram. I was only going into the office for two days a week, working from home on the other three, so it was unfortunate that it was a bit public when I fell apart.

'What's wrong, Gemma?' my line manager, Mike, asked. He was an older guy, in his fifties, and tended not to have an awful lot of understanding when it came to anyone displaying emotions. To be fair, I usually tried to act as professionally as possible and not give him, or anyone else, the excuse to blame anything I did, or said, on the fact that I'm a woman, let alone the mother of a two-year-old trying to juggle all the usual commitments. But I shouldn't really have been having sneaky looks at Instagram while I was working. Everyone did it, but if one of the directors had happened to come in at that moment, it would have been my emotional breakdown, not my social media habit, that would have looked unprofessional.

'Nothing,' I managed to reply. 'I'm... OK, just... got to... pop outside for a minute...'

I jumped up from my chair so fast, I knocked a pile of files off my desk and had to stop to pick them up, wiping the tears from my eyes as I did, knowing the other three people in our open-plan office were staring at me and beginning to look concerned.

I flew out of the door, down the corridor to the toilets, almost choking on my shock and dismay as I ran, and locked myself in one of the cubicles where I gave way to what I admit must have been pretty horrific howls of anguish. It wasn't until I'd managed to control myself enough to be merely sobbing, rather than sounding like an animal being tortured, that I heard someone on the other side of the door asking in a sympathetic voice:

'Are you all right in there? Is there anything I can do?'

I took some deep breaths to try to pull myself together, and managed to squeak some kind of response about being fine. I didn't recognise this person's voice, but I knew I had to get back to the office before my own colleagues turned up too and someone possibly started battering the door down.

There was silence outside my cubicle, so after taking a few more deep breaths I unlocked the door, went straight to the nearest sink and splashed my face with lots of cold water. When I looked up, dripping, the woman – I knew as soon as she began to speak that she was the one who'd called out to me – was standing against a sink a bit further along.

'I thought I'd better wait,' she said. Just that. No questions, no more attempt to intervene.

'Thank you. I'll be all right now,' I told her, just wanting her to go, so I could try to do something about the state of my face, and try to get myself together. I wasn't all right at all, I didn't know if I ever would be, but I needed to make some attempt at pretence, at least until I got home.

'What time do you normally take your lunch break?' the woman asked, not taking the hint and clearing off. 'If you can take it now, you probably should. It'll give you a chance to... redo your make-up. And so on.'

'I'd have to let them know. My colleagues. I'll have to go back and tell them – but I can't—'

'Got your phone on you? Call one of them. Say you're having lunch. It doesn't matter what they think.' She paused, tilting her head to one side, looking at me, making me feel uncomfortable. Then she shrugged and added: 'I'm just about to take my own break. Come on, wipe the make-up off.' She dived into a huge canvas rucksack-style handbag, rummaged around and produced some wet wipes. 'Then we'll go for lunch—'

'I can't eat!' I wailed, beginning to well up again.

'Just a coffee, then,' she said quickly. 'We'll sit outside in the shade somewhere to give your eyes a chance to settle down. Don't put the make-up back on yet. If at all.'

I looked in the mirror. Black mascara streaked down both cheeks. Red eyes, surrounded by splodges of black. I grabbed her proffered wet wipes and got to work, thanking her, wondering how the hell I was ever going to look presentable again, let alone feel like living.

I didn't even know the woman, didn't recognise her, had no idea whereabouts in the company she worked. But something about her matter-of-fact manner made me do exactly what she suggested: I called Mike's extension, told him I was taking my lunch break, ignored the tone of his response, and with my head lowered in case anyone else saw me, I followed my rescuer out of the building and round the corner to a little pub in a back street.

'There's a beer garden at the back. Secluded. And nobody from work comes here anyway,' she said, ordering herself a vegan wrap and decaf black coffee, and a cappuccino for me which I doubted I'd be able to swallow for the lump in my throat.

We went out into the beer garden, which was almost deserted, and sat at a table under an umbrella.

'OK?' she said.

'Not really,' I admitted. 'But thank you.' Trying to summon some kind of general social politeness, I added, 'Sorry. I don't know your name.'

'Crystal,' she said. 'I work in the design studio. You?'

'I'm Gemma. I'm... just... in accounts.'

'No *just* about it, is there? Every company needs people looking after their accounts.'

'Not as much as they need people designing their range in the first place.'

She smiled and shrugged.

I looked at her properly for the first time. I hadn't taken in her appearance at all, as I'd been too conscious of my own, but now I realised it was easy to guess she was a designer. She was probably around my own age – mid-thirties – but she wore her dark hair long and loose, with streaks of purple in it. She had massive jangly earrings, a nose ring, several tattoos on her arms which were almost covered up by the number of bracelets she wore, and her dress... well, I'd have called it a kaftan. We must have looked a strange pair – her in her hippy garb and me in my smart business suit, white shirt, black shoes... hair that had started off tied back in a neat ponytail but was now coming loose, and a face swollen from crying.

Our coffees and her food were brought to the table and for a while we sat in silence while she ate. I sipped my cappuccino, which made me feel sick, and tried to stop thinking about Jack. What he'd done to me. How I was going to live the rest of my life without him.

When Crystal finished eating, she sat back, wiped her mouth, and just looked at me for a moment before saying, 'I'm not going to ask. It's none of my business, obviously. But I'm a good listener, so if you need someone to pour it all out to – someone who doesn't know you, so isn't going to try to give you any advice that you don't want – well, feel free. Otherwise, I'm quite happy just sitting here relaxing while you try to calm yourself down. OK?'

I nodded, thanked her again. I sat for a little longer sipping the cappuccino that I didn't want, staring at the table, and suddenly I just couldn't stand it any more – not saying anything, not having been allowed to say anything.

'He didn't even have the guts to tell me himself!' I blurted out. 'I've been driving myself mad, waiting to hear from him: emailing him, getting no reply; trying to call him but his number's out of service – I've been so worried about him, and all this time the *bastard* has been shacked up with someone else, and his *brother* – who I've never even met – is the only one who had the decency to tell me! And even *he* just chose to disappear, delete himself, after he'd delivered the news – great, eh? Probably embarrassed. So what the hell am I supposed to do? I was supposed to be going out there with him, starting a new life—'

'Out there?' she asked quietly.

'Australia! He went out there to his family, and I was going to join him, with Poppy – our little girl – when he'd found a home for us. Then he just stopped communicating. Dropped off the internet – his email's not working, his phone's not working, all his social media's closed down, and I have no address for his parents; all I know is they live in the Sydney area. Do you know how many people live in the Sydney area?'

'No,' Crystal admitted.

'Nor do I. But a lot, obviously. And he's been gone for four months. *Four months*! And for half that time, I've had no idea what's happened to him. He might have drowned on Bondi Beach or been eaten by a shark for all I knew. I went to the police. Do you know what they said?'

'No.'

'They said he was an adult, he'd gone there of his own free will and he was within his rights to deliberately stop all communication. He's left me and his *child*! How could he, how could he *do* that to me? To not even tell me, not even have the guts—'

'So his brother didn't even tell you where he was?'

'No! Look, this is it.' I reached for my phone. 'This is what his private message on Instagram says. Let me read it to you, you'll never believe it, honestly, it's unbelievable: *Dear Gemma. I found you on here because I wanted to tell you, Jack is with someone else. I know he's changed his number and email. He doesn't know I'm messaging you but I think it's only right you should be told. He's got no intention of sending for you or the kiddie or seeing you ever again. He's my brother but I think he's a disgrace and our parents won't talk to him. Sorry to tell you but you'll have to forget him. I can't tell you where he lives* or give you any info. Don't try to contact him, you'll never find him. Or me. Sorry. Ryan.'

I stopped, swallowing back more tears, not wanting to start bawling my eyes out all over again.

'Forget him?' I managed to say eventually. 'I'm bringing up his *daughter*! How can he do this?'

Crystal got up, came to stand beside me, put her arm round me and stroked my hair as if I was her friend, as if she knew me.

'What a terrible way to find out,' she said gently. 'You poor thing.'

'We were supposed to get married!' I squawked. 'When I got to Australia – we were going to get married and have another baby.'

'What a good thing you didn't,' is all she said.

And I knew she was right, I knew I'd probably agree with her eventually, when the shock of it all had died down a bit. But right at that moment, I couldn't even begin to get there. Quite honestly, if it wasn't for the thought of my daughter, I could have just given up, gone home, laid down on my bed and stayed there forever.

But I had to carry on. For Poppy.

2

CRYSTAL

At that time, when I first met her, I knew nothing about her. She was just another woman who'd been treated like crap by a guy, and I empathised, of course I did, I felt sorry for her. She'd had the news at work and got herself into a state. I didn't want to interfere, and I certainly didn't want to make it all about me, so I just did what I could to calm her down. It made me angry to hear how completely callous her other half had been in the way he'd dumped her. What a cowardly thing to do – to just disappear while he was on the other side of the world, and not even have the decency, or the guts, to tell her. Even the brother didn't sound much better – sending that message, making it sound like he was being thoughtful and gracious in doing so, and then just erasing himself so she couldn't even respond. Didn't even give her the chance to ask any questions, or the satisfaction of a good rant.

I liked Gemma right from the start. Nobody deserved to be in that position, let alone when they had a child to consider. But I liked her spirit, too – her anger – even while she was so distraught – her fury at being treated the way her ex had treated her. It gave me hope, for her sake, that she wouldn't just fold up and go under, the way I had when I'd been put in a similar position.

Oh yes, I understood – only too well. That was why I knew I could help her. I'd been in a very dark place myself, and it hadn't been too long since I'd been able to start hauling myself out of it. I'd had a lot of help, and had finally been able to reach a kind of acceptance – well, acceptance of *most* of it, for *most* of the time. I was able to understand that there was only one person to blame for everything I'd been through, and that person was the bastard who'd walked out of my life at the very worst possible time he could have chosen, who'd told me there was somebody else and then just disappeared, leaving me... in chaos.

Well, it seemed Gemma was a victim of something

similar, so of course I empathised with her. From that very first day, all I felt was a completely genuine and heartfelt sympathy. I wanted nothing more than to be her friend.

And... names? Well, names can just be coincidental, can't they.

3

GEMMA

I'd been with Jack for four years; I'd met him at work, where he'd been a manager in the personnel department, before moving to a better job in a different company. For at least half the time I'd known him, he'd talked constantly about the idea of emigrating to Australia. I could understand it: his parents, followed by his older sister and her husband, and just a few months ago by his younger brother, had all gone out there to live and yes, from what he told me, they all seemed to be doing well. I'd never met any of his family – apart from the brother, they'd all been in Australia since long before Jack and I got together – and he didn't seem to communicate with them a lot. He wasn't the type of guy to chat to them on video calls, introducing me and showing off our baby girl. In fact, I often used to berate him about it.

'Surely you've sent your parents some pictures of Poppy?' I'd say. 'She's their grandchild! They must be devastated that they haven't met her yet!'

'They're not like that,' he'd say with a shrug.

I couldn't understand it. My own parents were both fanatical about their granddaughter. They'd been divorced for about ten years, but Mum only lived a few miles away, and came to see me and Poppy all the time. Dad had moved up to Manchester, but he called and messaged regularly, and loved to chat to Poppy on video calls. But in the end, I just had to accept that every family was different, that perhaps Jack would become closer to his parents and siblings if we finally did decide to move out to Australia ourselves, and that this was one reason why I really ought to consider the idea.

I didn't *want* to consider it. I didn't want to be separated from my own parents. Being an only child, I was acutely aware of how much it would hurt them both if Poppy and I went off to the other side of the world. But at the same time, I was tempted by the prospect of the better lifestyle Jack kept describing, the better opportunities for us, and more importantly, for Poppy. And then, one day when I was talking to Mum about it, she surprised me by announcing that if Jack and I decided to go, she'd follow us.

'You would?' I said, shocked. Mum had seemed so settled since the divorce, so independent, enjoying her part-time career that fitted so conveniently around her time with me and Poppy, and never seeming to have any interest in looking for another man. I'd never in a million years have imagined her, now in her sixties, wanting to uproot herself again and move across the world.

'Of course I would,' she said calmly. 'You and Poppy are the most important things in my life. Nothing else matters. I wouldn't want to live here without you.'

It was only then that I told Jack I'd go. And in no time at all, the plans were made. He'd go ahead of me, get a job and find a home for us all.

And... then he disappeared.

* * *

When I got home from work, on the day of his brother's message, the temptation to simply throw myself on the bed and give in to utter despair was still so strong I literally had to grit my teeth to make myself behave normally, like nothing was wrong, like it was an ordinary day. I'd picked Poppy up from the nursery and asked her about her day, admiring her splodgy paintings and encouraging her little smatterings of chat, her attempts to tell me what she'd done, watching her face light up when I reminded her the next day would be Wednesday – a *Mummy Day*. I chatted to her as brightly as I could manage while I prepared her tea, and made a supreme, almost super-human effort to enjoy bath time and story time.

As soon as she was asleep, I fell apart again.

Thank God, I didn't have to go into the office for the next few days. From Wednesday to Friday, I was self-employed, working in a completely different field from my accounting job in town – designing websites and writing copy. I'd been building this work up grad-ually since Poppy was born, and although some days were busier than others, it was still normally slow enough for me to be able to look after her myself on Wednesdays and Thursdays, working during periods when she was napping, or playing quietly, or in the evenings after she was in bed. But on Fridays, Mum usually had Poppy for me, giving me a whole day to catch up on everything.

That week, though, I made an excuse to keep Poppy at home with me. Fortunately I didn't have too much work on, anyway, and I knew that if I were to be face-to-face with Mum, I'd blurt everything out. And I couldn't. Not yet. Mum already knew I'd been worried that I hadn't heard from Jack recently; I'd told her this much, but had played it down, going along with her supposition that he must have been frantically busy, I hadn't told her how long his lack of communication had gone on, or even that I'd been to the police. Telling her that would have meant admitting I'd been more than just a bit puzzled, a bit concerned. And now I knew the truth, I had to try to come to terms with it all myself first before I could face her.

'Oh, darling, I'm so sorry to hear Poppy isn't well,' Mum said when I called her – making me feel even worse. What kind of mother pretends her child is ill? What if God, or the devil or someone, was listening to me and decided to make her really ill to teach me a lesson? 'I'd still be happy to look after her, though—'

'No, Mum, that wouldn't be fair, in case it's something infectious. There are all sorts of bugs going around at the nursery.' That much was true – it was always true. 'If she has got something nasty, I've probably already caught it from her, so we'll keep ourselves away from everyone else till after the weekend. Don't worry, we'll be fine.'

I don't know how I managed to lie so convincingly. The truth was I still doubted I'd ever be fine at all, and

I was in fact desperate to just throw myself into my mum's arms and tell her everything. Why didn't I? I can only say that the loss of control it would lead to actually scared me. It would be too easy to never recover from it – to completely collapse, to let her take care of me, treat me like a child, try to spare me all the pain, all the anxiety and problems that were to come. And I knew, despite the state I was in, that I couldn't let that happen. I knew I had to get through it... somehow.

So Poppy and I spent the next few days at home on our own, only going out for necessary trips to the shops, for little walks to the seafront, and short periods on the beach with her bucket and spade during times when I knew it would be quiet. And I spent a lot of time looking at the sea and thinking how easy it would be – if I didn't have Poppy – to just wade into the waves, out of my depth, and let myself sink.

'Mummy come in?' Poppy asked as we stood at the water's edge, looking at me with her head on one side and her hand held out for me to hold, to run and splash in the shallows like we often did, getting her used to the feel of the sea water on her bare feet, splashing her little legs, making her squeal.

I shook my head. 'Not today, Poppy. Let's go home now, it looks like it might rain.'

There was a brilliant blue sky above us, the sun already warming up for a fine summer day. But Poppy seemed to accept Mummy wasn't really feeling like a paddle. She'd sensed my mood and had been quiet and unusually placid during the past few days. She was two and a half, turning three that October, and could often be a handful, with a fiery, determined nature to match her beautiful red hair. I loved her with a passion I'd never expected to feel when I agreed, a little nervously, relatively soon after getting together with Jack, that it'd be a good idea to try for a baby. It was *his idea*, I recalled angrily as we started to walk home from the beach. *His idea, to have this child that he'd somehow managed to just leave behind like a piece of forgotten luggage, like a discarded wrapper, like a... like a... used condom!*

I think that realisation helped me a little. It was probably the moment that my anger at what Jack had done began to completely overtake the hurt and devastation. *How dare he? How DARE he do this, not just to me, but to his child?* From then on, every time I started to cry, to feel bereft, hurt, lost, sorry for myself, I reminded myself that I'd get over him – he wasn't worth my tears. But I'd never forgive him.

It became even easier to feel that anger as the days went by and the practical and financial reality of my

situation sank in. Jack had paid his share of the mortgage, utility bills and so on, into my account before he
left for Australia – to cover the first six months that he
was gone. We were sure it wouldn't even be that long
before I joined him. He earned more than me and paid
the larger share of all the bills, so now he'd gone, it
was only a matter of time before that money ran out.
Not only that, but because of his cowardly disappearing act, and his brother's equally cowardly refusal
to reveal his whereabouts, I wasn't going to get any
child maintenance out of him. I was on my own. Up
the creek without the proverbial paddle.

'What the hell am I supposed to do?' I muttered to
myself, looking at a spreadsheet I'd made of my income and outgoings which frightened me so much I
almost erased it all straight away.

'Mummy play with me?' Poppy said, getting up
from arranging her teddies on the floor and pulling at
my hand.

'In a minute, sweetheart,' I said distractedly.

'Play *now*, Mummy,' she insisted, tugging at me
again.

I turned to smile at her, even though the smile hurt
my face. 'You're a bossy-boots, that's what you are!' I
teased, reaching out to tickle her tummy and make her

laugh. 'All right, Mummy will play. Shall we get your tea set and pretend the teddies are having a picnic?'

'Poppy do it.' She ran to the toy box in the corner of the room and delved inside for the little plastic cups and plates. 'Mummy sit down.'

I knew when to obey orders. I sat cross-legged on the carpet – the giant at the party, between Big Teddy and White Bunny – and held out my miniature pink teacup for the imaginary tea Poppy poured into it, and ate my imaginary sandwich with as much pretend enthusiasm as I could manage in the circumstances.

And the day slowly slid away. And I pretended to forget about the spreadsheet, the mortgage repayments, the bills, for another day. But the anger at Jack remained. And it grew, and it festered, and it hardened, until I felt as if my heart was turning to stone. A heart made of stone can't hurt, I told myself. It was easier than being flesh and blood and feeling like I'd been ripped apart. I was going to be the Stone Woman; that was how I'd get through this. I hoped.

4

CRYSTAL

Gemma had mentioned that she was only part-time, so I knew I wouldn't bump into her again at work that week. The chances of bumping into her were pretty remote anyway. It was a big company, a big building, and we worked in completely different parts of it, on different floors. It was just coincidence that I'd happened to pop into the loos on her floor that day, en route from another department.

At home, on my own, I wondered about the coincidence of our experience. It was almost as if we'd been meant to come together. I pondered it over and over, getting angry on her behalf: angry with her ex for the way he'd treated her, just as I'd been angry when it happened to me. But no, I didn't want to slide back into that anger. I'd got over all this; I'd been getting better. Everyone had been saying I'd been making good progress. I was at a stage where I felt almost like a perfectly rational, undamaged person for *most* of the time.

But I'd not only felt compassion for Gemma, I'd really liked her, too. I could already sense that she was a nice person, a decent person who hadn't deserved to be treated so badly. I wanted to help her, if I could, just as I'd been helped myself when my world imploded. I can honestly say that was my only motivation at the time.

Or was it?

I didn't know much about Gemma yet, but there was one thing I did know: she had a child. A little girl. And looking back now, if I'm going to be totally honest with myself, I think I'd have to admit that this was already a factor, part of the reason I wanted to get close to her. Yes, I can't deny it: at that point in time, I envied everyone who had a child. I was curious about her daughter. I really wanted to meet her.

5

GEMMA

Needless to say, it wasn't easy walking into my office on the Monday morning. My colleagues actually looked quite relieved that I'd turned up at all. I could hardly blame them. It was hard, now, to imagine how I'd sat at my desk on the previous Tuesday afternoon, my face pink and shiny from crying, my head throbbing, my eyes so sore I could barely read anything on the screen, and my mind about ten thousand miles away, instead of focusing on profits, retail discounts and customer accounts.

'Are you feeling better, Gemma?' Mike asked, sounding, to be honest, like his curiosity was getting the better of his sympathy – while young Sophie, our office assistant, put her arm around me and purred in my ear that she'd spoken to the universe about me and could feel good vibes. I resisted the temptation to snap that the universe could stick its good vibes where the sun didn't shine, instead pasting what I hoped was a quasi-pleasant smile on my face and thanking everyone for their concern, offering an apology for being *unwell* the previous Tuesday and a promise to knuckle down to work now. I'd obviously practised this little speech at home, in the hope it would sound halfway sincere – although I knew it wouldn't. But it was all I could manage, and everyone got the picture and left it at that.

Towards lunchtime, I looked up from my work to see Crystal standing in front of me, holding a file.

'This,' she said very quietly, waving the file at me, 'is just an excuse, so I wouldn't feel so stupid in front of everyone if I'd got the wrong office.'

I would have laughed if I hadn't been turned to stone.

'Hello,' I said. I had to admit, it was nice to see her. She was a breath of fresh air in the quiet, studious atmosphere of the accounts office, with her outrageous hair (surely it hadn't been quite so purple last week?), her jangly bracelets and beads, and... well, I wasn't sure if her trousers had been scribbled over by a hyperactive child using a whole pack of coloured pens, and cropped off roughly around knee length by someone half-blind with blunt scissors – or if they were actually *supposed* to look like that. Her turquoise gypsy-style blouse, by comparison, was almost ordinary.

'Want to go for lunch again?' she said, without any beating about the bush. 'Like... now?'

I liked the fact that she hadn't asked, in front of the others, how I was feeling.

'Yes. That'd be good.' I glanced at Mike. 'If that's OK?'

'Sure.' He smiled at me. I think he was probably relieved to hear me speak. I'd kept my mouth shut and my nose to the grindstone, so to speak, all morning. 'Enjoy.'

* * *

We went to the same pub and sat in the garden again. This time, I ordered a sandwich too, not that I'd re-gained my appetite at all, but I'd got back into the rou-tine of eating, purely because of sharing mealtimes with Poppy. A two-and-a-half-year-old, even without a full range of vocabulary, can nevertheless manage a whole inquisition into why you might not feel like eat-ing, and the last thing I could have faced was questions about if I'd got tummy ache, if I'd been sick and what colour it might have been, or if I'd had runny poos.

'So,' Crystal said finally, once we were settled down with a coffee each. She fixed me with a meaningful look. 'How are you now?'

I shrugged. 'Trying to work out how to stay alive.'

'And you have to, don't you. For your little one.'

'Poppy. Yes.' I sighed. 'The thing is, I feel so angry now.'

'Good,' she said, nodding emphatically. 'So you should.'

'But I feel stupid, too. How could I have loved someone who ended up treating me like this? How could I possibly have believed he was a good guy, a decent, caring man who loved me as much as I loved him? And believed he was such a good father to Poppy, when he quite obviously couldn't care less about her? Was I blind? What did I miss? Surely there must have been signs?'

Crystal shook her head. 'I'm sure he did love you, and Poppy. Something must have happened to change him since he went to Australia.'

'Yes, he's met some other woman, that's what's happened, but even if he's so obsessed with her that he couldn't care less about me any more, how could he just cut me off like this with no communication, no financial support, no means of finding him? What am I supposed to do? How am I going to survive?'

Crystal reached across the table and laid a hand on mine. 'You will. You can. We do.'

I looked at her, understanding dawning.

'It's happened to you, too?'

She nodded. 'A few years back, yes. Something similar. I'm not saying it was as much of a shock as what's happened to you – I suspected my boyfriend was seeing someone else and it turned out I was right. But it still hurt. There were... circumstances... that made it very painful. But I've survived. So will you.'

'I don't know how.' I sniffed.

'You need to take whatever help you can get. Start applying for everything you're entitled to. As soon as possible.'

'I know. I've made a list of calls to make, things to apply for – income support, all that kind of stuff...' I dropped my head, trying not to start crying again. 'But I keep hoping it's all a mistake. That he'll suddenly call me and say—'

'Would you take him back? After this?'

I couldn't answer. My anger was telling me no. But my desperation, my hurt, my years of wasted love, were telling me that surely there was always room for hope, for regret and forgiveness?

Crystal, watching the look on my face, just nodded slowly, as if she understood. I supposed she did; she'd been there. In a strange way, this made me feel a bit better. Reminded me that I wasn't the only woman who'd been dumped like a sack of garbage. Not that I'd have wished it on her, or on anyone else.

'Have you got children?' I said, suddenly realising I hadn't asked much about her at all.

'No.' She looked away. 'Sadly not.'

It was my turn to just nod and stay silent. I didn't want to come out with the same old clichés that everyone probably told her: that she still had time, that she might meet someone else, or (worse) that she should make the most of her freedom. I could see from her face that it was a painful subject, that she'd have liked to have had a child, perhaps with the guy who left her.

But she quickly forced a smile back onto her face and she asked me, as our sandwiches were delivered to the table, to tell her about Poppy. I could feel my own face relaxing, the anxious frown shifting a little, as I thought about my little girl.

'She's two and a half, coming up for three,' I said. 'And, well, she can be difficult and demanding, of course – she's a toddler, it's her job! But... at the same time she's... just so sweet, so adorable and funny, she comes out with the cutest things and she's, well, I know all parents must say this, but she's the most beautiful child in the world, she's—'

'Have you got a photo of her?'

Crystal still had a smile fixed on her face, so I knew she was just being nice – polite – in showing an interest in Poppy, despite her own sadness, and this made me warm to her even more. I opened my phone and scrolled through the dozens of pictures of Poppy on there, determined to show her just one, a really good one, rather than prolonging the pain by making her look at them all. I found one of my favourites, taken just a couple of weeks ago: Poppy wearing her yellow dress with the matching sunhat, standing on the beach, holding her bucket and smiling at the camera.

'She loves having her photo taken,' I said, passing the phone across to Crystal. 'She's a real little diva!'

Crystal took the phone from me and gazed at the picture. She blinked a couple of times, looking, I thought for a moment, as if she might burst into tears.

'Oh!' she said. Just that. 'Oh!'

'I'm sorry,' I said, holding my hand out to take the phone back. 'I didn't want to upset you.'

'You haven't. I asked to see her. She's... absolutely beautiful.' She blinked again and quickly wiped her eyes. 'Sorry. It's just—'

'It must be hard. Seeing other people with children.'

'Yes.' She held on to the phone and looked at the picture again, shaking her head as if she couldn't quite believe how lovely my daughter was.

I felt bad then. She'd been so kind to me, trying to help me in my own distress, and in return I'd made *her* cry.

'Sorry,' I said again. And then, desperate to put things right, I came out with exactly the cliché I'd promised myself not to. 'Look, surely you don't have to rule it out completely, do you? Having a baby, I mean —' I stopped, immediately regretting it. Apart from being tactless, I didn't know the first thing about Crystal; I had no right to make assumptions. Just because she was sad about not having a child, it didn't mean she was on a desperate quest to have one now.

But fortunately she gave a little snort of laughter.

'Well, for one thing I feel like I never want to let another man into my life for anything other than servicing my car or my boiler – and definitely not for servicing *me*—'

'I know, I get that, I shouldn't have said—'

'And before you mention IVF or using a surrogate—'

'I wasn't going to. Honestly, I'm sorry, I just wish I hadn't shown you the photo.' I sighed, thinking that she probably wouldn't want to have lunch with me again. I was surprised to realise it mattered to me. I hardly knew her, but I liked the idea of having a friend from work, someone who wasn't exactly a colleague but was the same sort of age, as well as being in a similar situation as me.

'Don't be daft,' she said, putting a hand on mine, and managing a smile. 'I *wanted* to see your little girl. It's nice to hear about her, too. She's lovely.'

'Thank you.'

Crystal took a bite of her avocado sourdough roll and seemed to give herself a little shake before changing the subject, talking about her job, about the flat she lived in and the fact that her parents were both dead, her only close relative a younger brother who visited her from London occasionally, with a different girlfriend every time.

'I'm an only child,' I said. 'But my mum and I are close, and she only lives in Exeter so she helps out with Poppy. She has her every Friday so I can catch up with – everything.'

I explained about my self-employed work, and Crystal looked impressed.

'You design websites? That's quite a change – quite creative – for someone who works as a number-cruncher!'

'I suppose that's why I enjoy it: it's completely different. I was always comfortable with tech; I like fiddling around on computers. So while I was on parental leave, I thought it would be a good time to see if I could make a go of it. I write copy, too, if clients want me to – for websites, and media like newsletters or blogs.'

'Wow, quite an entrepreneur, aren't you! I'm glad. I was worried you were going to have a real struggle – on your own with Poppy – if you could only work here two days a week.'

'I *will* be struggling,' I said quietly, and I put my sandwich down, suddenly losing my appetite, thinking about the spreadsheet I'd made that I still didn't want to look at. 'The mortgage is in my name – it's my house; Jack moved in with me. My parents helped me get the deposit together, but of course, after I had Poppy and had to cut down my working hours, he paid far more than I did. Not only the mortgage repayments, but the bills, too. I don't know how I'm going to manage, to be honest.'

I could feel myself shaking, panic threatening to overtake me again. What the hell was I going to do? I'd have to sell the house, but I had hardly any equity in it.

'The *bastard* could at least have cared enough about his daughter to make some sort of arrangements, even if he didn't give a toss about me,' I went on. 'He ought to be paying maintenance.'

'The child support people can force him to, surely?'

'They'd have to find him first.'

'So that's what they need to start doing,' Crystal said, surprising me with the intensity in her voice. 'They need to find him; he needs to pay. You've got to get everyone looking for him, Gemma. Seriously, he might have gone AWOL but unless he's changed his name—'

'I wouldn't put it past him,' I said bitterly.

'Keep going with that anger. That's what you need, girl, to get you through this.'

'I'm angry, all right. With myself as much as anything – for ever thinking I loved him.'

But of course, I knew perfectly well that the trouble was. I *had* loved him. And if I hadn't done, I wouldn't have had Poppy.

6

CRYSTAL

That photo! That child! Oh my God. I almost wished I hadn't asked to see it. I didn't expect to react quite that way, but then, I hadn't expected Poppy to look like that; to be quite so stunningly beautiful. I'll admit it: it brought me to tears, seeing that beautiful little girl and knowing her father had turned his back on her, leaving her without a second thought. How could he *do* that?

Poor Gemma; I really felt for her. The anger that had almost destroyed me when I was deserted, came rushing back again. Her ex was not only a liar, he was a coward, running away from any confrontation, avoiding any consequences, not giving a damn about his responsibilities. I wanted him to be found, to be dragged through the court and forced to pay up. I wanted him to suffer. I was almost incandescent with anger on Gemma's behalf.

But I knew I needed to calm down. If I was going to be friends with Gemma – and I now wanted that desperately – then I had to keep my feelings to myself. To have me ranting furiously to her about her situation wouldn't exactly have helped her, it would have made things worse – and would probably have scared her off. She didn't need to know about my own story, my own suffering. Even if she asked me, it'd be best not to go into details. She needed me to be supportive, not make her feel worse!

Of course, that wasn't the whole reason I was going to be reticent about myself. If she knew everything, she'd have probably started to feel uncomfortable about me – about my motives, my reasons for wanting to be her friend. She might have not wanted me to meet Poppy. And I wanted that, now, of course. I so badly wanted to meet that little girl and spend time with her. And I could only do that by becoming Gemma's best friend – without her ever knowing my full story.

7

GEMMA

Mum called me several times that week but I still didn't tell her about Jack, even when she asked how he was. I said he'd been busy, thinking to myself that yes, he'd been busy all right, busy cheating and busy lying his way out of my life and into someone else's. But then it was Friday again – how had the world kept turning for ten whole days since I got that fatal Instagram message? – and I knew I wasn't going to be able to put it off any longer. I knew that when I saw Mum in person I was going to break down again.

'Get your shoes on, Poppy,' I told my daughter after breakfast. She'd been busy playing with the toy laptop Jack had misguidedly bought her at Christmas (personally, I thought kids started pleading for phones and tablets and laptops early enough, without us encouraging the interest. Or perhaps I was just finding fault with everything that reminded me of Jack, all of a sudden).

'Not a nurs'ry day,' Poppy said without looking up. I had no idea how she'd managed to work out, at such a young age, which days she went there and which she didn't, but she was usually right.

'No, not nursery today. Nanny's today. Come on, you can bring that with you.'

'Going to Nanny's!' she said happily, getting to her feet. She loved my mum – I guessed all children liked going to their grandparents, and getting all the extra attention and spoiling that we parents hadn't got the time or money to indulge them with. 'Come on, Mummy.'

She was putting her shoes on already and beat me to the front door, the miniature plastic laptop in her hands.

'OK, Pops, I'm just getting the car keys.'

On the drive to Exeter she always looked out of the window, singing to herself and guessing the colours of traffic lights and cars. She was good by now with blue, or *boo* as she called it, always pronouncing it in the same way you'd do if you crept up behind someone. She was good too with black and white, and with red, *lello*, and green, although understandably, shades of blue and green – like turquoise – confused her, and grey, brown and purple were a bit beyond her comprehension.

'*White* car!' she shouted as one passed us. '*Back lolly!*'

'Yes, black lorry, well done, Poppy,' I called back to her.

A bus passed, and instead of any comment on the colour, we got the usual hearty rendition of her favourite song: 'The Wheels on the Bus'. We always sang it together every time we saw one – and until very recently, Poppy had firmly believed a bus was actually called an *All Day Long*, because we'd sung that final phrase of every verse so many times. I already knew I wouldn't be too sorry when she finally got bored with the song. There were a lot of buses on the roads around Exeter! But at least it kept my mind, for now, off the conversation I had to have when we arrived.

* * *

Mum was bright and breezy, as usual, when she opened her front door to us, giving me a hug and a kiss and sweeping Poppy up into her arms.

'How's my little Poppy-Pops now?' she said, inspecting Poppy's face for signs of any lingering illness. 'Is she completely better, Gemma?'

'Oh yes, completely,' I said, and went on quickly before Poppy could start wondering what was supposed to be wrong with her. 'How are you, Mum?'

'I've got *this*,' Poppy interrupted, pushing the toy laptop into Mum's hands before she'd had a chance to answer. 'It's my fav'rite.'

'Your favourite for today, is it?' Mum laughed. 'Come on in, both of you. Have you got time for a quick coffee, darling, or do you need to get home and crack straight on with work?'

'I could have a quick one. Oh, look, Poppy. Nanny's got the doll's house out all ready for you.'

Mum kept some toys at her house, especially for Fridays, so there was always something different for Poppy to play with. She trotted over to the rug where Mum had put the doll's house, sat down and started to take out and rearrange all the furniture. I followed Mum into the kitchen and pulled the door half-shut behind us.

'I've got to tell you something,' I said – and already my voice was wobbling, tears not far away.

Mum turned, her eyes searching mine.

'What is it? Oh, darling, don't cry! Whatever it is, I'm here to help – come on, sit down, tell me all about it. It's not Poppy, is it? What was wrong with her last week? Did you have to take her to the doctor, or—'

'No – no, not Poppy, she's fine, Mum. I'm sorry, I need to tell you quickly, I don't want her to see me upset.' I wiped my eyes and blew my nose. 'It's Jack. He's... left us. I had a message; he's with someone else, he doesn't want us to go over there – it's—'

'*What*?' Mum demanded – and I put my finger to my lips, reminding her to keep her voice down. 'What the hell?' she went on. 'He can't stop you and Poppy going over there, surely? What, is he involved in some fling with some girl? Once you get out there, he'll—'

'We're not going, Mum. We can't. He doesn't want us. He's actually hiding from us – I don't even know where he is, he's changed his phone number, his email address, come off his social media, there's no way I can even—'

'That's ridiculous!' Mum exclaimed. 'I mean, I know you were getting worried that you hadn't heard from him recently, but – he's changed his number? Changed his email? He can't do that! He's got responsibilities!' I was glad, really, that she was so angry. If she'd started crying with me, it would have been too hard to pretend to Poppy, who might burst in at any moment, that everything was fine – as I'd been trying so hard to do. 'He can't hide away from everyone! We'll find him. Leave it to me, Gemma: I'll track him down, and when I do, I'll give him a piece of my mind. He can't just abandon you! And his daughter, for God's sake.'

'Mum,' I said wearily, 'Australia's a big place. Even the Child Support Agency' – yes, I'd contacted them the previous day – 'doesn't hold out very much hope. They say that if he's stayed in New South Wales, there's a *chance* he can be found – they've got a reciprocal arrangement, with Australia, apparently, but—'

'There's no *but* about it!'

'But,' I went on regardless, 'he's not stupid, Mum. He'll surely have realised that if he doesn't want to be tracked down, he'll have to move to another state; go completely off grid.'

She stared at me, shaking her head. 'I can't believe this. He always seemed so... well, you seemed so...' She stopped, lost for words. Then, shaking her head, said, 'You're surely not just going to let him get away with this? Did you have any clue? I mean, I know you hadn't heard from him recently, but did he hint at anything earlier, in his calls, or messages – anything to make you suspect he was carrying on with someone?'

'I haven't had any calls or messages,' I admitted, looking away from her. 'It's not just a recent thing. I haven't heard from him for weeks. Over a month.'

'Oh, Gemma,' she said, softening, holding out her arms to me.

'Don't. Please, I don't want to cry any more. I want to stay angry. Stay angry for me, please, Mum. It's the only way I can cope – by hating him.'

'I can't believe it, Gemma. I just can't believe someone can change so suddenly like this. *Surely,* whatever he says now, he'll get in touch with you soon, and you can at least talk it all over?' She paused, thinking about it, before adding, 'But how did you find out, if he's changed all his contact details? Did he contact you from a different number? Can't you—'

'His brother messaged me, without Jack knowing. The brother thinks he's a disgrace – but even so, he still closed his Instagram account, straight after sending me the message, so I can't get back to him. So, basically still loyal to his disgraceful brother, whatever he says.'

She nodded. 'I see.' I supposed the truth – that Jack really had dumped me without a second's regret – was beginning to sink in. 'And you've gone to the CSA. He hasn't set up any child support. You're going to need some help.'

'I'll... find a way to manage. I'll have to. Working extra hours or—'

'No. I'll help you, obviously. So will your father. Have you told him? Would you like me to?'

'No. I will, Mum – I'll call him. Tonight, when Poppy's asleep. I wanted you to know first. I'm sorry I couldn't tell you any sooner. I... had to pull myself together. And I'm not expecting you – or Dad – to help me. That's not why I'm telling you.'

'I know you weren't expecting it. But we will do, obviously. We'll pull together, Gemma, like we always have done. We'll have a meeting, the three of us. Sort out your bills, and—'

'I've made a spreadsheet,' I admitted.

'Of course you have,' she said, smiling. 'Ever the accountant – just like your father.'

Finally, I let her hug me, and we both tried – and somehow managed – not to cry.

'I'd better go,' I said. 'I've got a lot of work to get through.'

'I didn't even make the coffee!'

'It doesn't matter. It was just an excuse to come in here, so Poppy didn't hear.'

'I'd better check she's all right,' Mum said, bustling past me into the living room, back in nanny mode, putting on her nanny voice to sing out to Poppy that the doll's house looked *lovely*, weren't they *lucky* little dolls to have all their furniture tidied up so nicely?

'Thanks, Mum,' I said. 'Let's talk later.' I gave her a kiss, and bent down to hug and kiss my daughter. 'Bye, Poppy. Be good for Nanny, won't you?'

'Bye bye, Mummy.' She waved me off like a queen dismissing her courtiers.

'I'll bring her home after her tea,' Mum added quietly. 'So you can get as much work done as possible while it's quiet.'

'Thanks. I appreciate it.'

* * *

I thought about Mum as I was driving home: how she'd managed to stay on good terms with Dad after they'd decided to split up. I never really knew whose decision it was to divorce; they'd always kept to the narrative that it was mutual, that they'd simply wanted different things and decided they'd be better apart – but it had never really made sense to me. Neither of them had left for someone else. Dad had since had a girlfriend or two, but they hadn't lasted, and he'd even admitted after the last one, that he'd kept comparing her to Mum and it could never be the same with anyone else. So why? What had they achieved from the break-up? Mum said she liked her independence, but I'd never been aware of Dad stopping her from

doing anything she wanted. And it wasn't as if they'd
argued a lot. But I supposed nobody ever really knew
what went on in other people's relationships, even
their parents'.

Jack and I hadn't argued often, either. Just the occasional silly, minor dispute over whose turn it was to do
various chores, like everyone does – especially once
there's a baby to look after, making more washing,
more mess, more meals to prepare. Children do put a
strain on a relationship, I knew that, but Jack had always seemed to love Poppy so much, and had always
played his part as much as he could. He'd been gentle
with her, never seeming frustrated by her crying, always happy to pick her up and pace the floor to get her
settled. If we'd always been at each other's throats, if
he'd seemed unhappy with me or bored with life as a
parent, it would have made it all so much easier to understand. But this – the callousness of it, the absolute
lack of any care with which he'd apparently just *moved
on* – moved *beyond* us – it didn't make sense. It would
never make sense. I was never going to get over it, I
realised, and this did at least give me back the anger I
needed. He'd *ruined* me. That was the only way I could
think of it. I'd never be whole again.

8

CRYSTAL

I knew I had to take things slowly. I knew Gemma would think it was weird if I let her see how desperately I wanted to meet Poppy. But I was finding the days when I wasn't able to see Gemma, to chat to her and hear her mention Poppy, more and more slow and empty. It felt as if Gemma had come into my life at exactly the right time, just as I was feeling so much better in my own head, able to cope better with how it might feel to be in the company of a little girl like Poppy, when just a few short months earlier it might have made me slip completely out of control.

And anyway, I knew I had something to offer Gemma. Sympathy, understanding, a shoulder to lean on, perhaps even someone to offer some actual help in some way. She'd already said she felt better after talking to me, that it was good to be able to chat to someone who'd been through something similar. I obviously didn't want to talk about my past, but if I was too mysterious about it, she'd start to find it odd and unnatural. Friends always confide in each other, after all. So I decided it would be a good idea to gradually confide a little bit about my own life, without giving away the parts that would set alarm bells ringing. I wouldn't be giving her my real name, for one thing.

I suppose I'm making it sound like I had it all worked out. But I must admit that just occasionally, during those first few weeks, before I actually met Poppy, I did experience a few doubts. Was I being fair? However much I told myself I wanted to help her, was I really intending to *use* Gemma, to take advantage of her for my own selfish reasons – the pleasure of getting to know her daughter, of spending time with her, perhaps getting close to her?

Was getting friendly with Gemma actually going to be a dangerous path to tread? Would my therapist have recommended it? I knew quite well that I wasn't going to tell her, because the truth was, I knew it was crazy. So I worried about it, turned it over and over in my mind. But in the end, I knew I was still going to do it.

9

GEMMA

'I'm glad you've got your mum to help you. Support you. That must be a comfort,' Crystal said as she stirred her lemon and ginger tea. We were back at our usual lunchtime pub; without either of us having to say anything, it had become a routine for us to meet there for lunch on Mondays and Tuesdays.

I nodded, putting a hand on hers sympathetically. I knew why she was sounding sad about it. She'd told me her own mum had passed away only a few years earlier.

'You must miss her terribly,' I said. 'I don't know what I'd do without my mum.'

'Yes,' she said. 'Poor Mum – the diagnosis came completely out of the blue, but she went downhill quickly afterwards. Up till then she'd hardly ever been ill, in fact. She was really healthy, always down the gym...'

'How awful for you.'

'It was.'

We were both silent for a moment, contemplating the sandwiches in front of us and the unfairness of life. Then she suddenly went on in a rush, 'Especially given the circumstances. She died soon after my ex walked out on me.'

'Oh, no, you poor thing. Two awful shocks to contend with at the same time.'

'I didn't cope very well,' she admitted. 'Fell apart, to be honest.'

'I'm not surprised.' I looked at her, now picking up her hummus and carrot sandwich and taking a huge enthusiastic bite out of it before slurping some more of her drink. 'How did you manage to recover so well?'

'Oh, don't be fooled.' She laughed. 'The pain is still there, probably always will be. But someone suggested I should try a self-help group. I didn't really like the idea at first: talking about my problems to complete strangers – it didn't feel right. But I knew I had to do something; I was... sinking into a black hole. The doctor had given me antidepressants but I wanted to get off them. I didn't even feel like they were helping.'

'And did the group help?'

'Yes. The first one I joined was for bereavement support, and it did help me to face the fact that Mum had gone and she wouldn't have wanted me to be un-happy forever. But it didn't address the other issue.'

'Your ex. What was his name, by the way?'

'Simon,' she said, waving this aside as if it didn't really matter. I supposed it didn't, any more. 'So, someone else recommended another group, for people with depression. Then I tried one specifically for lonely people. And someone there gave me details of a group who based their philosophy on meditation and spiritual awareness.'

'And did that one help?'

It all sounded a bit mumbo-jumbo to me, but then, I'm an accountant. I've always been more likely to ad-dress my problems by making a spreadsheet than to go in for anything like spiritual awareness, and more likely to put on a smart suit and a brave face than to wear a kaftan, beads, smoke a spliff and chant. But somehow it all seemed right for Crystal, and I liked her for it.

'You worked your way through several groups to find the right one?' I asked.

'Oh, I kept going to them all for a while,' she said, smiling. 'But yes, I liked the meditation. It calmed me.

I still belong to the group. It's run by a therapist, but I like the way we all listen to each other and offer support. It's given me a better understanding of other people, I think. I can feel other people's suffering. I felt yours. I was drawn to you, to try to help you, when I heard you crying in the loos.'

'I'm really grateful,' I said. 'You've been very kind.' There was a pause, before I blurted out, 'But I don't think I'm up for... the meditation and stuff. Sorry.'

'Oh God, no, I'm not recruiting for the group, don't worry!' She chuckled. 'It wouldn't work for everyone, we're all different. You'll find your own new happy in time, Gemma.'

'Will I?'

I doubted it.

'Yes, you will. Things won't ever be the same, but there'll be a different kind of happy for you. Trust me.'

And for some reason – I did. I didn't know why; after all, I still hardly knew her. But I trusted her, completely. Far more than I could ever imagine trusting any *man*, ever again.

Fortunately for me, Poppy at this time was still at an age where she lived mostly in the moment, and didn't often ask about Jack. In fact, as time passed since he'd left for Australia, she'd asked after him less and less. But I still had a photo of him in a frame on my bedside table. I'd actually thrown it on the floor since I'd had the fatal message from his brother, three times in fact, and I was amazed the glass hadn't broken. Why had I put it back by my bed after that, despite everything? I don't know. Habit? Reluctance, even then, to face the truth? But the next time I was at home all day with Poppy, she was watching me making the bed when she pointed at the picture and, with her head on one side, asked plaintively:

'Where Daddy gone?'

I froze for a moment. I obviously should have anticipated this, but it was the first time she'd asked since everything had changed. Up until then, of course, I'd been able to answer her quite calmly, reminding her that Daddy had gone to find us a nice new house in a new country and we'd soon be going to join him there. She would nod, remembering being told this before, and she'd say, for reassurance, 'Mummy and Poppy go?'

'Yes, of course! We'll go together.'

'And Nanny?'

'Yes, Nanny's coming too.'

I'd make it sound like a fun outing, something exciting to look forward to, rather than going into detail about the long flight to the other side of the world, uprooting her from everything she knew; she was young enough anyway to cope with the change, probably much better than I would.

Except that now it wasn't going to happen. And I hadn't had the sense, with everything else I'd had to worry about, to think what I was going to tell her instead.

'Oh, Daddy's gone away for a while, to work,' I said as breezily as I could manage. 'Why don't we get your new book out and read a story—'

But the distraction tactic wasn't going to work so easily.

'Daddy gone 'way?' she repeated, still looking at the picture. It was my favourite photo of him, taken on the beach during the previous summer, on a warm sunny day. His hair was shining copper-red in the sunshine, the way Poppy's does, his bright blue-green eyes reflecting the colour of his emerald T-shirt, his mouth wide in a smile as he watched our little daughter playing, just out of sight of the camera.

I hurriedly choked back the tears that were threatening and told myself that photo *had* to be thrown away.

'Yes, darling.'

'Poppy and Mummy go too?'

What the hell could I say? I didn't want to lie to her, but... was I still, without even admitting it to myself, secretly hoping there was just a chance Jack might change his mind, finish with the new girlfriend, and send for us after all? Was I secretly thinking, despite everything I'd said to the contrary, that I might give in and take him back? Surely not. And yet...

'One day, sweetie. One day, we'll go,' I said.

Well, we might, of course, go to Australia one day – even though the thought of it made me feel physically sick at that moment.

'Nanny go?' Poppy persisted. But by now, fortunately, she was beginning to lose interest in the conversation; the idea of having her new book read to her suddenly took hold, and without even waiting for me to reply, she trotted off to her own room to look for it.

I grabbed the photo, stuffed it in my knicker drawer and swore to myself that I'd take it out of the frame and put it through the shredder as soon as Poppy was asleep. I knew there would be plenty of difficult questions to answer over the coming weeks, months, and years. But I wasn't ready yet. I'd keep the questions at bay for a little while longer.

* * *

By now, I'd spoken to my dad about the situation; in fact, I'd had several lengthy conversations with him about it. It was taking time for him to calm down. He was even angrier than Mum was, and not good at hiding it.

'Dad, I'm just as angry with Jack as you are,' I had to keep reminding him, but he ignored me, continuing with his rants, which usually went along the lines of Jack being a complete and total bastard, a despicable coward, a waste of space, a pathetic excuse for a human being who'd never deserved to set eyes on his daughter, and if Dad ever saw him again Jack would wish he'd never been born. I couldn't disagree with any of it so I didn't argue, but it did make me cry, because I hated hearing my normally mild-mannered, calm and rational father reduced to this seething spouting of hatred. It also had the effect of causing me, against my will, to imagine myself one day finding out that someone had treated my own daughter as badly as Jack had treated me, so I had to admit I understood my dad's passionate – and impotent – fury.

He'd offered to come down from Manchester to help me sort everything out, and it was only because I insisted I didn't want him around if he was going to make me feel worse with his uncontrolled anger, that he didn't actually turn up on my doorstep as soon as I'd told him what had happened. And for that reason, he eventually started to calm down. By the time we'd agreed that he could come for the bank holiday weekend at the end of August, I was so pleased to see him that I burst into tears anyway. But he did help me; his normal manner – when he wasn't consumed by such uncharacteristic rage – was to discuss things calmly and logically. I'd inherited my love of numbers and logic from him, but I wasn't in a logical frame of mind right then, so I really needed his help.

'Right!' he said in a business-like manner. 'Your mum and I have already talked about all this. And you're not going to have to worry about a thing, OK?'

'That sounds great, Dad, but unfortunately I *am* worried. The mortgage—'

'—is going to be taken care of. We're taking care of it, between us.'

'No. You can't do that!'

'We can. We've sat down together and worked it out, and there's no argument about it, we're taking over the payments. It's what we're going to do, until you've got yourself back on your feet – OK?'

In response, I just hugged him and started crying again. A few weeks had passed by then, since I'd had the news about Jack, but I still felt too weak with conflicting emotions to even attempt to argue about it. And in any case, I knew it was going to save me from going under.

'We'd do anything to help you, Gemma, we both would. You'd do the same for Poppy, wouldn't you?' he said, grasping my hand and sounding choked himself. 'If, God forbid, she ever found herself in trouble when she's grown up.'

But I couldn't bear to even think about that. The very idea of my precious little daughter ever being in any kind of trouble or pain was enough to start the tears flowing all over again.

I was still a long way from being OK; still, I suppose, very fragile, very needy. And most of my friends, sympathetic and kind though they all were, were too busy with their own families – children, partners, husbands – to listen to me constantly going over everything, trying to make sense of it. Looking back, it's obvious: Crystal was giving me exactly what I needed. A sympathetic ear. Understanding, from someone outside my family, someone who'd been through the same thing. A friend who listened and didn't judge.

No wonder we became so close, so quickly.

10

CRYSTAL

Gemma and I continued meeting every Monday and Tuesday for lunch. As I'd promised myself, I was taking things slowly. If I'd suddenly asked to see Poppy, Gemma would understandably have found it very odd. Instead, I let the conversation flow naturally into talking about her: what she and Gemma had done at the weekend, how she was getting on at nursery, when she was going to turn three, and so on. As far as Gemma was concerned, I hoped, I was just taking a polite interest.

'Has Poppy asked about her daddy?' I asked one day.

Gemma sighed. 'Yes. It was stupid of me not to anticipate it. Up till now I've told her he's gone to find us a new home, but I have to change the narrative now. I told her he was working away. She seems to have accepted that, but I know I'm going to have to deal with it properly at some point.'

'That's so difficult for you,' I said. 'But hopefully, as she's so young, she might not even remember him very well after a while.'

'That's what I'm hoping. It's not as if he's going to be fighting me for custody or demanding to see her, is it?'

'From what you've said, he isn't father material at all.'

'Well, so it turns out, no, he isn't.' Gemma sighed again. 'But it's come as such a shock, it's hard to actually believe it. I mean, when I look at some of the photos of the two of them together – father and daughter – he really did look as if he loved her. He really *behaved* as if he loved her. How can someone change so much, so suddenly?'

'Have you got any pics of them together on your phone?' I asked, as casually as I could manage. 'Or have you deleted them all? I think I would have done if it was me!'

'I've kept a couple of special ones,' she admitted, fishing in her bag for her phone. 'I ought to delete them but... somehow I just couldn't. Look. Don't you think they look like the perfect daddy and daughter?'

I had to admit that yes, they did. Jack was carrying Poppy on his back, holding her securely to keep her steady, and they were both laughing – her rosebud mouth wide, her little white teeth gleaming, her eyes sparkling, their matching red hair shining. It hurt my heart so much to see that photo, I had to keep my head down while I tried to control my breathing.

'It's a beautiful picture,' I managed to say eventually. And I added, to excuse anything she might have noticed of my emotional state, 'I feel so upset for you, love. It must be so hard.'

'Thank you,' she said, taking back the phone and stuffing it roughly into her bag. 'I need to try to move on, though. I need to delete it.'

And *I* needed to practise hiding my emotions. Because I was getting desperate, now, to meet Poppy in person. And I needed to be calm and in control when that happened.

11

GEMMA

One Tuesday, I was with Crystal as usual for lunch when she asked me, quite suddenly, what I was going to be doing at the weekend. We only normally saw each other, of course, on Mondays and Tuesdays.

I laughed. 'Same as usual. Housework, shopping, washing. Playing with Poppy. Mum might come over for Sunday dinner. Nothing exciting. Why? What are you up to?'

'Nothing exciting either.' She paused, then went on in a rush, 'I was just wondering whether you'd like to get together. On Saturday perhaps.'

'Oh.' I was a bit taken aback. We'd been getting on really well – so much so that I actually found myself laughing quite a lot, now, during our lunches together.

She brought me out of myself, and out of my depression, with her odd mixture of sympathy, self-deprecation and humour. But I suppose I'd put her firmly in the category of a work friend. The idea of seeing her outside of my days in the office hadn't occurred to me. 'Well... as you know, I've got Poppy. I usually put her to bed by seven o'clock so I can't go—'

'Oh, I meant during the day, really. I was thinking perhaps we could meet for a coffee or something? With Poppy, obviously – I'd love to meet her. What do you think? Not if you're too busy, of course. I'd understand.'

'Oh, right.' I thought about it, imagined taking Poppy out to a café, meeting Crystal, having a chat – like this – at the weekend. It would break up the endless monotony of chores and childcare, wouldn't it? Why not? 'OK – yes, that'd be lovely, actually.'

Her face broke into a smile. 'Great! Where do you want to meet? Somewhere near you, to make it easy for you.'

'OK, well, I'm at Bancombe, just down the road from Bancombe Bay. How about we meet at the beach café there?'

'Perfect, that's only a couple of miles from me. The weather's supposed to be nice, like this, all over the weekend, so sitting outside would be lovely. We could have a walk along the beach after we've had our coffee... oh, only if you've got time, of course,' she added quickly, her smile dropping slightly.

She'd sounded so excited by the idea of walking along the beach that for a moment, I wondered if – apart from her self-help group – she didn't get out much. But I was pleased to think she was looking forward to meeting up, so I smiled back and said yes, that sounded good, and I was sure I could spare the time, that it'd make a nice change.

'Great!' she enthused again, taking a sip of her elderflower cordial. 'It's a plan. I can't wait, Gemma!'

* * *

I thought about it from time to time during the rest of the week. *Can't wait*? Should I feel flattered, or puzzled? I did enjoy her company, and yes, we'd become good friends in a short time – I'd always be grateful to her for rescuing me at what had been one of the worst moments of my life. But surely she had existing friends of her own, even if only those from her hippy chanting group, to spend time with at weekends? She had no kids – no ties – why would she be so excited about a coffee at the beach café with someone tied to a toddler in a buggy? But in the end I decided to just be happy about it. I didn't exactly have a plethora of friends myself, queueing up to go out for coffee with me on a Saturday. I'd made the mistake of giving myself up almost completely to Jack and Poppy for company – and meanwhile some of my friends had two or even three children now and were even busier than me. Why not just enjoy this new friendship? We'd have more freedom and more time to chat on a Saturday than we did on working days.

* * *

Saturday was a beautiful sunny day, as September days often are in our part of the world, with just a gentle breeze blowing over the outside tables at the beach café. Poppy was in a happy mood, reminding me every few minutes about the ice cream I'd promised her. I found us a table overlooking the beach, and a few minutes later Crystal drifted across the terrace towards us, calling out hello and turning a few heads in her very wide floral cotton trousers and bright orange top. Poppy had been singing a little song to herself, swinging her legs as she sat on one of the chairs patiently waiting for her ice cream, but as I got up to greet Crystal she fell silent, looking anxious.

'This is Mummy's friend – I told you we'd be

meeting her, didn't I?' I reminded her as Crystal pulled up a chair opposite us. 'Her name's Crystal.'

'No,' said Poppy, hiding her face behind her hands.

I started to apologise, but Crystal brushed it aside.

'It's OK, Gemma. Poppy doesn't know me, does she?'

Poppy lifted one hand away from her face to take a quick peek at her and Crystal gave her a smile, but Poppy hurriedly covered her face again.

'She's not normally shy,' I said. 'She's quite out-going at nursery.'

'Nothing wrong with being a bit shy with strange adults. Let me get the coffees so you two can stay sitting together. And... what would Poppy like?'

The hands immediately flew away from the face and Poppy shouted, far too loudly for someone supposedly being shy, 'Ice cream p'ease!'

'I did promise her an ice cream,' I said, laughing. 'But let me get it... or give you the money, at least—'

'Absolutely not,' Crystal insisted as she headed for the counter. 'My treat. You can pay next time.'

I smiled to myself at the suggestion that there would be a next time. That we'd make a habit of this. I felt happy about it. I was already feeling more cheerful just from being in her company, my worries about money, work, and everything else fading into the background.

'What sort of ice cream – a cornet?' Crystal turned back to ask me.

'Perfect – a small one though. With a dish, please!' I'd had too much experience of dropped cornets to risk letting Poppy hold one without giving her a safe landing place for it.

'Of course,' Crystal said, as if this was a perfectly normal request.

'Have you got other friends with little children?' I asked her when she returned with the two coffees and empty bowl on a little tray and the ice cream in her other hand.

'Um... not really.' She smiled at Poppy as she put the cornet into her hand, and the bowl on her lap, every bit as if she did it all the time. 'There you are, angel. Hold it tight!'

'Not *angel*!' Poppy said indignantly, her shyness evidently completely forgotten now. '*Poppy*!'

'Say *thank you*,' I reminded her, and – after taking a good lick of the ice cream first – she looked up at Crystal and said, 'T'ank you, lady.'

'Her name's Crystal,' I reminded her – but Crystal laughed.

'It's not often I get called a lady. Enjoy your ice

cream, Poppy.'

There wasn't another sound from her apart from an occasional slurping noise as she devoured the cornet, while we sipped our coffees and chatted. Crystal was asking me about Poppy's nursery, and I started to explain that I'd always been happy with her two days there – using my free childcare hours – but that Jack and I had planned, before the decision to emigrate to Australia, that we'd have transferred Poppy from nursery to pre-school once she turned three, to give her more of a preparation for school.

'Anyway, the whole plan obviously got dropped because we thought we'd all be in Australia by now.'

'And you've decided to keep her at nursery now?'

'For now, yes. Apart from anything else, the original plan was for me to be able to get a full-time job because Poppy would've been at pre-school five days a week. But school holiday childcare isn't easy to find. My mum works part-time and it's nice enough of her to have Poppy every Friday.'

'And of course, you haven't had a chance to look for a full-time job because you didn't expect—'

'—to still be here. Or on my own. So she'll stay at the nursery. I don't know what I'll do when she starts school, though.'

I stopped talking, because I couldn't help noticing

how often Crystal was watching Poppy, smiling in a wistful kind of way, even while we were mid-conversation.

'I hope this isn't too difficult for you,' I said softly, remembering the way Crystal had talked regretfully about not having a child herself.

'Oh, no, of course not,' she said with a smile. 'It's just so nice to see her – to see both of you.' She lowered her voice as she added, suddenly looking quite emotional despite having denied it, 'She's *such* a beautiful little girl, Gemma. The colour of her hair. It's so striking.'

'Yes. Nothing to do with me, I'm afraid. I was a natural blonde when I was Poppy's age, but unfortunately blonde goes kind of mousy as you get older. You're lucky, I always think dark hair retains its colour for longer.'

'Poppy's got her father's colouring, then.'

'Yes, totally.' I gave a little snort as I went on, 'Probably the only good thing he's given her, as it turns out. I certainly hope she's not going to take after him in any other way.'

'She's lovely. You're very lucky.'

Crystal looked down at her coffee, pretending to be concentrating on stirring it. I wanted to retort that I wasn't lucky at all, that I considered myself very *unlucky* to have chosen a man who would treat me and his daughter the way Jack had done. But I'd heard the tremor in her voice, and I understood. I *was* lucky, because at least I had Poppy. Without her, I'd have given up. I'd probably have been on medication for depression, like Crystal had been, and I might even have ended up joining her self-help group.

I put my hand on hers – trying to ignore, for the moment, the way the remaining ice cream in Poppy's cornet was beginning to drip down the side, looking likely to miss the bowl and land on the ground – and said, 'You're right, I'm lucky to have her, of course. But at least, now, you've got a friend, one who understands.'

'Thank you, love. It *is* nice to have a new friend – I hope it's helping you, too?'

But before I could answer, Poppy suddenly started yelling.

'My ice cream!' She wriggled down from her chair, sending the bowl flying, and tried to pick up with her fingers the rapidly melting blobs of ice cream landslide that had landed by her feet. By the time I'd stopped her, she'd got sticky melted mess all over her hands, dropped the cone and trodden on it, and was heading for an almighty screaming fit.

'You can't eat it now,' I told her. 'Come here – let's just give your hands a—'

'I d'opped it! I wanted it!' she wailed as I set to work with the wet wipes.

'Come on, it doesn't matter, you ate nearly all of it, it was melting faster than you could eat.'

'But I wanted *that*!' she sobbed, pointing at the mess on the ground.

'Ah, never mind, Poppy,' Crystal said. 'How about we go down on the beach for a little while instead? The sea should be nice and warm.'

Her tears dried up instantly. 'Poppy can paddle? Mummy can paddle?' She gave me a hopeful smile and I couldn't help laughing.

'Yes, all right.'

I mouthed Crystal a thank you across the table. I always kept a little towel in my bag for impromptu paddling occasions, and there's nothing like a paddle in the sea to tame the wildest of toddler melt-downs.

'It never fails, does it – the promise of a paddle?' Crystal whispered to me with a grin as we left the café.

And I wondered again where she'd got her experience of children from. Perhaps she had little cousins, or neighbours with kids. Perhaps I'd ask her about it later. Or perhaps I wouldn't, because I sensed that questions about children were always likely to upset her. I decided that maybe she was just a natural, which made it all the sadder that she hadn't had any of her own.

And at least, after a good paddle and lots of splashing in the shallow waves down below the beach café, Poppy was in a good frame of mind again and the subject of the dropped ice cream was forgotten. And I think all three of us had enjoyed our morning.

'We should do it again,' Crystal said, waving goodbye to Poppy as we parted company.

'Definitely,' I agreed. I realised I was smiling. I was so unused to doing it now, it was hurting my face.

12

CRYSTAL

I couldn't stop thinking about Poppy for the rest of the weekend. Her pretty little face, her beautiful hair, her smile, her energy, her enthusiasm, her *spirit*. She was such a lovely child. She was exactly how I imagined she would be. And she took to me, I knew she did. I didn't even have to try to win her round, it was completely natural, as if we belonged together.

But I knew, too, that I couldn't allow myself to get carried away. It was obvious that Gemma had been surprised at how well Poppy and I had got on together. I was aware that it was quite unusual for a child to take so naturally to an adult they'd never met before. It was just proof, if I'd needed any, that Poppy and I had a close spiritual link.

But Gemma had enjoyed meeting up too. She'd said it gave her a nice break from doing chores, that it made a change for her to spend time with a friend – so it was quite logical to suggest doing it again the following Saturday, and she seemed really happy to agree. If she hadn't done, I'd have had to take a step back. It was still early days, and if at any time Gemma decided to pull back, for whatever reason – to want to spend less time with me – I supposed I'd have to accept it. Accept, perhaps, not seeing Poppy again. But now that I'd met her, I wasn't too sure I'd be able to.

Was I already getting in too deep? I thought about it, tried to rationalise it to myself. I was only trying to help, wasn't I? I wasn't doing any harm. I'd never want to hurt Gemma, or Poppy of course. But was it really the right thing to do – inveigling myself into their lives like that? Perhaps I should have just fronted up, come out with my full story, while I still had the chance. Before it went on for so long that it would become impossible to explain why I'd kept quiet about it.

But how would it have sounded, if I'd blurted out the truth at that point? Gemma would have thought I was some kind of stalker, that I had ulterior motives, that I was a threat, not to be trusted. No, it was better, I decided, to continue as we were. I was Crystal – it wasn't a complete lie, anyway, it was the name I'd been given in the self-help group – and she knew nothing about my past. I was just a friend, a childless, lonely friend who knew how it felt to be dumped. A kindly 'auntie' to Poppy and a support to her mum. I didn't see how I could be criticised for that, so I didn't understand why – in my darkest moments, alone in my bed at night – I still felt a pang of conscience. A pang I had to try hard to ignore.

13

GEMMA

'How's it going with the CSA?' Crystal asked me over lunch on Monday. 'Any luck finding your ex?'

'Not yet.' I sighed. 'They say it could take quite some time, even if they do manage to track him down. I've had to give them details of his family, but it doesn't help that I don't even know where *they* live. And even if they find them, can they force them to say where Jack's gone?'

'It's not right, is it? You'd think they ought to be able to... I don't know... put out a nationwide search for him, get him arrested, or something.'

I shrugged. 'I think it's best if I tell myself it's never going to happen – that I'll never get any money out of him. Then, if they do ever manage to find him and make him pay, it'll be a bonus.'

'You're a lot more sensible than I'd be. I'd probably be on a plane right now, on my way out there to find his family – his brother or whatever – and *force* them to tell me where he is.'

'I can't. I can't just take off like that, with Poppy – or leave her behind. And how exactly could I force them – supposing I could even find them?'

'I'd hire someone to beat them up if they refused to say where he'd gone,' she said.

I stared at her. 'No you wouldn't! You're not like that. You're all about peace and light and love!'

'That would all go out of the window, trust me, if I could find him for you. It makes me so frigging mad to think of him getting away with it – what he's done to you. He's Poppy's father. He's got responsibilities. How dare he just disappear out of your lives like this?'

I took a sip of my coffee, staring back at her in silence. She'd sounded furious there, almost more furious than I was myself about it. I suppose I'd convinced myself, by then, to more or less give up hope of getting anything from Jack – and to sustain the level of anger I'd felt at the beginning would have taken up way too much of my energy. It would have depleted what little I had left for Poppy, after working at my two different jobs. But even as I sat at the table now watching her, Crystal was pink in the face with her anger, shaking her head, as if her inability to do anything about my situation was eating her up. It was nice that she cared, but... well, I hadn't quite seen this side of her before.

'Honestly,' I said awkwardly, 'I'm not that stressed about it any more. What's the point? I mean, I agree with you, it's not right, of course it isn't, and I hate Jack for it, yes, I do. But I can't change the situation, so I have to try to accept it – at least for now, while I wait. The CSA might manage to find him, and if they don't, I've got to get on with it, haven't I? For Poppy's sake.'

Crystal let out a long breath of frustration. 'Yes, of course, I get that. Sorry, I don't want to make you feel any worse than you must do already.' She fell silent for a moment and then went on, 'But I hope you'll make sure Poppy knows, as she grows up, what a bastard her father was. That's what I'd do if my ex and I had had any kids – I'd make sure they knew the truth about him.'

'I... don't know how I'm going to answer her questions, yet,' I admitted. 'She's so little. She doesn't often ask after him.'

'Good.' She swallowed the remainder of her herbal tea, and finally gave me a smile. 'She's such a lovely

little girl, I can't bear to think of her being hurt – or
you, of course. To be honest, the way he's behaved, he
didn't deserve Poppy in the first place. He certainly
won't deserve any loyalty from her if he suddenly de-
cides he wants to see her in the future.'

'No. I suppose not.'

'He can hardly call himself a father,' she added
grimly.

'Well, I guess he's made up his own mind not to be
one any more.' Frankly, I was beginning to wish she'd
shut up about it. I didn't really need anyone to tell me
how badly Jack had behaved. 'Anyway – come on, we'd
better get a move on, we've almost gone over our lunch
break. Mike's going to give me his *stern* look when I get
back to the office.'

She grinned. Although she didn't really know
Mike, I'd told her about his frequently repeated
maxim that *a good manager is like a good father – kind
and fair, but stern when necessary.*

* * *

Crystal didn't say anything further to me about Jack
that week, and I tried to keep off the subject myself.
Her forceful anger had made me feel uncomfortable –
although on the other hand, I supposed it was nice of

her to feel such indignance on my behalf. My own feelings seemed to have faded into a kind of stunned apathy, almost to the point that I couldn't have cared less any more, about anything other than surviving, and keeping Poppy safe and well.

'You'll be fine,' Mum kept telling me. 'Your dad and I will make sure of it. You and Poppy are going to be fine.'

I wondered whether the reason she felt the need to say it so often was to reassure me – or reassure herself.

* * *

Crystal and I repeated our Saturday morning get-together that weekend. I told Poppy, as I was getting her ready to go out, that we'd be meeting *Mummy's friend* again.

'More ice cream?' she said at once.

'If you're good.'

'I be good. Mummy's friend get me ice cream.'

'Her name's Crystal, Poppy. And please don't ask her for an ice cream – that would be rude, OK? Mummy will buy one for you today.'

'I like C'ystal,' she said happily.

'CRystal,' I corrected her. 'With a R. Like in *crayon*.' I don't know why it felt important that she got my friend's name right; I suppose I just knew it would please Crystal.

'CRRRystal!' Poppy shouted back at me. 'I like Crystal. Come on, Mummy. Ice cream, yay!'

* * *

Crystal was at the café before us this time, with a cup of tea already in front of her.

'It was my turn to buy the drinks,' I protested.

'I was thirsty, sorry. Can I get you an ice cream again, Poppy?'

'Yay!' Poppy yelled. 'Ice cream!'

'I'll buy it,' I insisted. 'Will you sit there nicely with Crystal while I go to the counter, please, Poppy?'

'Come on, Poppy,' Crystal encouraged her. 'Come and sit next to me. I do love your T-shirt today. Isn't it a nice colour? Do you know what colour it is?'

'BOO!' Poppy shouted, and Crystal pretended to jump out of her skin, making Poppy fall about laughing.

Pleased to see that they were getting on OK, I left them to it and went to buy the ice cream and my coffee. When I came back, Crystal was in the middle of a deliberately slow and suspenseful performance of

'Round and Round the Garden' on Poppy's hand – much to her delight and anticipated excitement.

'...and tickle you under there!' Crystal finished with the usual flourish of tickling.

'Again! Again!' Poppy begged after she'd finished squealing.

'Hang on, Poppy, I've got your ice cream now,' I said. 'Quickly, sit up nicely on your chair before it starts to melt.'

I was happy, though, to see how well they seemed to have bonded. I thought Poppy had grown out of that tickling rhyme but obviously not. Crystal watched her, smiling, as she began licking the ice cream. She tucked the drip-bowl into a safe position on Poppy's lap and watched carefully for leaks on the edge of the cornet from Poppy's enthusiastic slurping.

'I remembered that rhyme from my own child-hood,' she told me with a grin – just as I was about to ask her how she knew it. 'And what's that other one – about a spider?'

'"Incy Wincy Spider"? Ah, we love that one, don't we, Poppy? She knows all the actions. No – don't try to do it now, Pops, you'll drop your ice cream! Afterwards!'

So as soon as she'd finished – without dropping any, this time – we had to have a session of 'Incy Wincy

Spider', and then 'Head, Shoulders, Knees and Toes', followed by 'I'm a Little Teapot'.

'This is great!' Crystal laughed. 'It's bringing it all back to me! I used to do all those with my mum when I was little myself.'

'The old ones are the best,' I agreed. 'You sing them at nursery, don't you, Poppy?'

'Again!' Poppy yelled. 'Teapot again!'

'Not if we're going to have time for a paddle,' I reminded her. 'Anyway, I think we've made enough noise here for today!'

'Not at all,' said an elderly lady at the next table. 'It's been lovely listening to you all enjoying yourselves, love.'

But the paddle was now firmly fixed in Poppy's mind, and without needing any more encouragement, she was on her feet, ready to head down to the beach, holding firmly onto her new friend's hand.

'Crystal paddle?' she asked eagerly. 'Paddle with Poppy?'

'Well, why not, if you'd like me to?' Crystal said. 'Come on, then. Hurry up, before the tide goes out!'

Both of them had their shoes and socks off and were heading into the shallows, still holding hands, before I'd even joined them on the beach.

'Look, Mummy! Paddle with Crystal!' my daughter called to me, ecstatic. 'Come on, Mummy paddle too!'

* * *

'I've had such a lovely time,' Crystal told me as we finally said goodbye a little later. 'Thank you so much for letting me spend time with you and Poppy.'

'No, thank *you*, for helping with her. She's really taken to you. Say goodbye to Crystal, Poppy.'

'Bye bye, Crystal,' Poppy said sadly.

'See you Monday,' I said.

'See you Monday,' Poppy repeated.

I laughed. '*You* won't, pickle! You'll be at nursery.'

'Have fun at nursery, Poppy,' Crystal said, bending down to give her a quick hug. 'See you again soon, though, I hope.'

'Next Saturday?' I suggested. 'If you're up for it?'

'Definitely. Let's hope it's nice enough for paddling again, eh, Poppy?'

'Yay! Paddling! Ice cream!'

We had to sing 'I'm a Little Teapot' all the way home. And I had to do 'Round and Round the Garden' six times before bedtime that evening. But it was well worth it, to see her so happy, and it was nice to know she was so at ease with my friend.

* * *

The following Saturday, though, it was pouring with rain. There was only outdoor seating at the beach café. I waited until half an hour before our usual meeting time to tell Poppy we wouldn't be going – and Crystal called me at the exact same moment to say we'd better cancel. I wasn't sure who was the most disappointed.

'I wanted ice cream!' Poppy was crying. 'Wanted Crystal.'

'Why don't you come here instead?' I said to Crystal. 'If we don't see you today, Poppy's going to have a meltdown.'

A little while later, Crystal's bright green car pulled up outside and she came up the front path wearing a shiny yellow mac over her flowing flowery dress. It was like opening the door and letting in a burst of sunshine. Poppy was immediately full of smiles again – especially when Crystal produced a bag of chocolate buttons from her pocket.

'Is it OK?' she checked with me before giving them to Poppy. 'I took a guess on children still liking these.'

'You guessed right.' I smiled. 'Poppy, let me put some of them in a little dish for you. Then we can save the rest for after lunch. Say thank you to Crystal.'

'T'ank you. What's this?'

This was Crystal's latest fashion accessory – a long leather thong hung around her neck, with a silver Tree of Life medallion dangling on the end of it.

'It's my necklace!' she said. 'Do you like it, Poppy?'

'Yes.' Poppy reached out and fingered it. 'Tree.'

I left them together while I went into the kitchen to make coffee. When I returned, Crystal was sitting on the sofa with Poppy, telling her a story about a fairy who lived in a tree. I sat down opposite them and just watched for a while – my friend and my daughter. They seemed so natural together. Crystal had her arm around Poppy and Poppy was leaning her head against her. It was probably the most peaceful I'd seen Poppy for days, as she'd started asking about her daddy again, unfortunately – asking questions I'd found impossible to answer. But now, well, I'd never seen her quite so relaxed with anyone before, other than my mum.

'You seem to have the magic touch,' I commented when Crystal had finished the story. 'You can put her to bed every night if you like!'

'Yay! Put me to bed!' Poppy said to Crystal, jumping up from the sofa.

Crystal laughed. 'Mummy was joking, Poppy. It's not even bedtime!'

But if it *had* been bedtime, I realised with surprise

– Poppy would probably have let her. And that, in it-
self, was something really unusual. I wondered, again,
how on earth Crystal had such a way with her. I supposed some women were simply complete naturals
with children, even without having any of their own.
Maybe she should re-train as a nursery worker or a
pre-school teacher, I thought; she'd be excellent at it.
But of course, if all she really wished for was a child of
her own, such a suggestion would only upset her. So I
kept quiet.

14

CRYSTAL

Poppy loved me already, I knew she did, and I loved her too, desperately. It made me feel so happy to know that I'd be seeing her again, that she'd be looking forward to seeing me too. It helped me through the days at work, and the long, slow evenings on my own at home. It helped to calm me, helped me to sleep. I even felt like I could pass up on the weekly meeting of the self-help group. In fact I was quite sure I'd be OK now without the group, but I knew from past experience what would happen if I didn't turn up: one of the leaders, either Jo, the therapist, or Malik, the yoga instructor, would get in touch to find out if I was all right, and try to persuade me to go back. And they wouldn't take no for an answer: they'd insist on visiting me at home, and talking through what I'd been up to, and they might ask why I suddenly seemed a bit *hyper*, as they liked to call it, and I knew what would happen: I'd start blurting something out about Gemma. About Poppy. And although I kept telling myself my conscience was clear, they'd somehow make me feel like I was doing something I shouldn't.

On the other hand, I was beginning to feel so bored by it all – all the talk of positivity and taking one day at a time and doing our breathing and yoga and looking for spiritual enlightenment – that when I went along to the group exactly as I always did every Monday evening, I found myself sitting in a corner on my own, yawning, wishing I was with Gemma. Helping with Poppy, playing with her on the beach, singing nursery songs with her. *She* was all the spiritual enlightenment I needed.

That was why I started to think that I could be far more useful to Gemma, far more helpful with Poppy, than just seeing them briefly on Saturday mornings. I could offer to look after Poppy sometimes, play with her, even take her out in her buggy for a little while, to give Gemma more time for her work. She'd already told me her mum looked after Poppy on Fridays, but she couldn't ask her to do more because she worked part-time. Well, I lived close enough to look after her for an evening occasionally, or at the weekend. It would make sense – Gemma was a single mum now, she'd admitted she was going to struggle financially, and I obviously wouldn't want any payment, it would be an absolute pleasure to spend time with Poppy. We would be doing each other a favour. But somehow I knew I'd have to be very careful in how I suggested it. I wouldn't want to give Gemma any cause for concern about my motives. After all, we still hadn't known each other very long – why should she trust me with her beautiful child?

But, then again... if Poppy trusted me, why shouldn't she?

15

GEMMA

'Poppy cried after you left on Saturday,' I told Crystal. It was Monday, and it was raining again, so we were sitting inside the pub instead of in the garden. 'It took me ages to cheer her up. You were a real hit!'

Crystal smiled. 'I've loved getting to know Poppy over the last few Saturdays. She's so sweet. But I'm sorry she cried after I left.' She paused, hesitating, fiddling with her plate and cutlery for a moment before going on quickly, 'I've got a suggestion to make, actually, Gemma. If Poppy has really taken to me, and if you wouldn't mind, I wondered if I could maybe come round occasionally... perhaps on days when you work at home, after I've finished work, or maybe at weekends... I just wondered if it would be helpful for you, if you're busy, to have someone around to play with her or... I don't know, just help out. But say no if you think it wouldn't be a good idea, I won't be offended, I only want to help.'

She lapsed into silence, and then, before I'd had a chance to answer, rushed on. 'I feel for you, that's all. On your own with Poppy. Because of what her dad's done. And I've been wondering how I can help.'

I was a bit taken aback. She'd sounded awkward, almost nervous – and why? I'd kind of assumed she'd come round to see me and Poppy again; it felt like we were good friends now, and I thought it was taken for granted that we'd continue to spend time together. I hadn't, of course, been expecting her to offer to help me in any way, but that was nice of her, so why sound so embarrassed about it? Perhaps she'd thought I might be offended?

'Of course you can come round,' I reassured her. 'And thank you for saying you'd like to help with Poppy. I don't normally need it, to be honest – I try to get as much of my work done as possible if she has a nap – she doesn't, always, now. Or in the evenings – and on Fridays, when Mum has her. But yes, sure, if you'd like to come and play with her, I'm sure she'd love that!'

'I know you're managing OK – sorry, I mean you're

managing *well*. I didn't mean to imply that you're not, obviously.' She sighed, shaking her head, seeming to have trouble expressing herself. 'But I thought that perhaps, if I could look after Poppy for you, just for an hour or so sometimes, it might give you a chance to get ahead of your deadlines, and maybe even approach some potential new clients. Build up your business a bit more.'

'Oh, I see. Well, you're right, it wouldn't hurt at all to acquire a few more clients. It's really nice of you to offer, Crystal. But only if you've got a bit of time to spare occasionally. You're working full-time yourself.'

'Yes, but I've got nothing whatsoever to do with myself in the evenings. Watching TV on your own gets boring, night after night. Honestly, an occasional hour or so of playing with Poppy before she goes to bed would seriously break up the monotony of my week.'

'OK, then.' I smiled my agreement. I could sympathise, when she put it like that. If I didn't have Poppy, I'd probably be climbing the walls myself, being at home on my own, night after night, with just the TV – or more work – for company.

'So how about this Wednesday?' she said. 'About half past five? I can come straight from work.'

'Um... yes, OK, that'd be good. I might still be

giving Poppy her dinner though. She normally has it around five, or five-thirty.'

'No problem, I can help with that, can't I?'

All her hesitation and awkwardness seemed to have suddenly vanished; she was sounding almost excited now. I couldn't help laughing.

'It's the first time I've heard anyone sound so chuffed at the thought of helping with a fractious toddler at the end of a long day. She'll be at her worst, you realise? Tired and grumpy, not all smiles like she was on Saturday, full of ice cream.'

'All the more reason why it would help you to have some backup. Seriously, Gemma, I just want to help. Give you a bit of support. What are friends for?'

'Ah, bless you. Well, if ever I can do anything for you in return, you must let me know, then, OK?'

'You are. You *are* doing something for me – letting me spend time with your daughter. It's going to be a pleasure.'

I thought about this later, on my way home that evening. It had seemed really odd, the way she'd approached her offer, all awkward and embarrassed. I couldn't quite make it out. But I supposed that if it did give Crystal some degree of happiness, to have an hour or so with Poppy now and then, and at the same time gave me the chance to start trying to expand my business, perhaps I should think of it as a mutual benefit. I'd seen the way she'd looked at Poppy, so longingly, and I did feel for her, knowing how much she'd have liked a child herself. And Poppy seemed to really like her, so where was the harm?

* * *

Crystal arrived straight from work that Wednesday, as she'd suggested – she must have left on the dot of five o'clock as she was with me by five-fifteen – and immediately took over from me, dishing up Poppy's dinner and shooing me out of the kitchen, telling me to get on with my work. It felt odd, just walking away, leaving someone else in charge of my kitchen and my daughter, but I did have quite a lot of work to get through so I obeyed, settling down at my laptop and closing the door behind me – as she'd suggested – to block out the sound of the chatter between them. After half an hour or so, though, I couldn't resist having a peek into the kitchen, to see Crystal washing up and Poppy sitting at the table, engrossed in crayoning on a sheet of paper from her 'craft drawer'. She looked up, saw me and gave a squeal.

'No, Mummy, no looking!' she said, trying to cover the paper with her arms.

Crystal turned round and smiled at me. 'It's supposed to be a surprise for you. It's not finished yet. Go on, get back to your work – we're fine, aren't we, Poppy?'

'Go on,' Poppy echoed. 'We're fine.'

'Well... I normally let her watch half an hour of TV – the children's programmes – before bed. Wind-down time.'

'Lovely. Well, if you find the right channel and put it on for us, Poppy and I can just finish off in here, then we'll swap rooms, OK?' Crystal stopped, looking at me thoughtfully. 'Didn't you say you normally work upstairs?'

'Well, yes.' I had a small computer desk in my bedroom, and it was true, that was where I usually worked. 'But I didn't want to shut myself away up there, while you're down here, in case—'

'In case we needed you?' She smiled. 'Honestly, we'll be absolutely fine. The whole idea is for you to be able to get on in peace.'

'We're fine,' Poppy mimicked again.

'Well, OK, then,' I said. 'But call me if you do need me for anything, all right?'

'Sure. We will.'

Feeling slightly redundant, I went back to the living room, turned the TV on to one of Poppy's favourite programmes with the volume low, then took my laptop upstairs and settled back down to work. I left my bedroom door ajar, so after a few more minutes, I was able to hear the volume raised just a touch, and hear Crystal and Poppy laughing together as they watched the cartoon. I had to make a supreme effort not to go downstairs and watch it with them. I went back to concentrating on my work, but when, a little later, I heard Poppy clambering up the stairs I immediately got up and went out to meet her at the top.

'Hello! Are you getting ready for bed now, sweetie?'

'Getting my PJs,' she said, rushing past me and into her bedroom.

'Ready for your story?' I asked. 'Which one shall we have tonight?'

'Want Crystal to read my story.' Poppy gave me a frown. 'Not Mummy.'

'I'll read it down here,' Crystal called up from where she was waiting at the bottom of the stairs, 'so we can leave you in peace.'

'No, honestly, I can take over now,' I said. 'I've had plenty of—'

'*Not* Mummy!' Poppy repeated, giving me a little push back into my bedroom. She was holding her pyjamas in a bundle in her arms and the smell of warm milk was wafting up the stairs.

'Wait at the top of the stairs, Poppy,' Crystal said. 'I'm coming up to help you.' She smiled at me as she appeared on the landing. 'I don't want her falling down the stairs, carrying her PJs. Have you chosen a story book, Poppy, or would you like a made-up story?'

'Made up!' Poppy's eyes were bright with excitement. She looked back at me and frowned again. '*Not* Mummy.'

'Go on, Gemma, get on with your work, we're having fun! I'll get her ready for bed and clean her teeth, don't worry.'

I felt dismissed but I just shrugged. 'OK. But be very good, all right, Pops? I'll come and kiss you goodnight when you're in bed, then.'

'OK.'

To be honest it was difficult to concentrate on working, after that. From downstairs I could hear the low murmur of Crystal's voice as she told her story, and the occasional giggle from Poppy in response, and a little later I heard them coming back upstairs, heard all the familiar bedtime sounds – the bathroom tap running, the loo flushing, the blinds being pulled closed in Poppy's bedroom, even the creak and bounce as she threw herself onto her little low bed. Then the night light being switched on and the murmur of voices – *Good night, sleep tight.* And ridiculously – instead of feeling grateful for the heaven-sent opportunity I'd been given to have an hour or two to myself, to concentrate on my work... I felt left out. Replaced. Almost... dared I say it? *Jealous.*

Telling myself not to be so childish, I closed my laptop and got to my feet, meeting Crystal as she came out of Poppy's bedroom, and – whispering a *thank you* – tiptoed into the bedroom myself and sat down on the bed. Poppy was pretending to be asleep already, but I put my arm around her and planted a kiss on her forehead.

'Night night, my angel,' I murmured. 'See you in the morning.'

She opened her eyes. 'Crystal be here?'

'Not in the morning, sweetie, no.'

'Owh,' she complained, pulling a face. 'Not fair.'

* * *

'I can't thank you enough,' I told Crystal when I joined her in the kitchen, where she was wiping down sur-faces and putting things away.

'Oh, honestly, I've loved every minute of it. I should be thanking you! Poppy is such a little darling. Oh, look, this is the picture she made for you. She was supposed to give it to you, sorry – she must have forgotten.'

That says it all, I thought, slightly resentfully, as I looked at the picture: an almost-square red shape with black circular squiggles underneath it.

'Poppy was singing "all day long" to herself while she was crayoning,' Crystal said, looking mystified.

I nodded and smiled. At least this was something Poppy and I shared just between us. 'It's a bus,' I said.

'Ah yes. I can see it now. Very artistic!' Crystal smiled back at me. 'Did you get plenty of work done?'

'Well, yes, quite a bit. But some of it was thinking time,' I said, as if I had to excuse myself for the little I'd done. 'I'm planning an advertising campaign.'

'For one of your clients?'

'Well, actually – for myself. You're right, I need to attract some new clients if I want to expand my business. And I do need to do that, now I'm the only wage-earner.'

'Excellent idea, Gem. Well, in that case, the more I can do to help you out with Poppy, the more you'll be able to work on the campaign, and in time, the more clients you can take on.'

'But in that case I'll have to pay you—'

'Absolutely not,' she shot back. 'Pay me for enjoying myself?'

I stared at her. She meant it – I could see she did. She was actually offering to help me with Poppy – to help me to get more work – simply because it made her happy. I felt my earlier resentment slip away. How ungrateful of me to begrudge such absolute kindness. What was the matter with me? I should feel nothing *but* gratitude. It was *wonderful* that Poppy and my new friend seemed to have developed such a rapport in such a short time. Only a pathetic, immature version of a mother would be jealous. Only an idiot would re-sent such an opportunity.

I turned back to face her, smiling.

'I'll tell you what, then,' I said. 'I'm going to get us a takeaway, OK? It's not much of a payment, but...'

'Well, OK. But only tonight – not every time I come to help. That'll be too much. Maybe next time we can cook together.'

'You're on.' I gave her a hug. 'Thank you so much. I'm so grateful.'

'Me too,' she insisted. 'Same time tomorrow, then?'

16

CRYSTAL

Poppy, sweet, beautiful little Poppy! It was an absolute pleasure to spend time with her during our evenings together. I was loving every minute of it, feeling quite at a loss on the evenings that I didn't go to Gemma's house, when I had to go back to my usual routine of sitting at home on my own with the TV. Gemma seemed to enjoy my company too; I'm glad we agreed on cooking together. The takeaway on the first night was really nice, of course, but it was even more fun, chopping vegetables and meat for a stir fry, chatting while we worked together, sitting at her kitchen table to share the meal and then washing up together. I was pretty sure it made a nice change for her, too, and I must have tired Poppy out, playing games with her before she went to bed, because we didn't hear a thing from her all evening. And of course, while I was keeping Poppy amused, Gemma was able to get on with some more work.

I thought she was glad, now, that she'd agreed to let me help out. Let me spend time with Poppy. I still needed to be careful not to get too pushy, though. If it was up to me, I'd have seen Poppy every day, but I realised Gemma would find that a bit weird. Anyway, I had to go to my group on Monday evenings. I needed to keep going, even though I didn't actually think I needed it any more; I felt so much better, so much calmer and more settled now. I had something to live for, something special in my life, in between the scheduled trips, marked in red in my diary. The trips that I looked forward to so much, the trips that always then ended up distressing me so much, bringing me back down, tumbling down, into the black void of depression all over again. Perhaps now, now I had Gemma and Poppy in my life, I would be able to manage it all a bit better the next time. I might have been able to endure however it turned out on the day, without getting myself into such a state.

The therapist who sat in on our Monday evenings and insisted on quizzing me every week about my state of mind, had actually agreed that I seemed to be improving. Of course, she didn't know what I was up to – but I was improving, that was surely what mattered.

I liked to think my relationship with Gemma and Poppy was of mutual benefit, helping both of us – all three of us. Perhaps it was fate that I found her that day, crying in the toilets.

17

GEMMA

'Have you got any plans for the weekend?' Mum asked me that Friday when she brought Poppy back home in the evening.

'Only meeting up with Crystal tomorrow morning as usual,' I said.

She nodded, looking at me in silence for a moment as if she wasn't sure whether to comment or not.

'That's the usual thing now, is it? Every Saturday? The beach café and the beach?'

'Well, yes. While the weather's still so nice, why not? If it rains, I suppose she'll just come to my place, like last time. She came round a couple of evenings in the week, actually. Looked after Poppy for me so I could get on with some extra work—'

'Did she?' Mum was frowning now, and sounding a bit worried. Or maybe hurt. 'Gem, you should have told me if you needed some more help. I mean, I'm pleased to hear you've got plenty of work, but *I* would have looked after Poppy for you, you know that.'

'You already have her all day on Fridays. And you're working yourself, three days every week.'

'I could help out at weekends, though, couldn't I? I was going to ask you if you wanted to come for Sunday dinner, but if it'd be more helpful, I could just have Poppy again so you can—'

'No, Mum – we'd love to come for dinner on Sunday, wouldn't we, Poppy?'

Poppy, who'd rushed in from Mum's car to give me a hug, was now sitting on the sofa with one of her teddies, singing to herself. She just looked up at us and nodded, obviously totally unconcerned about where she was going to have Sunday dinner.

'There's no need at all for me to have any more childcare,' I told Mum firmly. 'Crystal and I just like spending time together, and she happened to offer to look after Poppy occasionally, so—'

'At your house. Not at hers?'

'At mine, yes.' I frowned. 'What's wrong with that? She's being nice.'

'But you've hardly known her for more than five minutes. Are you paying her for this?'

'No, Mum, she won't take any payment, but I treated her to a takeaway and we cooked together on the second day. She just enjoys playing with Poppy and, well, Poppy seems to like her too, so it gave me the chance to start working out how to build up my client base. It'll be really great if I can get a few more clients; I need the extra work now.'

'Well, if you do get really busy with new clients, I'll definitely help you out with Poppy for another day a week.'

'If I get that busy, Mum, I might be able to pay for another day at nursery. Seriously, at the moment it's just the occasional favour from a friend, OK? She's lovely, you'd like her. I might not have known her that long but we get along together really well.' I didn't know why I felt so defensive about it. I turned back to Poppy. '*You* like Crystal, don't you, Pops?'

'Yes!' She jumped up, looking excited. 'Crystal put me to bed!'

'Not tonight, baby. Another time, perhaps.'

'Owh, not fair!' Poppy slumped down on the sofa again. 'Want Crystal.'

'You see?' I said to Mum, laughing.

'Well...' Mum shrugged and gave Poppy a smile. 'What can I say?'

'Anyway, we'll definitely see you on Sunday, then, if you're sure.' I gave Mum a kiss. 'Thanks again for today. As always.'

'You're welcome, love. Yes, see you both on Sunday. Bye, Poppy-Pops.'

'Bye bye!' Poppy waved and carried on singing to herself. It was 'The Wheels on the Bus'.

'*All day long!*' I joined in, sitting down next to her and giving her tummy a tickle. 'How about getting into your PJs now, miss?'

'Crystal put me to bed?'

'No, Poppy, not tonight!' I laughed. 'Another time soon, OK?'

* * *

As it happened, the next day it was pouring with rain. Crystal called, sounding disappointed. It definitely wasn't a day for the outside tables of the beach café, nor for a paddle.

'Well, we could go somewhere else,' I said. 'Or you could just come round to mine again – it's a bit boring for you, but—'

'Oh, are you sure?' she said, immediately brightening up. 'Of course it's not boring, it'd be lovely to see Poppy again. And you, of course!' she added as an afterthought. 'I'll bring some cakes.'

'You don't need to—' I began, but she'd already ended the call.

Half an hour later she was at the door, dripping rain from her rainbow-patterned poncho. I'd been feeling a bit low, looking out at the relentless downpour, and starting to think about the approaching winter. The thought of being on my own during the winter was so much more depressing than in the summer. But once again, as soon as Crystal walked in, everything seemed brighter. Her crazy clothes, the colours, designs, and mismatched jewellery she wore, the purple highlights in her hair, the whole aura of *different* she gave off as she breezed in, calling out to Poppy, grabbing her and swinging her around in her arms – it was enough to lift anyone's spirits.

'Here are the cakes,' she announced, putting a carrier bag down on the table. 'Sorry they're not homemade, I didn't exactly have time. I hope they're not too full of horrible additives and colourings and, well, sugar, but—'

'Ah, we won't worry about that too much; it doesn't hurt to have an occasional little treat – thank you, love,' I said, giving her a hug. 'It's so nice to see you.'

Poppy by now was almost hysterical with excitement about the contents of the bag, so I opened it and took out a packet of gooey-looking chocolate cupcakes, a lemon drizzle cake and some Bakewell slices. Poppy's eyes were almost out on stalks.

'You shouldn't have bought all these!' I remonstrated. 'You'll have to take some of them home with you.'

'I don't really eat cakes,' she said with a shrug.

'So why...?'

But she was too busy chasing Poppy out of the kitchen to answer me. I shook my head. I'd have to make sure I returned her generosity another time. Meanwhile, I made coffee, put a selection of the cakes on a plate and called Poppy to come and sit at the table.

'Do you mind if we sit in here?' I said to Crystal. 'She'd make a terrible mess if I let her loose with a cake in the living room.'

'Of course I don't mind.' She pulled out a chair. 'This is so nice, being in here together, warm and cosy while the rain pours down outside. Lovely, isn't it, Pops?'

'Lovely,' Poppy agreed, reaching for one of the chocolate cupcakes.

'Ask nicely first, Poppy,' I reminded her.

'Please can I have?' she said, looking beseechingly at Crystal. The buttercream from the cake was already all over her fingers.

'Of course, sweetheart.' Crystal helped her take the cake out of its wrapper, and I got a knife to cut it into halves. 'There you go!' She laughed as Poppy licked her fingers first. 'That's the best bit, isn't it?'

We sipped our coffee in silence for a while and I persuaded Crystal to have a slice of the lemon drizzle cake so I wouldn't feel guilty for eating one myself.

'I've had a response from one of the potential clients I approached the other day,' I told her. 'They want me to quote them for some work: a new website and possibly a social media campaign.'

'Wow, Gemma, that's amazing!'

'Well, I'm not getting ahead of myself. I've got to pitch the quote for the website right, first. I presume they'll be getting other quotes.'

'Well, I'll be keeping my fingers crossed for you. You're going to be busy, aren't you, if you get the work.'

'Yes. But I'll manage. I can easily fit in more work in the evenings after Poppy's in bed.'

'And tire yourself out completely? I'd be more than happy to look after Poppy sometimes at weekends. Just say the word. Poppy, how would you like me to come and play with you sometimes on a Saturday, like today, while Mummy does some work?'

'With cake?' Poppy asked, wiping chocolatey fingers across her face.

'We don't *ask* for cake, Poppy,' I reminded her gently. 'Sorry, Crystal.'

But Crystal was smiling so lovingly at my daughter I couldn't help but feel my heart melt. She seemed to love her so much – and despite her wishing she had her own children, she wasn't coming across as being jealous or resentful – far from it. She seemed almost childlike herself in some ways, as if she and Poppy were just two little friends. And Poppy seemed to love her, too. I felt a bit bad, knowing Mum had already offered to look after Poppy more often if I needed it, and I knew how much she absolutely adored her little granddaughter. But Crystal lived nearer, and it seemed that spending time with me and Poppy had given her a new purpose in life, whereas – whatever Mum said about having plenty of spare time – she was a busy lady, with lots of her own friends and activities she enjoyed.

'OK,' I said. 'If I do get inundated with new work, I'll let you know. Thank you.'

* * *

The rain stopped a little later, and although it was still grey and chilly outside, we decided to go for a walk to work off the calories from the cake. Crystal asked to push Poppy's buggy, and kept up a running commentary to her about the passing traffic, the flowers in people's front gardens, the clouds in the sky and whatever else we saw as we headed towards the park. I remembered doing this all the time when Poppy was a baby – trying to be the perfect mum who gives her child the very best start in life. But my own life had gradually got in the way, and these days I was ashamed to realise I probably didn't talk to Poppy so much while we were out, or engage her as well as Crystal was doing. I supposed it was a novelty for her, but even so, it made me determined to try to do better.

When we got to the park, Poppy wanted to get out of the buggy and run ahead of us.

'She'll be fine,' I reassured Crystal, who'd started to run after her. 'She won't go too far ahead.'

'Oh, I just wanted to run with her!' she said. 'Come on, Pops, let's have a race!'

I watched in a kind of wonder for the rest of the morning, as Crystal played with Poppy in the playground, pushing her in one of the baby swings and catching her at the bottom of the little slide, and chatted to her about the ducks on the duck pond, choosing their favourite duck. When we reached the little café at the other side of the park, Crystal looked at me, raising her eyebrows, and whispered that it was a long time since we'd had coffee and cake, and perhaps somebody might like some lunch? I was amazed to see that it was nearly one o'clock.

'Yes, OK, but I'm paying: no arguments,' I insisted.

'Cake?' Poppy said, seeing the display at the counter. And then, catching sight of someone holding a cornet, 'Ice cream!'

'No,' I told her firmly. 'A drink and a sandwich, Poppy. They do special little sandwiches for children. You've already had cake today.'

Her eyes started to fill up with tears and her mouth started quivering. She stamped her feet and I sighed, guessing we were now in for a full-blown tantrum.

'Hey, Poppy, do you know what happens if you eat too much cake or ice cream?' Crystal said, crouching down to her level.

'No.' Poppy stared at her, interested, holding fire on the crying fit.

'Your tummy gets fatter, and fatter, and fatter...' Crystal was tickling her tummy as she spoke, and Poppy couldn't help but start to giggle. I took the opportunity to order her a sandwich. 'And in the end...'

'Does it burst?' Poppy asked excitedly.

'It might do! It might get *so* fat, it goes BANG!' Crystal clapped her hands together hard, making Poppy jump and then double up with laughter.

'BANG!' she shouted as Crystal led her to a table in the corner. 'BANG, BANG!'

'All right, let's do it a bit more quietly,' Crystal said hurriedly. 'How does it go? Whisper! It's our secret! *Bang, bang!*'

'It's amazing,' I whispered as I sat down at the table with a tray of drinks and sandwiches, 'how something like that can seem funny to a two-year-old.'

And it was amazing, too, I found myself thinking as I smiled at my little girl tucking into her sandwich without another word of protest, how brilliantly my friend seemed, instinctively, to be able to handle children. And it was just so, so sad that she hadn't any of her own.

18

CRYSTAL

It was the best day I could remember for such a long time. Definitely the best since, well, since everything that happened. I actually forgot about it all, completely, for those few hours. I started to feel like I belonged somewhere again, like I had a family of my own. And although that was exactly why I knew this whole thing was dangerous, it made me so happy, and helped me to get through the rest of the weekend and the next few evenings on my own. So I refused to think about the danger.

If I'd been honest with people about it – people at the self-help group, for instance – then I know they'd have warned me, told me it wasn't a good idea – that, yes, it was dangerous. Not dangerous to anyone else, obviously; no, just to me. To my mental health, my recovery, my chances of... possibly... one day coming out the other side of the nightmare I'd been living through. Of getting my life back. Of regaining everything that really mattered to me. But of course, I didn't tell them. If anyone asked me what I'd been doing lately, I fobbed them off, told them I was doing what I normally did: working all day, sitting on my own every evening and weekend, watching the TV. To keep everyone happy, I occasionally mentioned that I'd had lunch with a new friend at work. They liked that. They liked to think I was making an effort.

But I was getting closer and closer to the date marked in red in my diary, and I'd already had a phone call reminding me about it – as if I needed a reminder. Every time I thought about it, I felt myself go weak and my heart started racing. I didn't even know if it was excitement or dread: probably a mixture of the two. There'd been so many times I'd looked forward to these trips and then the whole thing ended up being a disaster, as usual, as always. And instead of coping with it the way I'd been schooled by everyone to do, I'd got myself into a terrible state, putting my recovery back all over again, as well as my hopes of ever getting things back to normal.

But then again, what was normal for me, now? Normal had gone forever: it had gone when that bastard turned his back on me. And chose the very worst moment of my life to do it.

19

GEMMA

I was finding the dreary autumn weather and the darker evenings depressing. I noticed, more than any previous year, how everything was dying or closing down: the leaves withering and falling, the sea and the sky grey and bleak, the beach, the seafront and cafés quieter and sadder-looking as the summer visitors all went home. Added to my depression was the fact that I'd had no luck yet with the CSA tracking down Jack or even his family. Had they *all* disappeared? Really? Just to save Jack from having to pay what was due for the care of his own child? It didn't seem credible.

I only really cheered up when Crystal was around. I soon heard that I'd not only won the job with the company who wanted the new website, blog posts and regular social media updates, but I'd also got another website creation job for a small local business. This was on top of my existing clients, so it was really helpful to have Crystal around for the evenings, entertaining Poppy and getting her ready for bed. That next Saturday, the weather was good enough for Crystal to take her out for a brisk walk down to the beach, where they ran around and played to warm themselves up, leaving me in peace to get on with my work. In the evening, after she'd put Poppy to bed, we cooked another meal together and Crystal stayed over, on my sofa. She claimed it was so comfy she preferred it to her own bed.

The only problem with all this was that I knew it was upsetting Mum. She was still hurt that she wasn't the one I was asking to care for Poppy.

'But you're still having her for a whole day every week!' I reminded her once again while we were having a cup of tea together on the Friday morning, when I dropped Poppy off. I'd happened to mention that Crystal was coming round that evening, and now I was wishing I hadn't.

'And I've told you, I'll keep her for the evening if you need to work!' she protested. 'I'll keep her overnight – I'd love to. And I obviously wouldn't want anything in return—'

'Nor does Crystal, Mum. The only reason I treat her to a meal is that I don't want to take advantage of her – and anyway, we enjoy each other's company. We're both on our own—'

'So am I,' she said quietly.

'Oh, Mum!' I gave her a hug, feeling bewildered by her attitude. She'd never before seemed jealous of me or Poppy spending time with anyone else. 'You've got such a full life, so many friends, and clubs that you belong to, quite apart from your job.'

'None of them are as important to me as you and Poppy are.'

'I get that, and I'm grateful for it, honestly. But can't you be pleased for me, that I've got a new friend?'

'I don't even know her, Gemma. I haven't met her. It all seems to have happened so suddenly.'

I sighed. I was beginning to lose patience, but didn't want to show it.

'Yes, well, my life changed pretty suddenly, didn't it? If Jack hadn't done a runner on me, I might not have needed a new friend so badly. She came along at exactly the right time, that's all.'

Mum nodded. 'I know. I suppose that's what worries me, if I'm honest. It's... so much, so soon, that's all. I mean, you're letting her take Poppy out on her own. Are you quite sure you trust her?'

'What? Of course I trust her, Mum. And Poppy loves her.'

She shrugged and forced a smile. 'Well, I'm sure you know what you're doing. And of course, I'm glad you're feeling happier.'

'I'm not, not really. But Crystal helps. As do you, obviously. And I'm grateful to you both.'

We left it there, but it played on my mind. It was the nearest thing to an argument I could remember having with my lovely mum for such a long time. It upset me that she seemed to disapprove of my friend without having even met her.

'I think she's a bit jealous of someone else being involved with her granddaughter,' I said to Crystal that evening over dinner after Poppy was in bed. 'It's not like her at all.'

I knew I probably shouldn't have been talking to her about Mum like that, but I'd been worried about it since the conversation with her, and couldn't help blurting it out.

Crystal seemed to think this over before replying.

'She doesn't know me, Gem. Perhaps it would help if I were to meet her? Introduce myself?'

'I suppose so. I just hadn't thought it should be necessary. I thought Mum would trust me not to let anyone unsuitable take care of Poppy.'

'Well, I suppose it's only natural for her to be concerned. You're her only daughter, Poppy's her only grandchild, and she doesn't know the first thing about me.'

'Yes. I guess so.' I took another mouthful and chewed it thoughtfully before making a decision. 'Right, I'll ask her to come over and have lunch with us tomorrow. Is that OK with you?'

Crystal put her fork down and sat with her head lowered for a moment, biting her lip, before replying without looking up at me, 'Sorry. I can't make it tomorrow. I was going to tell you: I can't do this weekend at all.'

'Oh. OK.'

I admit I was a bit surprised. Crystal had been spending the whole of every Saturday with me for weeks now. It had become such a routine that I suppose I'd come to expect it. Of course, she was perfectly entitled to have a life of her own, and to have other things to do at weekends that didn't involve me – it was just that she'd always made it sound like she didn't. That, in fact, being with me and Poppy was all she wanted to do, and as often as possible. She never talked about having any other kind of social life, apart from the self-help group. Perhaps she was going to spend time with some friends from there. Or perhaps she was going to see her brother – she'd mentioned that he occasionally came down from London to see her.

But she didn't say so, and I didn't want to appear nosy, or needy, by asking. We sat in an awkward silence for a few minutes, Crystal still not meeting my eyes, and when she jumped up and took our dirty plates to the sink, I took it to mean that the conversation was over. Perhaps, despite being the one who'd suggested it, she *didn't* really want to meet my mum – or not yet, anyway. I dropped the subject.

The following day, when there was no visit from Crystal, I was shocked by how odd it felt. Although it had only been a few weeks, our Saturdays together had quickly become such a fun part of my life that I suddenly felt almost bereft without her. I told myself not to be ridiculous. I would just have to do all the usual things with Poppy – the usual things I *used* to do pre-Crystal – and try to fob off her questions about why Crystal wasn't there. But Poppy wasn't having it.

'Crystal day! Going to the park!'

'Not today, Pops. Crystal isn't coming today.'

'Yes. You said Saturday, Crystal comes. You said!'

'She *has* been coming on Saturdays, yes, but today she can't. She has to... go somewhere else, OK?'

Poppy stamped her foot. 'No, *not* OK. I want Crystal.'

'We can still go to the park, all right? I'll take you instead.'

'I want to go with Crystal,' she insisted, and promptly threw herself on the floor and started crying. I really didn't have the patience for it, but it was my own fault, I told myself, for letting her get too attached to Crystal so quickly. It stood to reason that there would be days when Crystal couldn't come round, and I couldn't have Poppy going into meltdown over it every time.

After she was finally in bed that night, I had my dinner and then got on with some work for an hour or so before watching TV, but I felt suddenly lost, alone, and lonely. I found myself dwelling on my situation, thinking about Jack and what he'd done to me, and it made me even more aware of how different my life would have been by now if Crystal hadn't come into it.

But there was something else nagging at me, too, something I was trying not to admit to, even to myself. However hard I'd tried to fight it, I couldn't keep denying it now: I was jealous. It hurt. Hurt that my little girl would rather go to the park with my friend than with me. I was shocked that this had happened so fast – so fast I'd hardly even noticed. I'd just been pleased that they got along so well together, pleased that I had a new friend, one who not only seemed to love Poppy but was also happy to look after her for me. And somehow I'd let it get to the stage where already, Poppy seemed to love her more than me.

Jealousy is such a destructive emotion. And being alone and miserable on a Saturday evening felt so much worse than on all the other days. I gave myself a little shake. Poppy was no different from me: we both enjoyed Crystal's company, both felt happier when she was around. I shouldn't be cross with Poppy for expressing her feelings when I'd been feeling exactly the same – lost and lonely because Crystal wasn't there.

20

CRYSTAL

Afterwards, after the weekend was over, I wished I could have just gone to Gemma's as usual: played with Poppy, taken her out to the park or the beach, and perhaps met Gemma's mum, too, as she'd suggested, and had lunch with her – instead of spending my weekend the way I did.

As always, I'd built it up into such a big deal in my mind. It wouldn't be quite right to say I was looking forward to it, because past experience had taught me that it never worked out the way I'd hoped. But I'd convinced myself that this time, finally, was going to be the time when it was different. And that even if it *didn't* work out, this time I'd remain calm, no matter what; that I wouldn't fall apart and cause a scene.

I was feeling nervous but resolute on the Saturday morning as I set off on the journey. Resolute, because however nervous I felt, I was so determined to make it a good experience. I'd brought a little present with me, as usual, and if it wasn't accepted I wasn't going to be upset. I was still going to be happy that I'd at least gone there, made the visit, made contact.

As it was quite a long journey, we always stayed overnight in a B&B so we didn't have to drive home on the same day. I often thought it must be nice for Sarah, who came with me. Like a little mini-break. Or it might have been, if she didn't have to cope with someone who turned into a raving nutcase on every occasion. That was me, the raving nutcase.

In my room in the B&B, waiting for Sarah's knock on my door to say she was ready, I looked at myself in the mirror and gave myself another talking-to. This time, I told myself, it was going to be different. This time, when we got there, I was going to stay calm no matter what, no matter how hurtful, how distressing it was. I was better now; meeting Gemma and Poppy had helped me, I would cope, I'd prove to everyone that I could handle it.

But as it turned out, I couldn't. I fell apart, just like I always did. I came home a wailing, snivelling wreck, and no amount of cajoling and comforting, repeated assurances that I mustn't give up, it'd all work out OK in the end – none of it was going to help, because I'd failed, yet again. My carefully wrapped present had been thrown across the room and the visit had to be written off, as always. A disaster, as always. And I was left wondering – as always – whether it would ever be any different.

21

GEMMA

The next Monday when Crystal and I had lunch together, she was unusually quiet. Even her clothes were less flamboyant than usual, as if she'd dressed to reflect her mood – a long, plain brown skirt and cream blouse, and a black cardigan thrown on carelessly when we left the building. I thought perhaps she was tired after her weekend – presuming she'd been to see her brother or perhaps had him to stay with her, and maybe they'd had a couple of late nights. But when she remained almost silent while we were eating, I asked her if she was feeling OK.

'Yes,' she said abruptly. Then, looking up at me, she shook her head and apologised. 'Sorry, I'm just... I've just got a bit of a headache, that's all.'

'Oh, you poor thing. I've got some Paracetamol in my bag if you—'

'No, it's OK, thanks.' She forced a smile. 'I'm just not very good company, sorry.'

'No need to apologise. Did you have a good weekend, though? Poppy and I missed you.'

She shook her head again. 'Not really. I wish I'd spent it with you and Poppy.'

'Oh.' I stared at her. She looked upset, and not just in the way someone with a headache might do. It was something else, obviously – something about the weekend. I put a hand on hers. 'I'm sorry to hear it wasn't fun—'

'Far from it,' she muttered, toying with her couscous salad.

I didn't know quite what to say. I didn't want to be nosy, to ask questions – she'd surely tell me if she wanted to – but she'd been there for me whenever I'd been upset about Jack, and I wanted to be an equally good friend in return.

'Is there anything I can do?' I asked gently. 'I can see something's upset you, love. You don't have to tell me, obviously, but you know I'm here for you if you want to talk it over.'

'Thanks,' she said gruffly, and I was surprised to

see there were tears in her eyes. It was so unlike her, I jumped up and went to put my arms around her. But she quickly wiped her eyes on the sleeve of her cardigan and muttered that there wasn't anything I could do. 'It's just something I have to live with,' she added quietly, almost as if she was talking to herself.

She sighed, and nibbled a forkful of lettuce, looking like she was trying to convince me she was OK now – but it was pretty obvious she wasn't.

'You've helped me so much, Crystal,' I said, sitting back down and talking to her quietly. 'So I hope you know, that if ever you needed any help or advice yourself, or just someone to confide in – someone to have a moan about things with – I'll always do what I can, and whatever it is, it'd never go any further. OK?'

She nodded without meeting my eyes. And then, to my surprise and dismay, she suddenly threw down her fork and began to cry properly.

'Oh, Crystal, what is it?' I said, feeling quite alarmed now. 'Please tell me – there must be something I can do to help.'

She shook her head, almost violently. 'There isn't. And I can't tell you – you'd hate me if I did.'

'Don't be ridiculous, of course I'd never hate you! It doesn't matter what it is—'

'Oh, Gemma, *please* stop being so nice to me. Please don't make me feel any worse, any more guilty than I already do!'

I sat back in my chair, shocked. 'Guilty? Why on earth would you feel guilty?'

'Because you don't know the truth about me. I've been lying to you, Gemma.'

'Lying to me?' I stared at her. 'What are you talking about?'

But she just kept her head down, sniffing over her salad, wiping her eyes, blowing her nose, doing anything, it seemed, rather than look at me or answer.

'What do you mean?' I asked again, more insistently. 'Lying about *what*?'

Finally, slowly, she seemed to have got herself together. She took a few deep breaths, and looked up at me. There was something in her eyes I didn't quite recognise. Was it fear? Regret? Anxiety? Whatever, I had a feeling she was wishing she'd never let those words about lying out of her mouth.

'My name's not really Crystal,' she said – and stopped, waiting for me to ask the obvious question.

'OK,' I said slowly. 'So what is it?'

'Suzanne. Suzie.' Again she stopped, just looking at me, waiting, as if she was expecting a reaction.

'Right.' I stared back at her. 'But you call yourself Crystal? Is that it?'

'Yes.'

For what felt like ages, we sat and stared at each other. She'd stopped crying, but her face was expressionless, and I was finding the whole exchange frankly quite odd. Did it matter that she called herself by a different name? Was that a crime?

'Is it... your middle name, or something?' I asked eventually, as the awkward silence was going on for so long I was beginning to feel almost freaked out by it.

'No. It was the self-help group. Everyone who joins is given a kind of pseudonym, in case they don't want people to know who they are. Most people who join have been going through some sort of crisis, and some are... kind of shy about revealing themselves, you know?'

I nodded. 'I see. Yes, I get that.' She was talking more normally now, sounding... somehow relieved, as if she suddenly felt she was on safe ground. The words were almost rushing out of her.

'There's a woman called Breeze, and a young girl called Sunshine, and a man called Flint, and – well, if they want to reveal who they are, it's up to them, but we all use our Planet Earth names at the meetings.'

'Planet Earth names. That's rather nice.'

'So that's why I got called Crystal.'

'Well, it's a nice name anyway.' I smiled. It was quite obviously not just her name that she was feeling upset about that day, and I had no idea why she should feel guilty for not telling me. 'Presumably you preferred it to, um, Suzie.'

'Yes, I did. So I decided to keep it.'

'And are you happy for me to still call you Crystal?'

'Yes. Everybody does, now.'

'Well, that's fine, then, isn't it? I wouldn't exactly call it a lie.' I laughed. 'Lots of people call themselves by different names.'

'Yes, but – well, look, now we're getting to be such good friends, I just felt a bit bad about not telling you my real name, that's all. Sorry for making a fuss. It... as I said, it wasn't a good weekend, and I suppose I'm just feeling a bit down.'

'Ah, I'm really sorry your weekend was a disappointment. And I won't ask any questions if you'd prefer to keep... whatever happened... to yourself.' I paused, and then suggested as brightly as I could, 'Why don't you come round tonight and we'll watch a film or something?'

'Thanks, Gemma, but it's Monday, though. The group meeting. If I don't go, they... get worried.'

'Really?' I frowned, and then shrugged. It was nice

that she had a supportive group, but it seemed a bit extreme that she couldn't even miss a meeting occasionally. 'Well, OK – you're welcome another night, then. Whenever you want, you know that.'

'Thanks.' She was smiling now. 'Perhaps I'll come on Wednesday, if that works for you. It'll cheer me up to see Poppy again.'

* * *

All that evening, after I'd put Poppy to bed and while I was supposed to be finishing off a blog post for a client, I sat in silence, puzzling over that strange conversation. Crystal had been so upset – something had obviously gone very wrong for her at the weekend, something she didn't want to talk about. But the whole thing of lying to me about her name was just bizarre. She'd looked almost scared, there, for a minute, as if she half expected me to be furious about it. And the way she cheered up – as she always did – at the very idea of seeing Poppy... it was a bit over the top. Of course, it was really nice that she loved Poppy the way she obviously did, and I'd schooled myself sternly about my jealousy over the way Poppy loved her back. But I was also starting, just a little, to feel a bit used. I was starting to wonder if Crystal really wanted to be my friend as much as she said she did – as much as I thought she did – or if all she really cared about was being Poppy's honorary 'auntie'.

And then I remembered how much she'd helped me, how kind she'd been to me when I found out about Jack, how supportive and sympathetic she was, how nice it was of her to look after Poppy so that I could work. She was a good friend, of course she was. OK, so she had some kind of hang-up about her name – what did that matter? Perhaps she needed my support and sympathy now, and I needed to step up and give it. She could come round any time she liked, even if all she wanted to do was play with Poppy. If it made her happy, who was I to begrudge her that? I definitely needed a friend myself. We were our own mutual support group, and it was petty of me to feel jealous of her love for my daughter, just as much as it was childish to feel jealous of Poppy's love for her.

* * *

Crystal was a bit quiet again when we had lunch the next day, but was quite obviously making a supreme effort to pretend everything was OK. And when she came round on the Wednesday evening, she seemed pretty much back to her normal self. She swooped on

Poppy, picking her up and swinging her around joyfully as if she hadn't seen her for months, and took her to play a game, waving me off almost dismissively to go upstairs and get on with my work. I heard the two of them laughing together downstairs and began to wonder if I'd imagined the distressed state she'd been in on the Monday. Again, I had to rein in my pathetic feeling of being left out, missing out on the fun, wishing *I* was the one who made my daughter so happy and excited instead of being boring old mum, there to feed her, mop up the tears when she was unhappy and calm her when she was cross.

As we cooked a chicken curry together, Crystal suddenly switched from talking about Poppy and how clever and sweet and beautiful she was, to quietly telling me:

'I'm sorry about being a bit miserable the other day. It was an overreaction to something. A silly argument with someone – you know how it is – I took something too much to heart.'

It hadn't looked, to me, at all like just being *a bit miserable*. But it was obvious she wanted to play the whole thing down; she was probably embarrassed now and just wanted to forget it and move on. And for me to do the same. So I went along with it.

'Ah, no need to apologise,' I said lightly. 'It can be

really upsetting to have an argument with someone, can't it? As I've already told you, I'm always here for you if you want someone to share stuff with.'

'I know, and I'm grateful. But honestly, it's just too silly, and I'm over it now.'

'Good.' I smiled at her. I'd come to the conclusion that whatever had happened at the weekend must have been about her brother. It was probably wrong of me, because she'd now made it clear she didn't want to talk about the *silly argument* she'd had, but my curiosity drove me to ask, in as innocent a voice as I could manage, 'So how's everything else going? Have you seen your brother lately?'

As soon as the words were out of my mouth I regretted them. If my hunch was right, I was risking upsetting her all over again, stirring up the memory of the argument she'd been trying to suppress. But she just looked back at me blankly for a moment before answering that no, she hadn't seen him for months, probably wouldn't even hear from him until Christmas, which was nothing unusual.

So it wasn't her brother. I told myself, finally, that I had to stop speculating; whatever had happened, it was none of my business. Crystal had obviously completely forgotten – or had deliberately forgotten – that she'd pretended the whole upset had been about not telling me her real name. It was so obviously nothing to do with that, but I wasn't about to bring it up again. Nevertheless, that aspect of it was still puzzling me. Why on earth would she have thought it was such a big deal not to tell me her real name? Perhaps I'd never know.

22

CRYSTAL

Oh my God. I nearly ruined everything. I'd told myself I'd be able to hold it together when Gemma and I met for lunch, but as soon as she asked about my weekend, assuming it had been a jolly jaunt somewhere, or a get-together with my socially inept and lazy brother who hardly ever even bothered to call me, I just fell apart. And the more Gemma, bless her, kept fussing over me and begging me to let her help, the worse I became. Quite apart from the way I felt already about the weekend, she was making me feel worse by being so nice, so caring, so desperate to support me in return for... well, for what she saw as my support for *her*; but of course most of what I did was because of how much

I wanted to see Poppy; because of... yes, because of my love for Poppy.

So the more she said, the more she tried to comfort me, the worse I felt. I told her I was feeling guilty, I told her I'd lied to her. I was so close to telling her the truth about myself, I had no idea how I managed to stop at just the point of revealing my real name. And that was bad enough. It could have given everything away, ruined everything. But as soon as I'd said it, as soon as the name *Suzie* was out there, and the shock of saying it out loud had frozen me into silence, I knew it was still OK. Safe. There was no recognition on her face – no alarm, no sudden memory of what the name meant to her. She'd never heard of me. Thank God.

I explained how I'd come to be Crystal – no need for any lies there, it was all true, I even called myself Crystal at work. I did prefer the name, and discarding my real name in nearly every area of my life had helped me, just a little bit, to move on. Even my brother, when he remembered – when he even remembered I was alive – had got the hang of calling me Crystal.

Of course, there was still one area of my life where I remained Suzanne: on any official papers. So there were people who still called me Suzanne – but fortunately, they were the people Gemma wasn't ever likely to meet. Not if I had anything to do with it.

23

GEMMA

It was nearly the last day of October, when we'd be celebrating Poppy's third birthday, and this year, she understood the whole process a little more. I'd been talking to her about it, and almost every morning from about two weeks before the date, she'd been asking me, 'Is my birthday yet?'

Finally the day arrived and when she bounced out of bed on the morning that I was able to tell her yes, it was her birthday today, she was now three years old, she promptly went into a huge fit of excitement.

'It's my birthday, it's my birthday,' she sang, jumping up and down on the spot. But when I brought her present into the room, she went quiet and stood, awestruck, staring at me as I handed it to her.

'Is it for me?' she said, and I laughed.

'Yes, of course, sweetheart, it's your birthday present. Do you want me to help you unwrap it?'

'No! I do it.' She'd become very independent recently, wanting to try to do everything herself, including getting dressed, which sometimes ended in tears because it could take her so long, I'd have to hurry her up. Luckily her birthday had fallen on a Thursday so there was no work or nursery to rush to. I wouldn't have wanted a tantrum on her birthday.

She sat down on the floor with the parcel on her lap, and tore at the wrapping.

'Oh!' she said, looking at me in amazement. 'It's like at nurs'ry.'

I'd been told, often, of how she had to be cajoled into taking off the princess outfit in the dressing-up corner at nursery, before home time, or because other children wanted a turn wearing it. So I'd managed to find one almost identical online.

'Do you like it, Poppy?'

'Yes!' She was already stripping off her pyjamas. 'It's BOO! Can I wear it today?'

'Of course. I knew you'd want a *blue* princess dress, Poppy. And it's a Mummy day today so you can wear it all day if you like. Let me brush your hair before you put your crown on!'

I'd worked hard, during the previous few evenings, to get ahead with my work so that I could take the whole day off to spend with Poppy. Mum was coming for lunch and we were going out to the park together in the afternoon. All morning, Poppy played with her dolls and teddies, being their princess, arranging them in rows so she could parade in front of them and tell them to sit up straight and listen to her commands. Mum arrived at midday with a beautifully wrapped present for her. I decided three was the most delightful age so far: still young enough to be overawed by the whole ceremony of being given a present, without having unrealistic expectations. Mum had bought her a walking, barking, toy puppy dog, and the way Poppy reacted, you'd have thought she'd been given the moon and all the stars.

'A doggy!' she said, looking awestruck – and when she stroked the toy and it gave a little bark, her eyes widened in stunned delight. '*My* doggy!'

The postman had already delivered her present from Dad, a rainbow-coloured unicorn backpack, with a set of sticker books inside, and she'd reacted with such excitement, trying it on (on top of her princess outfit) and announcing solemnly *I take this to nurs'ry*.

'Well,' Mum said as we went into the kitchen to prepare lunch and I rebuked her for spending out on the toy puppy, 'it wasn't very expensive, and after all, there's no Daddy to make a fuss of her now, is there.'

Just as we were sitting down to lunch – I'd made Poppy's favourite sausage-and-ketchup sandwich, plus some more civilised sandwiches for me and Mum – there was a ring at the doorbell.

'Postman?' Poppy said, her eyes lighting up at the idea of yet more presents or cards.

I laughed. 'No, Pops. The postman's already brought everything. Let me see who it is.'

And it was Crystal, standing on the doorstep wearing a bright, luminous long blue dress decorated with stars and moons, and holding a large present wrapped in blue, with a blue bow on top. BOO, Poppy's favourite colour – she'd remembered, I thought, but at the same time I was staring at her in confusion. What the hell? One o'clock on a Thursday? Surely she should have been at work.

'Surprise!' she sang out. 'I took the afternoon off. Hope you don't mind? I *had* to come and see the birthday girl! Where is she? Hello, Poppy! Happy birthday, three-year-old! Wow, you're a *princess* today? That's *so* beautiful!'

'I... didn't know you were coming,' I stuttered, ushering Poppy back to the table, as she'd come running out holding a quarter of sausage sandwich which was threatening to drip ketchup. 'Um... my mum's here...'

'Oh!' Far from looking embarrassed, Crystal followed Poppy – uninvited – through to the kitchen. She smiled at Mum. 'Hello, I'm Crystal. How lovely to meet you.' She turned to me. 'Shall I put the kettle on, Gem?'

Flustered, aware of the look of surprise and, I thought, flash of annoyance, on Mum's face as she said hello back, I just nodded and mumbled a thank you. Crystal put the wrapped parcel down on the table and smiled at Poppy again.

'For you,' she said. 'But not until you've finished your lunch, OK?'

'But don't rush,' Mum told Poppy in a slightly less-than-happy tone. 'Or you'll get tummy ache.'

Poppy's eyes rested, gleaming, on the blue parcel as she proceeded to pretend not to rush eating the rest of her sandwich. Meanwhile, Crystal had filled and turned on the kettle and was asking who wanted tea or coffee.

'Um... would you like a sandwich?' I asked, having not catered for another guest but feeling awkward and embarrassed despite how unexpected her arrival was. 'I've got some cheese left, and a couple of tomatoes—'

'Oh God, no, I didn't expect that, don't worry about

me. But I've brought a' – she dropped her voice to just above a whisper – 'C – A – K – E. It's in the car, I thought I'd better not bring it in yet. I guessed you might be having lunch.'

'We've already got one,' Mum said somewhat icily.

I glanced at her in surprise. Although it was a little awkward, especially as it was Mum who had brought cake number one, it wasn't like her to be so... well, frankly, rude.

'But thank you,' I told Crystal. 'That's so nice of you. Maybe we can have a slice of yours first, Mum,' I suggested, thinking quickly, 'and a slice of yours later, Crystal, after we've been to the park?'

'I won't be able to manage a second slice,' Mum said, sniffing. 'And we don't want Poppy spoiling her birthday by being sick, do we?'

'Not being sick!' Poppy protested, shoving the last mouthful of sausage sandwich into her mouth.

'Not yet, Pops,' I said as cheerfully as I could manage. 'But you will if you don't slow down.'

I was now feeling anxious about the mood of the whole day being spoilt. I'd already promised Poppy the outing to the park, and Mum was looking forward to coming with us, to doing all the usual things with Poppy – the little slide, the baby swing, the balancing logs, the miniature climbing frame – all the play equipment for younger kids that the birthday girl adored. It would be incredibly difficult not to include Crystal in the outing, and now that she'd turned up, Poppy would be upset too if she didn't come along. But I had a horrible feeling Crystal wouldn't just rival Mum for Poppy's affection – she would take over.

Poppy finished her sandwich as Crystal made the coffee, and she sat, wriggling with impatience, staring with unconcealed excitement at the blue parcel. Finally, Crystal picked it up and put it in front of her, kissing her on the head and wishing her a happy year of being three.

'I like three,' Poppy said earnestly, as she began to tear at the wrapping paper. Then she sat back, giving a gasp of surprise, as the paper fell away to reveal – well, she quite clearly didn't know what it was.

'It's a robot,' Crystal said. 'Look, here's the remote control. You can make him run across the floor, sing three different songs—'

'He's BOO,' Poppy said in delight. 'A BOO wobot. What's a wobot?'

'Robots, for three-year-olds?' Mum said disparagingly with another sniff. 'She's already been given a walking, barking, dog – I think that's more appropriate for her age.'

'Look, Pops,' I said quickly, talking over Mum. 'Put

him on the floor. Now, if you press this button... whoa! Off he goes! Isn't that clever? Oh, and look at his eyes flashing!'

'You can press *this* button to make him come back, Poppy,' Crystal added. 'And if you want him to sing a song—'

Mum was collecting the sandwich plates and taking them to the sink, her shoulders rigid with disapproval. I looked at Crystal apologetically. Of course, Mum must have felt she'd been outdone, but I wished she hadn't made it quite so obvious.

'Look, let's take the robot into the living room, Poppy,' I suggested. 'You can play with that *and* your new doggy. And we'll get the cake ready,' I said as Crystal shepherded Poppy out of the kitchen. 'Thanks for bringing it,' I added quietly to Mum.

'Well, it looks like it's surplus to requirements now,' she said.

'Not at all.' I dropped my voice to a whisper. 'I'm sorry, Mum. I didn't realise Crystal was going to turn up today.'

'Can't be helped, I suppose,' she said curtly. 'Now then, I've brought candles. Shall I get some clean plates out?'

* * *

The singing of 'Happy Birthday', the blowing out of the three candles, and the cutting and consuming of the pink-and-white sponge cake all went peacefully enough. I'd spent a few days talking to Poppy about this process, reminding her of how I'd helped her with the blowing out the previous year when she was a bit too little to manage it, and she made a good job of extinguishing all three candles herself.

'So who's ready to walk off their cake?' I suggested after we'd all finished.

'Park!' Poppy said, jumping to her feet. 'Going to the park now! Nanny coming!' She looked at Crystal. 'Crystal coming?'

'Oh, I don't know,' Crystal said, smiling. 'I mean, I feel like I kind of butted in on all this – I didn't know what you had planned—'

'Don't worry, we understand if you need to get home,' Mum said – and suddenly I lost my patience. Crystal might have turned up unexpectedly, but she was trying to be polite now, and Mum was being downright rude. Hadn't she complained that she'd never met my new friend – well, now she had the opportunity to start getting to know her, but she was acting as if she'd already made up her mind, and not in a good way!

'Crystal come!' Poppy said, her voice rising ominously. 'I *want* Crystal to come!'

'Yes, of course you must come, Crystal,' I said firmly. 'The more the merrier, eh, Poppy, for your birthday treat?'

This year she was still little enough to just want me, Mum, and Crystal – and surely that was something for us all to treasure and share together? By her next birthday, she'd probably want to have little friends from nursery or pre-school or wherever I'd managed to afford for her to go, to come and have a birthday party. Mum was feeling jealous and resentful, and although I kind of got that, I *wanted* her to spend some time with Crystal, to get to know her and realise why I liked her.

To be fair, I think Mum took the hint from my tone and the look I directed at her, as she seemed to pull herself together and make an effort to be a little more congenial, but I could tell she was disappointed with the way the whole day had turned out. I tried not to feel the same. Yes, it was awkward, and I wished Crystal had spoken to me beforehand instead of just turning up, but the only thing that really mattered, I told myself, was that Poppy enjoyed the day, not how offended the situation made any of us adults feel – we were old enough to know better.

So the outing to the park went reasonably well, and when we arrived home Crystal asked if it would be OK (*'as long as your mum won't be upset?'*) if she brought in her own cake from the car now, as it would be a bit daft to take it home with her and she'd never manage to eat it on her own. I smiled and said yes, that would be lovely.

She carried the cake inside in its box, and already I could see that it was twice as big as Mum's. Not only that but, as she lifted it from the box, I could also see that it was iced in blue and white, not pink. Poppy was tired now from her exertions in the park and I thought that perhaps she wouldn't take much notice of the colour anyway. But as I carried in the cake – without candles this time; even Crystal must have realised that it would be going a step too far if she'd have tried to rival Mum in this too – Poppy jumped up, a huge smile on her face, and said:

'Yay, BOO cake! Not pink! I like BOO best!'

* * *

'I'll take the rest of my cake home, shall I?' Mum said as she was getting ready to go home. Crystal had at least had the sense to be the first to leave, shortly after we'd all – apart from Mum – had a slice of the blue

cake. 'I won't want to eat any more of it myself but perhaps the birds will enjoy it.'

'Oh, Mum!' I said, exasperated. 'Don't be like that!
Crystal wasn't trying to compete with you, or anything
like that; she didn't know you'd be here!'

'So why didn't she ask, like anyone with an ounce
of common sense would do? And honestly, what on
earth was she wearing? With those boots? And the tattoos? What does she think she looks like?'

'She's just a bit of a hippy, that's all. It's her style. It
suits her. She's a really nice person; I wish you'd give
her a chance. She's been a good friend to me, and she
loves Poppy to bits.'

'And she hasn't got any children herself, you say?'

'No. Unfortunately not. As I've told you, that's why
I feel for her.'

'Hmm.' Mum pulled her jacket on and picked up
her handbag, preparing to leave.

'What do you mean, *hmm*?'

'Just be careful, Gemma, that's all I'm saying,' she
said. 'What exactly is she after?'

'She's not after anything, she's just being a *friend* to
me, and to Poppy. And she's not replacing you, Mum,
whatever you might think, so please stop worrying and
try to be nice to her. For my sake.'

'It's for your sake that I'm worrying. And not because I think she's replacing me, either. Think about it, Gemma, that's all I'm saying. She hasn't got kids, she wishes she had one, and she loves yours *to bits*?' She headed for the door, shaking her head. 'I'm just saying,' she repeated, turning to give me a serious look, 'think about it.'

24

CRYSTAL

I didn't really blame Gemma's mum for being upset. I should have let Gemma know I was going to go round there, but it was a last-minute decision. I'd bought the present, and the cake, and had planned to call on her after work, but then I thought it would be a bit late for the cake, and I was so excited to see Poppy on her birthday that I suddenly decided to ask for the afternoon off and go straight there. We weren't too busy in the design studio and it wasn't difficult to take the time off, and – well, to be honest, I just didn't think it through.

As soon as I got to Gemma's place and saw the strange car outside, I guessed whose it was. Of course her mum – Poppy's grandma – would be there on her birthday. I should have realised. Perhaps I should have also realised that I wouldn't be particularly welcome: the unexpected guest; the bad fairy at the birthday party, from Gemma's mum's point of view, anyway. In that particular scenario, three was company – their little family, together for Poppy's birthday – and four was going to be a crowd. I should have turned the car around and headed home, or I should, at least, have called ahead and asked if it would be OK to pop in. Instead, I decided to just go right on and brazen it out, *knowing* it was going to be awkward, but too desperate to see my little Poppy, to care.

I should have taken the hint and gone home instead of going with them to the park, but I didn't, because Poppy was quite obviously so pleased to see me, despite Grandma being there, and well, I suppose I took a mean, perverse, kind of pleasure in that.

So I'd blown it, as far as my chances of being popular with Grandma went. And yes, I regretted it afterwards. I'd have liked to meet her in a more congenial way; at a more appropriate time, by prior arrangement like a normal, sensible, polite friend instead of an overexcited, slightly unhinged 'auntie', desperate to hug Poppy on her third birthday. It wasn't nice of me to have upstaged her – she'd have resented that, from a random stranger she'd never even met before. And more importantly, it wasn't nice of me to put Gemma in such an awkward position.

I decided to suggest to Gemma that we arranged for me to meet her mum again at a better time, fairly soon, and I'd apologise and hopefully we'd all be able to move forward. I wanted to get along with her. I had no reason to resent her or feel jealous of her. Because I already knew that I was more important to Poppy than anyone else... other, of course, than Gemma.

25

GEMMA

The day after Poppy's birthday was a Friday, and I'd been hoping that when I took Poppy to Mum's as usual, we might have moved on from the awkwardness of the day before. But no, Mum wanted to debate, all over again, the way Crystal had turned up without asking, bringing an 'inappropriate' present and a 'pretentious' cake, and she probably would have continued in that vein if I hadn't said, with a sigh, that Crystal was my friend whether Mum liked her or not, and I had hoped she'd be pleased for me that I had a good friend on my side.

Mum went silent for a moment, looking hurt, and then put on a very deliberate fixed smile and said that of course, she was pleased, and I should forgive her for being so concerned about me and Poppy but that, as I should know, it was only natural for a mother to worry.

'I know that,' I said, giving her a hug, desperate to calm things down and be back on our usual good terms. 'And I'm grateful for your concern, but honestly, Mum, there's no need. OK?'

'OK,' she said, the fixed smile looking as though it was hurting her face. 'Well, at least I've got Poppy to myself today. And if you're busy, Gemma, *please* let me keep her here for the night for a change. I'll give her dinner, put her to bed upstairs – you know I keep a few clothes and a pair of pyjamas here for her. We'll read lots of stories, we'll have fun. And I'll bring her back in the morning.'

I hesitated. I suspected Crystal would want to come round this evening, hoping to see Poppy again, but if I said this to Mum right now, it wouldn't go down well. And to be fair, I did have quite a bit of work to catch up on, and Mum had offered so many times recently to keep Poppy overnight on a Friday that I really didn't have the heart to say no. Poppy would love to stay with her nanny anyway – it had been a while since she'd done so.

'OK. Thank you, Mum, that would be lovely.' I gave her a kiss. 'I hope she behaves herself.'

'She always does, with me,' Mum said with a smile, sounding almost smug about it.

I really hoped we weren't going to get into a situation where the people who loved Poppy were competing against each other for her affection. How had it come to this?

* * *

I thought about it on the drive home. I'd been irritated by Mum's attitude the previous day, and when she urged me to *think about it*, I'd dismissed it out of hand, cross with her for casting aspersions about my best friend. Just because someone would have liked kids of their own, that didn't mean they were about to run off with their friend's child, for God's sake. OK, so Crystal did seem to be slightly over the top with her enthusiasm for Poppy, but wasn't it lovely that the feeling was so obviously reciprocated? Poppy didn't always take to people so instantly or enjoy their company so completely. As far as I was concerned, it was a win-win situation, and I hadn't felt any need to worry about it whatsoever... until now.

Not that I was worried about it, really. Not at all. I was just concerned about the effect it was having on Mum; on my relationship with Mum.

All right, I suppose since Mum made that comment, I'd been a *bit* worried. But only because she'd sowed that tiny seed of doubt, of concern, in my head and now I kept pondering over it, swinging from still feeling cross with Mum for planting that doubt in me, to wondering if I was missing something. Being naïve, if you like. *Was* it quite normal for a childless woman to strike up such an intense friendship with someone so quickly... when she seemed more interested in spending time with their child than with the mother herself?

No! That wasn't true – she liked spending time with *me*, too, didn't she?

By the time I arrived home I'd talked myself into a complete circle of doubt and confusion. I didn't want to doubt Crystal. I *didn't* doubt her. She'd shown no sign of wanting to steal Poppy away from me. It was ridiculous to even think like that, even for a minute. I *wouldn't* think like it. I trusted Crystal.

But did that mean I didn't trust Mum?

I threw myself into my work, refusing to look up even to take a coffee break, and didn't stop for lunch until two o'clock – when I ate a sandwich while scrolling through the news feed on my phone so that I didn't have to think about anything. Mum had sent me a photo on WhatsApp of Poppy eating chips at her local café, grinning through a mouth smeared with tomato ketchup. *Someone isn't going to want a big dinner!* she'd written with a laughing-face emoji. Mum was usually pretty careful about sensible meals, not too many treats, not giving in to toddler whims, and so on, and I couldn't help wondering if she was doing a bit of extra spoiling, to compensate for what she'd obviously felt was her failure to be the most popular guest at the birthday party.

Stop it! I told myself, putting the phone down and getting on with my work again. I was beginning to think *I* was the one with the problem, imagining ulterior motives everywhere.

* * *

It felt strange not having Poppy home for her dinner, and to be honest I felt nothing but relief when, at half past five, the doorbell rang and there was Crystal on the doorstep, smiling and cheerful as usual in a bright blue stripey cloak that billowed out with the breeze.

'Hello, love!' she said. 'Sorry, I've done it again, haven't I – turned up without calling you first.' She didn't sound the least bit apologetic. In fact, she laughed as she went on, 'It'd serve me right if you weren't in! Hope I'm not interrupting anything?' She dropped her voice and added, as I held the door open for her to come inside, 'Is your mum here?'

'No,' I said, struggling to get my face to decide whether to smile or not. I couldn't help being pleased to see her, but I hoped she wasn't going to be sarcastic or rude about Mum – about the awkwardness of the previous day.

'Oh. I know she usually brings Poppy back about this time, so I thought it might be an opportunity to... well, you know...' She shrugged. 'Apologise, I suppose.'

'No need to apologise,' I said. 'It was just a little bit awkward.'

'Yes. My fault entirely. I shouldn't have turned up uninvited like that. I thought perhaps if I saw her today we could clear the air.'

'Well, yes, I'd like you to meet each other at a... less awkward time,' I agreed. My face had decided to smile. 'But in fact Mum's kept Poppy for tonight.'

'For dinner? Oh, that's nice for her. For Poppy too.' She smiled back, and my face began to relax completely. 'And it's given you a bit more time to yourself. Lovely.'

'Yes. She's keeping her all night. She hasn't done that for a while, and—'

'All night?' Crystal said, stopping halfway into the

room, halfway out of her coat, her face suddenly changing. 'What – sleeping at her house?'

I laughed. 'Yes, of course. She's often stayed over in the past. Poppy's got her own little room there, with a princess duvet cover and her own pyjamas and toys and everything—'

'Oh. Well, that's nice.'

Crystal's whole tone had changed. She looked as if – as my grandad used to say when I was little – she'd lost a pound and found sixpence.

'Of course it is. She's Poppy's nanny. Poppy loves staying over with her.'

'Yes. Of course.' She was still standing halfway into the living room. 'Well, I suppose there's no point me staying, then.'

I felt my mouth drop open in surprise. *No point staying*? Really?

'But... I thought... we can still have dinner together, can't we? Like we usually do after Poppy's in bed? You can stay over, if you want – have a glass of wine?' I gulped, not wanting to sound too desperate. 'Unless you've got something else on, I mean.'

'Well, I suppose...' she began reluctantly. 'But, well, normally I come round to help out with Poppy, you know, and then we have dinner, but, well...' She sounded awkward, almost miserable about it. 'I guess you don't need me, so—'

'But Crystal, come on, you're my friend, I look forward to seeing you – it isn't *just* so you can help with Poppy.' I stared at her, waited for her to meet my eyes, then added more quietly, 'Is it?'

'No, no, of course not,' she said quickly, colouring slightly. 'Of course we're friends, and – sorry – yes, of course I'd still like to have dinner with you.' She smiled. 'And yes, if you're sure, maybe I'll stay over, too, then I might get to see Poppy when she comes home in the morning.'

'Right.'

I went ahead of her through the living room and into the kitchen, my heart suddenly pounding as if I'd been running, my thoughts flying chaotically through my head. However much Crystal had tried to deny it, it was pretty obvious from her reaction that she'd really only come round to spend time with Poppy. Not me. Even now she'd agreed to stay, it was only in the hope of seeing Poppy in the morning. I felt hurt, and disgruntled. It even crossed my mind for a split second that I should tell her I'd decided I was too busy tonight after all. Instead, I just put the kettle on and banged a few cups around, trying to calm down, conscious of her standing silently behind me.

'What have I said?' Crystal asked after a couple of minutes, sounding genuinely puzzled.

'Nothing.' I turned to face her, shaking my head. I was being ridiculous. It was *nice* that Crystal loved Poppy so much. At least she'd agreed to spend tonight with me, even if she was disappointed not to see Poppy. Instead of getting upset about it I should concentrate on the two of us having fun this evening while I had the chance of a relaxed, child-free evening. 'I'm just making tea,' I went on. 'Want a cup? Or shall we get straight into the wine?'

* * *

I didn't want to overdo the drinking, as I'd need to be fit to look after Poppy when she came back in the morning, but it was really nice for once to be able to indulge in a couple of glasses of wine. I woke up later than usual, remembering with a smile how Crystal and I had laughed uproariously, late into the night, about – amongst other things and in no particular order – people at work, various antics Crystal and I had confessed to getting up to when we were teenagers, and boyfriends we'd had in the past and why we'd finished with them.

Crystal was already in the kitchen, making toast, and looking a lot brighter and breezier than I felt.

'We had a good night, didn't we?' she said with a grin as she plonked a cup of coffee in front of me.

'Yes. I told you about Claude. How embarrassing.'

'The French boy you met on the school exchange trip, who tried to smuggle himself onto your coach to come home with you. That was hilarious – the way you described your teacher finding him trying to hide under your seat!'

'And your story about the guy you dated, who worked for the circus—'

'Training the elephants! I loved those elephants!'

We were almost helpless with laughter again as we went over all the silly stories that we'd shared the previous evening. By the time we'd eaten toast, drunk two cups of coffee each and just about managed to stop laughing, Mum was at the door with Poppy.

'Mummy's in her jamas!' Poppy exclaimed, eyes wide with shock.

'Sorry, Pops, I had a bit of a lie-in!' I pulled her towards me for a hug. 'Did you have a lovely time at Nanny's?'

'Yes! Look! Jam tarts!' She held up a cake tin, shaking it so the contents thumped against the tin's lid. I imagined broken tarts with jam everywhere – not that it mattered, when she'd obviously had such a nice time helping to make them.

'Yummy!' I said. I looked at Mum. 'Thanks so much for having her. I must admit I didn't realise how much I needed a night off.'

'I hope it gave you a nice rest, love,' Mum said, smiling. 'Did your friend come?'

'Crystal. Yes, she's here – we've just been having a late breakfast. Come in, Mum. She's in the kitchen.'

'Crystal here?' Poppy squawked, immediately running ahead of us into the kitchen.

'Poppy!' Crystal was shouting, picking her up in her arms as we joined them. She gave Poppy a kiss before planting her back down and turning to Mum. 'Hello again, Mrs – um...' She paused in her obvious attempt to be polite, looking at Mum expectantly. But Mum shook her head, managing a smile.

'Call me Jane, please. Hello, Crystal. Did you both have a good evening?'

Mum sounded so formal, it was almost to the point of being unfriendly.

'Yes, we did, thanks, Jane,' Crystal said. 'And I'm glad I've seen you. I just wanted to apologise for barging in on the three of you on Thursday. I should have realised you'd want Poppy to yourselves on her birthday, but I was so excited to see her.'

'Well, she does seem keen to see you, too,' Mum said in a slightly grudging tone.

I waited, but Mum didn't go on to accept the apology and neither of them seemed to know what else to say to each other.

'Want a coffee or anything?' I offered, but she shook her head and said thank you but she'd better get off home and leave us to it.

I waited again, this time half-expecting Crystal to say she'd be going herself – but no, she just turned to talk to Poppy and then followed her into the living room as if they were two kids ignoring the adults and going off to play together.

'Well, thanks again for having Poppy all day and all night,' I said to Mum to break the awkward silence.

'I've loved it,' she said. 'Well, I'd better leave you to it. Have a nice day. I suppose Crystal's staying for the day? Or the weekend?'

'I don't know – we haven't discussed it yet. She might have something else on.'

'OK. Well, have fun. I'll see you next Friday as usual, I suppose?'

'Of course, Mum – if that's OK.' I sighed, and then added quietly, 'Don't be like this, please. You know how grateful I am to you.'

She just gave me a nod and a smile, and turned to leave.

'Bye bye, Poppy-Pops!' she called into the living room.

'Bye, Nanny,' came the response. I wanted to call to Poppy to come out and say goodbye properly but I knew that it would, somehow, make it even more hurtful to Mum that I'd had to ask her. Tearing her away from her new best friend.

'I'll call you,' I promised as I kissed her goodbye.

Then I sat down at the kitchen table on my own, looking at the detritus from our giggly breakfast, listening to my daughter squealing and laughing with Crystal and feeling... somehow, weirdly sad.

26

CRYSTAL

Well, I tried, didn't I? I apologised to the grandma – Jane – and all I got for it was a frosty response, an icy stare and a stony silence. Frosty, icy, stony, that just about summed her up. But she was Gemma's mum so I had to try to be nice. I know it upset Gemma, the way her mum reacted. We'd had such a laugh together the previous evening, and first thing in the morning too, but after Jane had gone, she didn't seem to be able to snap out of her miserable mood. Even Poppy asked her, '*Whassa matter, Mummy*?', and Gemma had just sighed and said she had a headache. But I knew her mum's attitude had upset her. And it was sad to see her like that again. I mean, she'd been sad and depressed –

obviously – a lot of the time when we'd first met, because of her ex and what he'd done, but recently I'd been seeing a change in her, like she was starting to come to terms with things and even starting to enjoy her life again, just a little. I'd like to think I might have helped with that, even if only a little bit. And now it felt like, because of the mistake I'd made, alienating her mum by turning up on Poppy's birthday, she was upset again.

'Cheer up,' I said, going into the kitchen and sitting down opposite her, when Poppy eventually began to tire of playing horses with me on the living room carpet, jumping on my back. 'Shall we go out for a walk? The fresh air might help your headache—'

'Actually, Crystal, if you don't mind I've got some work to finish off today,' she said without looking up to meet my eyes.

'Oh, no problem, I'll take Poppy out for you, then, so you can get on in peace. I'll put her warm coat on her and—'

'No. Sorry, I didn't mean...' She tailed off. 'I kind of need to have a day with Poppy on our own, if you don't mind. She was with Mum all day yesterday, and all night, and, well, I just feel like I want to spend some time with her today. I think she needs a quiet day too, to look at her birthday presents and get over all the excitement she's had and, well, just kind of wind down, you know?'

She still hadn't looked up at me. I didn't know what to say; I felt like I was being dismissed. On one level, I knew what she was saying made sense: I got it, she and Poppy just needed a quiet day. But I could have had a quiet day with them too. I could calm Poppy down, sit with her and read stories with her or play a quiet game instead of jumping around like we'd been doing. No – she just didn't want me around. Perhaps she was upset about the awkwardness between me and her mum. Well, I was the one who'd made an effort, wasn't I? I think she knew I'd be hurt, because of the way she was sounding uncomfortable about it, avoiding my eyes and pretending she was going to do some work.

'OK,' I managed to say after the silence had gone on for just a minute too long. 'All right, well, I hope your headache soon feels better, and – well, I'll just get my things, then, and say goodbye to Poppy.'

Even while I was putting on my coat and hugging Poppy – who clung to me and asked me to stay – Gemma stayed sitting at the kitchen table, staring at nothing, saying nothing.

'Bye, then!' I called out before I opened the front door, still hoping there might be a last-minute reprieve, a change of heart, a sudden cheery, *Oh, all right, don't go, let's have a nice day together*... but there wasn't.

'Bye,' she said tonelessly. 'See you at work on Monday.'

I let myself out.

27

GEMMA

I spent the rest of that weekend trying to persuade myself there was nothing to worry about. It wasn't that I had any doubts, myself, about Crystal; I was just so worried about Mum taking such an obvious dislike to her. She'd never been the kind of mum to disapprove of my friends, or boyfriends – even back in my teenage years when it was fair to say some of them weren't particularly sensible choices. She'd told me since that she and Dad took the view that if they tried to stop me seeing someone that they thought was unsuitable, it would just make that person seem even more appealing to me, and I might have tried to see them in secret. So instead of speaking out, they'd just watched the situation carefully and waited for it to run its course. It went without saying that they approved of Jack. But if that made them bad judges of character, what did it say about me? I'd thought he was wonderful.

By the Sunday morning, I'd talked myself out of my despondency. Mum still didn't really know Crystal, whereas I did, and I knew she was a kind, caring person who'd had her own problems. All she wanted was to spend time with me and Poppy – and if it sometimes seemed like Poppy was the priority, well, where was the harm in Poppy having another adult to lavish love and attention on her? She didn't have her father around any more, after all.

So Poppy and I spent the rest of that leisurely weekend on our own. She spent most of it wearing her princess costume, and it was nice to hear her chatting to herself as she played little make-believe games of being a princess, ordering her dolls and teddies to bring her imaginary treasure.

* * *

Crystal and I went for lunch as usual on the Monday, and I apologised straight away for the way I'd dismissed her.

'Don't be silly, I understood, completely,' she said.

'Look, I realise it's got a bit… kind of full on, our friendship, right? We've been seeing a lot of each other—'

'Yes, but I'm grateful for that, honestly. I think I was just tired on Saturday, I needed a bit of quiet time, that's all.'

She smiled and nodded. 'Well, any time you want a break from me, you must just say so. I realise I can be a bit… well, a bit much. A bit loud and over the top and—'

'Not at all. You're exactly what I needed, exactly what I still need. I honestly don't know how I'd have got through these last few months without you.'

It was only as I was saying this that I realised how completely true it was. However lovely, however helpful and sympathetic my mum had been, I'd have drowned in my own despair had Crystal not been around to cheer me up, to keep me sane and keep Poppy happy.

'Well, it works both ways, love. I feel so much happier myself too. I don't think I even realised how lonely I was before.' She paused, and then added in a rush as if she didn't really want to say it, 'I'm sorry your mum doesn't seem to like me much.'

'No, it's not that – she, well, she's hardly even met you.'

'I know, but we've got off to a bad start. I'll try to put it right. I know how much she means to you.'

I smiled. She was so considerate, and really, was it too much to ask for Mum to make an effort?

'Thanks. I think she's just got used to having me and Poppy to herself, that's all. When Jack was around, I didn't really have time for a special friend.'

Special friend. I saw the reaction in Crystal's eyes, and I was glad we'd had this conversation – cleared the air. I was even convinced that Mum would come, in time, to appreciate Crystal as much as I did – maybe even as much as Poppy did. It was ridiculous to imagine Crystal could ever have any ulterior motives. She was my special friend.

* * *

That evening, a little while after I'd put Poppy to bed, I had a call from my dad. It was unusual; he was more likely to call, or video-call me, at weekends so he could chat to Poppy too. He hadn't done so that weekend but I hadn't been concerned. He was often busy with his golf club friends, and of course, he'd spoken to Poppy on the morning of her birthday.

'Is everything all right?' I asked him, a little anxiously.

'Yes, of course, love. Well...'

I heard the anxiety in his hesitation.

'Well, what?'

'I'm just a bit concerned, to be honest, about what I've been hearing from your mum.'

I sighed. 'And what have you been hearing, Dad?'

'She's very worried, Gem, about this friend of yours.'

'I know she is, and frankly, I'm a bit annoyed that she's been bothering you about it,' I said. 'She seems to have got it into her head that Crystal's taking her place. It's ridiculous. I never imagined Mum would get jealous about me having a friend.'

'It doesn't sound like jealousy to me. It sounds like genuine concern. She says this Crystal is spending more and more time at your place, spending more and more time with Poppy—'

'Yes, she is! She is, Dad, because she's been helping me out, looking after Poppy so I can spend more time working, getting new clients – and it's paying off, and I, for one, am grateful and I can't understand why Mum doesn't see it the same way. Unless she's jealous that I'm letting someone else spend time with Poppy, which is ridiculous because I'm only thinking of Mum. I don't want to keep asking her, when she's got her job, and her own friends and clubs and—'

'Hey, all right, calm down, nobody's criticising you for anything.'

I didn't realise I'd raised my voice. I took a breath.

'Well. Sorry, but it's a bit annoying. Mum's offended Crystal and as I say, she's been a good friend to me.'

'I think your mum's the one who's been offended,' Dad said quietly. 'I understand Crystal turned up on Poppy's birthday and deliberately out-did her on the present and the cake.'

'Deliberately? That's nonsense; she couldn't possibly have known what present and cake Mum was bringing. And anyway, the whole thing is a farce. Crystal recognised that she should have called me first about the birthday, and she apologised to Mum about it on Saturday. She just got excited about seeing Poppy.'

'That's exactly what we're worried about,' he said. 'I understand she doesn't have children of her own...'

'What's that got to do with anything? Surely you don't think she's only coming to see me so that she can steal Poppy from under my nose, do you – because yes, that's what Mum hinted at. Like no childless woman can possibly be trusted around other people's children? What do you think she's going to do, exactly? Sneak Poppy out of the house while I'm upstairs working? Run off with her while she's taking her for a walk to the park?'

'Do you let her take Poppy out on her own for walks?'

'Yes! Yes, of course I do, because she's my best friend, I trust her, and Poppy adores her! Dad, honestly, this is completely ridiculous. Mum's only saying all this stuff because she felt hurt about the birthday thing – and yes, I get it, she was upset, and I was a bit cross too, but it was just a bit thoughtless of Crystal to turn up like that, that's all. Please tell me you're not seriously thinking she's some kind of monster. She isn't. You haven't even met her.'

'No. Perhaps I should.'

'Fine, come down next weekend – why not? Poppy would love to see you, so would I. I'll ask Crystal to come round on Saturday afternoon. For you to interview her,' I added sarcastically.

'Don't be like that, sweetheart. Yes, I'd love to come down on Saturday. But you know I'm only concerned because I love you. And Poppy.'

I exhaled my anger out.

'I know. All right, I suppose I'll want to inspect all of Poppy's friends before I'll trust them. Anyway, it'll be lovely to see you. Message me when you're leaving, OK? And drive carefully. Love you, Dad.'

I sat in silence for several long minutes after I ended the call. This was so unlike my dad. He'd brought me up to believe the best in everyone, and yet here he was, after one disgruntled call from my mum, convincing himself that Crystal was... what? A child-napper? Unbelievable! Was it really so unusual for a woman without kids of her own to become attached to her friend's daughter? And in such a short time?

Well, OK, and even if it *was* unusual, that didn't necessarily make it a bad thing...

Did it?

* * *

Poppy seemed to have suddenly become more grown up since her birthday. I knew, of course, that children's development was like this; it had happened before that she'd suddenly taken a massive step forward after months of seeming to be much the same. But it felt like, having turned three, she'd left babyhood behind and was now starting to behave like a proper little girl. She was fiercely independent, and wanted to choose what she wore every morning as well as dressing her-self – sometimes resulting in bizarre combinations of colour, or totally unsuitable clothes like summer dresses on cold days, or sandals when it was raining. It was becoming more and more difficult to talk her round on occasions like these, and it sometimes resulted in us being late for nursery and work. It was embarrassing to have to tell Mike that I was rushing into the office at the last minute because of a tantrum over a pair of socks, or an argument about the suitability of shorts and T-shirts in November – but fortunately, he'd had kids himself so he was pretty understanding.

Even more noticeable was the rapid improvement in Poppy's vocabulary. She was coming out with new words every day – some of them far more sophisticated than I'd have expected – and speaking in full sentences more often than not, chatting away non-stop. So it was a surprise when, one evening when I collected Poppy from nursery, she was uncharacteristically quiet.

'What's up, Pops? Are you tired?' I asked her as I strapped her into her car seat.

'No, I'm *not* tired,' she retorted. 'I'm *cross*.'

'Oh, dear – why?' I wondered if she'd had a fight with one of the other children, or been told off for some minor misdemeanour.

'Because everyone's got a daddy. But I haven't.'

My heart sank. 'You have got a daddy, sweetheart. He's away, that's all – and anyway, I'm sure not *everyone* has got a daddy. Lots of daddies don't live with their children, so—'

'He's been away for *ever*,' she said, ignoring me. Her voice was wobbling. 'Why doesn't he come back?'

'Well, he's very busy...' I began, as I started the engine. 'And—'

'Freya's daddy takes her to nurs'ry. And Mina's daddy—'

She was starting to cry. And my heart was starting to break.

'Well, I know Naomi definitely hasn't got a daddy living with her, and Alfie's got two mummies instead of a daddy. You see? Your daddy—'

'My daddy's not ever coming back,' she said, sobbing properly now. 'Is he, Mummy?'

I turned the ignition off again. I got out of the car, opened the back door and sat on the back seat next to my baby girl. Undid her straps, pulled her out of her car seat and onto my lap, holding her close while my tears mingled with hers. I asked myself why I'd been hiding the truth, trying to protect her from what, in the end, she was going to have to know. I wasn't being fair. She needed to know, to understand, and instead of helping her to come to terms with it I'd been protecting myself from having to have this conversation.

'I don't know, sweetheart,' I finally admitted,

stroking her hair, the beautiful red hair she'd inherited from the bastard who'd inflicted all this pain on us both. 'I don't know if he's ever coming back. He might not. He probably won't. But we'll be OK on our own, darling; you and me together forever, all right? We'll miss him, but we can be OK without him. We've got each other, that's all that matters now. And I love you enough for both of us, more than enough – more than a hundred daddies could ever love you. All right?'

She nodded, her face still a picture of misery. 'More than a hundred?' she repeated.

'More than a thousand, more than all the daddies in the world.'

She wiped a hand across her eyes. 'I *knowed* he wasn't coming back,' she said now, loudly, angrily – and the tone of her voice told me everything I needed to know. She'd be OK. She was cross with him, as much as missing him, but she'd needed, more than anything, to be told the truth.

'Are you ready to go home now, Pops?' I said, giving her a final cuddle and helping to wipe her tears away. 'I've got chocolate biscuits for your snack.'

'Yay, chocolate biscuits!' She shifted herself back into her car seat. 'OK, Mummy, let's go home.'

My beautiful, feisty daughter was going to be fine. And so was I.

'Stuff you, Jack,' I muttered to myself as we headed off home. 'We don't need you.'

28

CRYSTAL

The date for the next of my monthly visits was fast approaching – it was the following weekend, and all I wanted to do was to take my mind off it, to not have to think about it until I really had to. If I did, I'd start getting my hopes up again, as always, even though I knew it was pointless. I should never have got hopeful at all; it was easier to cope when it turned out exactly the same way as always – a disaster.

So I was spending as much time as possible with Gemma and Poppy. Gemma trusted me so completely by now, despite her mother, that I quite often took Poppy out for walks on my own if she was busy working. I loved pushing her around the neighbourhood in her buggy, chatting to her about the things we saw, or holding her little hand while we strolled down to the seafront to watch the waves.

There was just *one* good thing, though, about the date of this month's visit. It clashed with Gemma's dad coming down from Manchester and Gemma had told me he particularly wanted to meet me. I supposed Jane had been talking to him about me. According to Gemma, they still chatted on the phone to each other all the time. I found that odd, to say the least. Why split up if you're going to keep on chatting to each other? Well, anyway, I was quite relieved that I wouldn't be around, so I wouldn't have to be interrogated by Daddy.

The problem was that I'd have to tell Gemma, and I'd been putting it off because I knew she wouldn't be pleased. I'd have to come up with an excuse.

I didn't understand why he needed to meet me anyway. It wasn't as if it was going to make any difference to him who was spending time with his daughter and granddaughter, while he was living up in Manchester. No, it was obviously just a plot by Jane to get me out of Poppy's life. I don't know why I let her jealousy bother me. Poppy loved me, and that was all that mattered. Nothing, and nobody, was going to come between us.

29

GEMMA

It was Saturday morning; Dad was on his way down from Manchester, expecting to have lunch with me and Crystal, and at the last moment I had a phone call from Crystal saying she couldn't make it. She'd forgotten she had a dentist's appointment.

'On a Saturday?' I said.

'Yes. It's... an emergency, they've fitted me in—'

'I thought you said you'd forgotten about it.'

'Well, what I meant is that I forgot to tell you I had a terrible toothache,' she said, sounding awkward. Of course she was awkward – it was such an obvious lie. How can you forget you've got a toothache? How can you forget you've got an urgent appointment?

'Can't you come round after your appointment?'

'Oh, I'm really sorry, Gem, but I think I'm just going to have to take it easy for the rest of the weekend. The pain has been keeping me awake every night and, well, if the dentist has to take the tooth out, or do one of those root canal treatments, I'm going to be so sore once the anaesthetic wears off. I don't think I'd be very good company.'

'Right.' I knew I didn't sound very sympathetic. I couldn't understand why she would lie. She'd normally have done anything to spend time with Poppy, so it was quite obvious she just wanted to avoid meeting my dad. 'Well, sorry about your tooth. But if you do feel OK afterwards, or if you're better tomorrow, give me a call. Dad was really hoping to meet you.'

'I know, and I do feel bad about it. Sorry, Gem. But have a good time with your dad.'

* * *

I was still feeling irritated about it when Dad arrived, but I didn't want him to know Crystal had made a silly excuse to get out of the meeting. He was already thinking the worst of her so I didn't want to give him good reason to continue doing so.

'She sounded like she was in a bad way,' I said, repeating her lie. 'Thank goodness she's got an emergency appointment but she thinks she'll be out of action all weekend.'

'I see,' Dad said, quite obviously not buying it. 'And I don't suppose she's too upset about not having to meet me.'

'Oh, she sounded really disappointed—' I began. And then I stopped, sighing. Dad was giving me a look, and I knew the meaning of that look all too well. 'OK,' I said. 'To be honest, no, she didn't. In fact, I think she might have been making an excuse.'

'Yes, that's how it sounds.' He was still giving me the look. Then he spread his hands and shrugged. 'Well, she's your friend, I suppose you know her well enough. But from what I've heard, she's been spending every weekend and most week nights here with you, and yet she can't be bothered to meet your family.'

I could feel myself going into sulky-teenager mode. I was thirty-four, I hadn't lived with my parents since I'd gone to uni at the age of eighteen, but any hint of criticism or disapproval from Mum or Dad still had this effect on me. Even if I *had* agreed with every word Dad was saying, it would still have got my back up, still have made me determined to argue back in support of Crystal.

'It's not like that,' I insisted. 'For a start, she hasn't

been here *every* weekend. In fact she spent a whole weekend with someone else just a few weeks ago. Last month. And when she is here, it's because she wants to help me. I can't see what you could find to criticise in that.'

'I'm not criticising, love,' he said quietly. He hadn't even taken his coat off yet. He unzipped it now and hung it up behind the door. 'Come on, let's just enjoy our time together. I don't see you often enough.'

'I know. Sorry.' I hugged him, wondering what I was apologising for. I felt torn between resentment of his implied criticism, and the truth – that I secretly agreed with him. Not with his worries about Crystal spending so much time with me, or more to the point, with Poppy, but with his assessment of her excuse for today. Why did she have to make an excuse? Why wouldn't she want to come? She could have just called round for half an hour if she really didn't want to spend any longer – just to be polite, just to appease Dad. Or – if there was even a grain of truth in the toothache story – she surely could have agreed to come the next day, once the dentist had done whatever was necessary?

I kept going over and over it in my mind throughout the rest of the day, while I was making lunch, listening to Dad chatting about his golf club

and his neighbours in Manchester while he sat enjoying a cuddle with the granddaughter he adored but
didn't see nearly enough of. The feeling was mutual –
Poppy adored her grandad too, and I wondered if she
was hugging him even more intensely now because
she'd understood that her daddy wasn't coming back. I
felt bad then for getting cross with Dad about Crystal.
It was only natural for him to be concerned – he'd
never met her, he'd heard all these stories from Mum,
probably exaggerated, about how much time she spent
with me and Poppy, and now all he could see was that
she appeared to be refusing to come and be introduced to him. I felt the frisson of irritation again and
determined to have it out with her next time I saw her.

* * *

I put sandwiches, a bit of salad, and crisps on the table
and sent Poppy to wash her hands. Dad was silent for a
moment and then said, quietly, 'I know we said we
wouldn't keep talking about it. But I just wanted to say
I'm sorry if you think I'm being interfering – about
your friend. If you think that's all I came down for.'
    'Well...' I hesitated. 'No, OK, I get it, Dad, but hon-
estly, there's no need for you to worry. Mum took of-

fence over a couple of things, that's all. Crystal did apologise.'

'Yes, I know. But look, your mum's an easy person to get on with. She nearly always likes people. She's got over being offended about Poppy's birthday, it isn't that. She's just worried about the amount of time this girl's spending with Poppy, the way she seems to have – in her words – almost taken her over.'

'And you both seem to think that just because she hasn't got a child herself, she's planning to run off with Poppy.' Despite my best intentions, I was getting riled again. 'Dad, don't you realise how ridiculous and far-fetched that sounds?'

'Perhaps it does to you. Because she's helping you, and being a friend just when you needed one.'

'Exactly, Dad.' I was trying not to raise my voice. Poppy would be back in the room any second and the last thing I wanted was for her to hear us arguing. 'I can't understand why you can't both just be pleased for me.'

'We are. I mean, we would be. But you're on your own now, with Poppy, and frankly, you're a bit vulnerable. And this girl could obviously see that, and she's stepped in and—'

'I washed my hands,' Poppy yelled as she ran into

the room, holding her hands out to show me. 'Can I have some crisps?'

'Yes, but a sandwich first, please.' I pulled out her chair. 'Come and sit down.'

I looked at Dad and forced a smile. 'Can we drop it now, please? And just have a nice weekend together?'

He nodded.

The subject of Crystal wasn't raised again for the rest of the day. We had a lovely afternoon playing some of Poppy's games and – during a dry spell of what was a horrible windy, rainy day – having a quick walk down to the beach and along the seafront. By bedtime, Poppy was tired out from all the excitement and thought it was wonderful that her grandad read her bedtime story for her.

'Why do you have to live far away?' I heard her ask as he was settling her down for the night.

'Well, that's where my work is, sweetheart,' he said.

'My daddy went far away. But he isn't coming back.'

Dad was silent for a moment. I pictured him giving Poppy a cuddle, or perhaps stroking her hair. Then he said, his voice sounding a little husky:

'Well, *I'm* coming back, that's for sure! I'll come back as often as I can, my little princess – so whenever we say goodbye you can be sure I'll soon be saying hello again.'

* * *

Mum had invited us all round for Sunday dinner the next day, and as we set off for Exeter I braced myself for the possibility of another round of Crystal-related discussion. She'd already called Dad to ask how he'd got on with her the previous day, so she knew about the *dentist* story. And she didn't waste any time bringing it up.

'Honestly, it's just such bad manners,' she said, shaking her head in disgust as we worked together in her kitchen, peeling potatoes and carrots. 'You can't tell me she really couldn't have called in, even for just half an hour, however bad the supposed toothache was.'

'No. I know, Mum. I don't know why she didn't. Perhaps she felt... I don't know, maybe a bit intimidated.'

'*Intimidated*?' Mum shrieked, dropping a potato into the sink in her disgust. 'Intimidated by your father? He's never intimidated anyone in his life – not even you, when you were at your worst!'

'What do you mean, *at my worst*?' I retorted, genuinely interested.

'You know. When you were that difficult age. About fourteen, fifteen, when you thought you knew it all, like all teenagers. He could always get round you, never had to raise his voice. Anyway, don't change the subject. Why on earth would you say Crystal was intimidated?'

'Not by Dad himself. Just by the undercurrent. Don't look at me like that, Mum, you know what I mean. There's been an undercurrent of mistrust from you, where Crystal's concerned, and she was probably nervous that Dad was going to be the same – which he would have been, let's face it.'

'Oh, nonsense! He's just been anxious about you, that's all, and wanted to meet her to set his mind at rest. Now he's even more anxious because he thinks – quite rightly in my opinion – that if Crystal can't have the decency to come and see him, when he's driven all this way specifically to meet her—'

'Well, thanks. And there was I thinking he'd come *all this way* to see me and Poppy,' I said, trying to lighten the tone. I really didn't want to spend any more time going over the whole thing.

'You know what I mean.' She shot me a look. 'It was rude, Gemma, that's all I'm saying. Letting you down at the last minute.'

'Well, if it was actually true that she needed an emergency appointment, she couldn't exactly have—'

Mum plonked the potato she'd just peeled onto the chopping board and attacked it so viciously with her knife that I actually flinched.

'We both know,' she said in a tone that wasn't going to allow for any disagreement, 'that it wasn't *actually true*, though – don't we?'

I didn't need to reply.

* * *

Dad and I had driven to Mum's in separate cars, as it was much easier for Dad to head straight home from Exeter after lunch. He gave me a hug goodbye, promised to come back again soon, and then picked Poppy up in his arms and showered her with kisses.

'Don't go 'way, Gandad,' she said, tears coming to her eyes.

'Remember what I told you,' he said, soothing her. 'I'm coming back. Soon, OK?'

'She's got a bit funny about people leaving,' I told Mum quietly while I helped her load the dishwasher – Poppy having been coaxed out of her tears by being allowed to watch a mermaid cartoon on Netflix. 'Ever since I told her about Jack not coming back.'

'Yes. And I'm not surprised, poor little love. I suppose she's transferred all her affections to Crystal, now.'

I sighed. How was everything coming back to Crystal again?

'No, not all to Crystal,' I said. 'To me, to you, to Dad, to her nursery teachers, *and* to Crystal. OK?'

'Mummy,' said a little voice from the kitchen doorway. 'Why do you sound cross?'

'I'm not cross, sweetie,' I said, forcing a laugh. 'I'm just—'

But fortunately, before I could think of a good excuse for what, without a doubt, must definitely have sounded like crossness, she went on with no regard to the abrupt change of subject, 'I wish I was a mermaid, Mummy. I want a fishy tail.'

'But then you couldn't run away when I chase you like this!' I said, pretending to try to grab her as she squealed and dashed off around the house.

If only everything could have been as easy to answer as that.

30

CRYSTAL

It was a stupid excuse. I didn't think it through. An emergency appointment – I thought Gemma would understand that. Unfortunately, she understood only too well. It was no excuse for not simply going round for a brief chat, no excuse for not going on the Sunday, after I'd supposedly had the tooth treated. No excuse at all. Even if Gemma pretended to believe me, I knew she didn't. And more to the point, her dad wouldn't have done, either.

If I'd been in a better frame of mind I'd have thought of a better cover story. And I'd have told Gemma at a sensible, polite, decent time – the week before, not on the day. But of course, I wasn't in a good frame of mind, not at all. I never was, when I was in the lead-up to one of the visits. I often got to the point where I was even thinking of cancelling. Just not going. Would it have been any worse than going through the agony of how it ended up, every single time?

But it would have. It would have been worse, much worse, and not just for me. It would have been worse for the person who really mattered. Because, however long it took for things to change – if they ever did – there would come a time when we could at least look back and know that I'd made the effort. I kept trying, every month without fail, going through the same pain, the same *purgatory*, never completely giving up hope. But this time had been no better than all the others – it never was, no matter what I hoped for, no matter what everyone said to encourage me. It was always just as awful. All that pain, all that heartache – and none of it was my fault. That was what I'd never be able to forgive. None of what happened was my fault, but it ruined my life, ruined *me*.

Gemma thought Jack had ruined her life by leaving her – and I sympathised, I really did, because I knew how that felt. But she had no idea how much worse it could have been. She had no idea of the truth about me. And if I'd told her, it wouldn't have just been her parents who wouldn't trust me. I doubted whether she'd ever have allowed me to see my little Poppy again.

So I'd just have to go on with the lies, the half-truths, the feeble excuses – even though I didn't like myself for doing it. Poppy had saved my life. I couldn't give her up now.

31

GEMMA

'Before you say anything,' Crystal said, as soon as we met up the next Monday lunchtime, 'I'm sorry, OK? Really sorry I had to let you down at the last minute like that. I know what you must think.'

'So I presume it wasn't true?' I said. I could hear the snappiness in my voice. I was giving her the benefit of the doubt – but I suspected that even now, she was going to lie. Anything other than admit she hadn't wanted to meet my dad.

'Not *completely* true,' she said. 'But I did have a terrible toothache. It came on suddenly, and, well, I just couldn't think straight. I did try to get a dentist's appointment but it was no good, I couldn't get in anywhere. So I just took some strong painkillers and went to bed.'

'So why wouldn't you tell me that?'

'It sounded pathetic,' she said, with a sigh. 'I thought you'd think it sounded like... well, like an excuse.'

'So how is it now?' I couldn't hide the scorn in my voice. We both knew she was still lying. Why couldn't she just admit it?

'Much better, thanks. I didn't sleep all night for the pain, so I stayed in bed yesterday, too, but today, it's OK. Isn't that amazing?'

'Yes. Amazing.'

She fell silent. Then, 'You don't believe me, do you?'

'Should I? Look, I'd have preferred it if you'd just told me right from the start that you didn't want to meet my dad, OK? Why leave it till the last minute and make up some pathetic story? You didn't have a toothache at all, did you?'

For a minute I thought she wasn't going to answer. We were walking towards our usual lunch stop, and we'd already crossed the road and turned the corner. Then, 'I'm sorry,' she said again, grabbing my arm, bringing me to a stop. 'Please don't hate me.'

'Don't be stupid, I don't hate you, but I am annoyed. Disappointed. I'd just rather you were honest with me. I could have understood, in a way – although my dad isn't scary, he's lovely. But perhaps you felt like you were going to be interrogated or something – after all, my mum hasn't exactly been welcoming—'

'I did think that, a little bit,' she admitted. 'I was a bit nervous, yes. I wish I *had* been honest with you, Gem, but I didn't want you to hate me.'

'What's all this about hating you?' We started walking again. In a weird way, I felt better now she'd admitted to lying, annoying though it still was. 'There's no need to talk like that, is there? I was just cross that you cried off, at such short notice. All it's done is give Dad even more of an impression that I shouldn't trust you.'

'Is that what he thinks?' she said, sighing.

'Yes. Frankly, yes, and since we're being honest with each other now – so does my mum. They're both suspicious of you, and now you've made it worse.'

'I'm an idiot,' she said quietly. 'It was true that I couldn't make it this weekend, but I didn't know how to tell you. I thought it would have sounded... feeble. But I had something I couldn't get out of.'

I waited, but it seemed she wasn't going to tell me what it was. She didn't have to, of course, but I couldn't help wondering. *Like the last time*, I thought. Again, she was unavailable for a whole weekend but didn't want to talk about it. Well, that was her business, I supposed.

'Well, you're right, you're an idiot,' I said, a bit more affectionately, as I pushed open the pub door. 'We've been friends for long enough now, haven't we? You should have just told me you couldn't make it – I won't ask why, if you don't want to tell me – but please, don't go making up stupid lies about dentists ever again if you want us to stay friends, OK?'

'OK.' She linked her arm through mine. 'I'm really sorry, Gem. Thanks for being so nice about it. I don't deserve you.'

'All right, all right, don't overdo it. There's an empty table at the back, look. Go and grab it while I order the food. What are you having?'

'I'll have a lentil curry today. I'm hungry.'

'After your weekend not eating because of the toothache, I suppose?' I teased, and she gave me a grimace in response.

I was glad we'd made up, glad we could move on. But at the back of my mind, I still had a niggle about the way she'd felt the need to lie, and more to the point, to let me down. Let my dad down. Make things worse for us both.

'So tell me why you think your parents are suspicious of me,' she said when I went to join her at the table. 'What have I done? Is your mum still upset about Poppy's birthday?'

'No, it's not that.' I paused for a moment, wondering how honest to be with her. But really, I thought she needed to know. 'It's... well, look, perhaps it sounds a bit daft, but the truth is, they're worried about how close you seem to have got with Poppy. Over such a short time.'

'So they're jealous, that's all. Because I'm spending more time with Poppy than they do? Don't they understand that I'm doing it to help you?'

'Yes, I keep explaining that. But they're not jealous – well, Mum might be, a bit, but it's not just that. They're suspicious because... oh it's ridiculous, really, but they seem to think you might run off with Poppy or something. Steal her from me.'

There was a silence. Crystal bent her head and looked down at the table. She was upset, and I wasn't surprised. I touched her hand and went on, softly, 'I keep telling them it's ridiculous.'

'You don't think that, do you?' she asked without looking up.

'No. Of course not. And anyway, if you'd wanted to steal Poppy from me, you've had plenty of opportunities to run off with her – when you take her out for walks. Do you think I'd let you take her out if I didn't trust you with her?'

Our meals were brought to the table then, so we both fell silent for a few minutes. I started on my soup, but Crystal just toyed with her curry, lifting forkfuls of it and putting them down again.

'Your parents only think that about me because I haven't got a child of my own, don't they?' she said eventually, looking up to meet my eyes. 'They think I'm so desperate that I'd make friends with you just to steal your daughter. I'm really hurt that anyone could think that of me.'

'Well,' I said, trying to spare her feelings, 'perhaps it's just that they find it strange how quickly we've become friends, and how well you've got on with Poppy. Don't worry about it, and please don't be hurt. *I* trust you, and that's all that matters. But please make an effort to meet them both properly and show them you're... not what they think. For my sake, OK?'

She nodded. 'OK. I will. Now, what's the latest about Jack? You said you've heard from the Child Maintenance Service again?'

'Yes.' I blinked back surprise at the sudden change of topic, but I guessed she just didn't want to talk about my parents any more. Not that I really wanted to talk about Jack, or his disappearing act, either. 'Apparently neither Jack nor his family can be traced in New South Wales. The Australian authorities are suggesting the entire family might have even moved to another country.'

'*What*?' she gasped.

'Unbelievable, isn't it?'

'You don't think they've come back here, to the UK, do you?'

'The CMS will find them if they're here. No, I bet they're still in Australia or New Zealand somewhere, living under false names or something, but it seems ridiculously extreme, doesn't it? The whole family in hiding – just to avoid Jack paying maintenance for his daughter? I can't get my head around it.'

'Sounds like they must have more to hide from than just the CMS, if you ask me.'

'I've been wondering the same thing.' I put down my soup spoon and turned to look out of the window. It was raining, dark and cold – depressing weather for a depressing conversation. 'I never really knew Jack at all, did I? I was in love with... a myth. A pretence.'

'It must feel that way,' she sympathised – and then reached over the table to squeeze my hand. 'Keep hold of that anger, love. Don't be sad. Get your own back by having a good life without him.'

I nodded. 'I know. I'm trying.' I smiled at her. 'I couldn't do it without you, though.'

We went on to talk about other things, and while I was glad to drop the subject of Jack, there was also no more mention of my parents and their suspicions, which I found quite strange since she'd professed to be so hurt by it all.

* * *

The following evening, as I was getting Poppy out of the car outside my house, one of my neighbours from along the road, a middle-aged woman called Amanda, happened to walk past and called out hello.

'Haven't seen you for a while,' she commented. 'Or your other half. Are you both keeping well?'

'Oh.' I felt my face drop. I only knew a few of the neighbours, and not well enough to have felt like broadcasting the news of our separation to any of them. 'Well unfortunately we're not together any more,' I said, and turned away, wanting to leave it at that.

'Oh, I'm so sorry to hear that,' Amanda gushed. 'I did wonder... what with your sister having moved in with you.'

'My *sister*?' I stared at her. 'Oh – you must mean

Crystal. She's not my sister, she's a friend. And she hasn't moved in. She's just... spending quite a bit of time with me. Helping me, actually.'

'I see.' She nodded. 'Well, that's nice, and I'm glad you've got someone to help you. She's always up and down here with your little one, isn't she? Hello, dear!' she added to Poppy, and then turned back to me and went on, half under her breath, 'Such a shame for her – her daddy leaving. Bye, love.'

'Bye bye, lady,' Poppy called after her as she walked down the street.

I was seething. Nosy old bag. I was sure Crystal hadn't told anyone she was my sister, Amanda had just said that as a ruse to find out exactly who she was, not that it was anything to do with her.

'Lady in the sweet shop,' Poppy said as I opened the front door.

'Lady? The lady we saw just now, Pops? She lives along the road. You've seen her in a shop?' I said, surprised.

'Sweet shop. Gives me buttons.'

I was frowning now, confused. 'That lady – Amanda – you've seen her in the sweet shop? What, the shop round the corner? And she gave you chocolate buttons? When was this, Poppy?'

'Yesterday.'

To Poppy, everything in the past was 'yesterday' so it really didn't tell me anything. I wasn't sure if she was making this up, or...

'Was it when you were out with Crystal?' I guessed.

'Yes. When I goes with Crystal. In the sweet shop.'

'And... hang on, has this happened more than once? The chocolate buttons?'

'Yes, in the sweet shop!' she said, sounding impatient now. 'Play with me now, Mummy?'

There was no point questioning Poppy any more, but I pondered over it during the evening, while she was in bed. It sounded innocuous enough for Amanda, if it was her, to see Poppy with Crystal in the post office and buy her some chocolate buttons. Poppy called it the sweet shop because I often treated her to sweets when we had to queue in there. Nice of her, but out of the ordinary. So it seemed odd that Crystal hadn't mentioned it. And odd if it really had happened more than once. It made me feel a bit uncomfortable: I could have thanked her, if I'd known about it. *Why* hadn't Crystal told me about it? She couldn't have forgotten. It would have been quite unusual for someone to give Poppy sweets like that – she'd surely have mentioned it, asked me about Amanda, whether I knew her, whether she knew Poppy?

For some reason, then, I went back to thinking

about the conversation we'd had over lunch. When I'd told Crystal of my parents' concerns about her, and the way she'd abruptly changed the subject. I'd assumed it was because she was upset – she *looked* like she was upset – but was she actually just being dismissive? Thinking it was all a fuss about nothing? I'd assured her I thought my parents were being ridiculous, but wasn't I – if I was completely honest – wondering just a tiny bit whether it *was* strange how much time she wanted to spend with Poppy, how often she came around, how she seemed to have made me depend on her so quickly. I knew it was all a bit unusual, but I talked myself out of thinking that. I talked myself into accepting it because I liked her, I needed her, I needed to trust her. Surely I wasn't wrong – was I?

32

CRYSTAL

I couldn't say I was surprised, obviously, that I'd now upset Gemma's father as well as her mother. It was unforgiveable, as well as stupid, to leave my excuses for the weekend until the last possible moment and then invent something that was palpable nonsense. My only excuse was that it was *that* weekend, and I couldn't think straight. But now I felt like I might have made Gemma start wondering about me too. Hearing her parents express doubts about my motives – however much she said they were being ridiculous – I was worried now that some of it might have stuck.

So, I was going to have to make time to meet up with both of them: the dad the next time he was down from Manchester (and I just hoped it wouldn't be on the same weekend the following month, or I'd have to find a better excuse), and Jane, the mum, whenever she deigned to meet me again. Although God knows why she'd want to, as she hadn't exactly seemed eager to get to know me each time we'd met up so far.

It crossed my mind briefly that perhaps I should just tell Gemma the truth. Explain why I had one weekend every month booked up, sacrosanct, when I couldn't see her, her parents, or anyone else. But no – if I did that, I'd have to wave goodbye to being allowed any more time with Poppy. And I couldn't let that happen, not now, now that it was going so well... helping me so much. I shuddered, literally shuddered, to think how I'd cope if that was taken away from me.

I wouldn't have minded if the weekends marked in red in my diary had ever turned out to be a success – if I didn't always come back afterwards feeling worse than when I went away. That previous weekend I'd cried so much I felt like I'd almost have preferred to spend it facing the inquisition from Gemma's father. The next visit would be a pre-Christmas weekend... and any normal person would have been looking forward to it.

But I wasn't normal, was I? Nobody *normal* would have had to do what I did – no matter how much they all tried to tell me now that I couldn't have done anything different, that I'd had no choice at the time. Everything would come good in the end, they all told me: I just had to be patient. But it was so hard, and I'd had to be patient for so long. And I'd never, ever, be able to forgive the person whose fault it all was.

33

GEMMA

Crystal turned up a couple of evenings later, offering to play with Poppy while I did some work – but I said I'd rather she had a cup of tea and a chat with me. Poppy had been amusing herself with some toys but as soon as she heard Crystal's voice, of course, she came running out of the living room, holding up her arms to be picked up, wanting Crystal to go and play with her. So rather than cause an upset just before bedtime, I left them to it, got Poppy's milk and pyjamas ready, and let Crystal put her to bed – a bit early, but Poppy wouldn't know that.

'So what did you want to chat about?' Crystal asked when she was finally settled down. She looked at me warily. 'Is there something worrying you?'

'Not exactly worrying, no – but it is puzzling me.' I turned to look her straight in the eyes. 'Have you been telling people you're my sister? People you've met when you're out with Poppy?'

'What?' She looked genuinely surprised. 'No, why would I do that? What makes you think I have?'

'A neighbour of mine down the road said she'd seen you a lot, out with Poppy, and she thought you were my sister. Perhaps she was just making assumptions, but—'

'Perhaps,' Crystal agreed, with a shrug. 'Or... well, I sometimes refer to myself as *Auntie Crystal* when I'm talking to Poppy, so if this person overheard me say that, she could have assumed that meant I was your sister.'

'Yes, I suppose so. Poppy said this woman – Amanda – saw you with her in the post office, and gave her some chocolate buttons. Is that right? It seems a bit odd; I don't know her very well.'

'Oh!' Crystal's face cleared in recognition. 'Yes, I know the woman you mean; she works in the post office, doesn't she?'

'Does she? I didn't know that – I've never seen her in there.'

'Just at weekends, apparently. We always have a

chat when I take Poppy in there to choose some sweets.'

'Well, thank you, but you shouldn't keep buying her sweets,' I said. It sounded like she'd been making a habit of it, rather than an occasional treat. But that was beside the point, really. 'Poppy seemed to think Amanda herself had given her chocolate buttons.'

'Well, yes, she did – just once. Or maybe twice. I think she probably felt a bit sorry for Poppy—'

'Sorry for her? Why?'

'Well, she asked after you, and Jack, so I told her about Jack leaving, and—'

'*What*?' I stared at Crystal. 'That was *not* for you to tell her. I don't want you talking to my neighbours, telling them private things about me—'

'But she asked!' Crystal said, looking stricken now. 'I couldn't very well just pretend Jack was fine, still living here, when he isn't, could I?'

'That's for me to decide, not you. Apart from anything else, that nosy cow fronted up to me the other day and pretended not to know, asking after him again like she was fishing for more information – which I *didn't* give her because it's frankly none of her business! She's probably gossiping about me now with all the other neighbours, and everyone who goes into the post office—'

'Oh.' Crystal looked down. 'Oh, Gemma, I'm really sorry. But surely she wouldn't gossip about you, she seemed so nice—'

'I hardly even know her! I don't want her giving Poppy sweets, OK? Trying to get round you, probably trying to worm more information out of you – making assumptions that you're my sister. In fact, I don't want you to take Poppy into that shop any more. I don't like the idea of it. Poppy will start expecting it, and it's not good for her.'

Of course, I often bought her sweets in there myself but that wasn't the point. I was working myself up into a frenzy of annoyance, thinking about Amanda giving out chocolate button bribes in exchange for gossip, thinking about Crystal telling all and sundry my personal business. How dare she?

'Sorry,' she was saying again, shakily. 'I won't go in there any more then, I promise. Please don't be angry with me, I didn't mean any harm, please don't stop me from taking Poppy out for walks—'

I stared at her. She was on the verge of tears.

'I didn't say anything about stopping you taking her out. Don't get upset about it... Just – look, please just don't talk to anyone around here about me, or about my personal business, that's all I'm saying.' I lowered my voice a little and added, trying to sound less confrontational – although God knew, it was me that should be upset, not her, 'All right?'

She sniffed and nodded. 'Yes. Of course. Sorry.'

'OK, well, let's just leave it there.' I felt awkward, as if I'd been unreasonable. After all, she *was* doing me a favour. But no – she'd overstepped the mark, and I'd needed to make it clear I wasn't happy about it. But the panic on her face, and in her voice, when she thought I might stop her from taking Poppy out – it was quite startling. Far from her just doing me a favour. I'd suddenly been faced with the reality of exactly how much of a favour *I* was doing *her*... just by letting her look after my daughter. And I felt a little shiver of apprehension.

Crystal stayed for dinner that evening, and we talked about other things – a stilted conversation, like people who'd only just met. I felt shaken, and she was quiet and despondent. She didn't come round the following evening – a Friday – which was unusual, and I wondered if I'd upset her so much that she'd been frightened off. But on the Saturday morning she appeared as usual, bright and smiling, seemingly back to her old self, wearing a long, bright red corduroy dress decorated with yellow sunflowers.

'Got it from one of those pre-loved clothing websites,' she said cheerfully when I complimented her on it, looking down at my boring denim jeans and grey jumper and making the obvious comparison. 'You should try them. Lots of designer outfits on there, at rock-bottom prices.'

I could hardly tell her that, good though the dress looked on her, I'd never go out wearing anything like the clothes she chose. But just looking at her made me feel more cheerful, and it was a sunny day despite being absolutely freezing cold, so when she suggested taking Poppy out for a run around the park, I said I'd go too. Her face fell for a moment and I guessed she was wondering if I didn't trust her after our contretemps during the week, but I gave her a hug and said I was up to date with all my work and just fancied a walk in the sunshine.

Poppy was excited by the prospect of the park – it was the first bright day for a while so it had been a couple of weeks since she'd been there.

'I can walk. Big girl now,' she said, refusing to sit in her buggy but taking hold of Crystal's hand as we set off.

'She'll change her mind halfway there,' I said quietly to Crystal. 'It's still too far for her—'

'I know. She always does.'

It rankled a little – this implication, whether it was intended or not – that Crystal knew as much about Poppy as I did, if not more. But I swallowed it back. I wasn't going to start finding fault with everything she did now, all of a sudden, just because of one incident that had annoyed me. Sure enough, Poppy asked to get into the buggy well before we reached the park, but jumped out, excitedly, once she spotted her favourite play equipment.

'Swings!' she yelled, racing towards them.

'Stay back, Pops!' Crystal warned her, running after her. 'Someone's in one of them, don't get too close.'

She grabbed Poppy just in time to stop the child in one of the baby swings from accidentally kicking her over.

'Thanks,' I said, catching up with them. 'Poppy, I keep telling you about this, don't I! You must stay clear – wait for one of us to bring you to an empty swing.'

'No harm done!' said the mother of the little boy. 'I'd have grabbed George's swing and stopped it, if Poppy had got too close. Hi!' she went on, to Crystal. 'Haven't seen you over here for a while.'

'No – well, the weather's been a bit grim, hasn't it?' Crystal replied. 'Come on, Poppy, I'll put you in the one next to George, OK?'

I looked from Crystal to George's mum and back, waiting to be introduced, but Crystal seemed to be almost pretending I wasn't there.

'Hello,' I said, eventually, when the other woman turned to give me a questioning look. 'I'm Gemma – Poppy's mum.'

'Oh!' The woman coloured slightly, looking from me to Crystal, who had her back to us, securing Poppy into the swing. 'Oh – I see. Um... I thought...' She tailed off, gave an awkward little laugh, and then went on in a rush, 'Well, um, it's nice to meet you. I'm Nicky, and this is George – he's the same age as Poppy and we often see her over here, don't we, George? When she comes with her... um, with...'

'My friend. Crystal,' I said, to help her out. Crystal still had her back to us.

'Your friend. Right,' Nicky said a little faintly. She looked with a puzzled expression at Crystal's back view, but didn't say any more, turning instead to her little boy, who was urging her to push him higher.

Crystal pushed Poppy, Nicky pushed George, we all laughed as the kids squealed excitedly for more, and none of us said any more. Crystal didn't look me in the eyes again until after we'd finished with the swings, moved on to the baby slide and climbing blocks, said goodbye to Nicky and George, and walked back to look at the ducks.

'I think Nicky must have assumed I was Poppy's mum,' she said, in the tone of someone who was pretending to think something was very funny.

'Yes. I can't imagine why she assumed that,' I said drily.

I told myself, as we walked home, with an overtired Poppy singing softly to herself in the buggy, that it didn't mean anything. Anyone would assume, if they regularly saw a woman with a child in the park, that the woman was the mother. But that didn't quite explain why Nicky had looked so confused, had seemed so flummoxed by it, and had stared at the back of Crystal's head as if she'd expected something from her.

She'd expected an explanation. Because it was pretty obvious what had happened there, and I didn't like it. I wanted to confront Crystal about it, but what was I going to say? That I didn't believe Nicky had just made an assumption, at all – that I suspected Crystal was claiming to be Poppy's mother? She'd just deny it; there was no way I could prove it, and it would seem petty to push the point.

But I wanted to know why. *Why* was she passing herself off as my daughter's mother? What could she gain from it? Was it just a game of pretend for her, a chance to act like the mother she so wished she'd been? Or something else entirely?

* * *

I worried about it all the rest of the weekend. Mum had invited Poppy and me to her place for dinner and I was aware that I was quiet, listening to Mum chatting about plans for Christmas and what Poppy and I would like as presents, wondering whether Dad would join us for Christmas dinner – as he usually did – or whether he might want to spend the day with friends from his golf club.

'He's not seeing the young lady he went out with last year, any more,' Mum said, sounding quite unperturbed by the whole thing. 'I don't know why he bothered, to be honest. He told me he found her boring.'

'Perhaps he just liked having a bit of female company. Going out for dinner and so on,' I suggested. The last thing I wanted to have a discussion about was my father's love life. It seemed bizarre to me that they still got on so well together, spent birthdays and Christmases – and once or twice even a holiday – together, despite being divorced. So to me, there could only be one possible reason for Dad having dated a couple of seemingly younger women since the divorce, and it had nothing to do with enriching his mind.

'Are you all right, darling?' she asked as I sat in silence staring at my apple crumble while Poppy made short work of hers. 'You're very quiet today.'

'I'm fine, Mum.'

'Have you seen Crystal this weekend?' she asked, pretending to sound casual.

'Crystal took me to the park!' Poppy said.

'Yes – yesterday. We went together, didn't we, Pops?'

'Me and George went on the swings!' she told Mum excitedly.

'George?' Mum raised an enquiring eyebrow at me.

'A little friend Poppy's made at the park. He was there with his mum.' I felt myself frowning, just saying it, just remembering. 'She'd... got to know Crystal.'

'When Crystal takes Poppy to the park on her own?' Mum said, her mouth going into a disapproving line.

'Yes.' I looked down at my dish. 'Actually, Mum, I'm really sorry but I'm too full up for dessert. I should have said no.'

'Not to worry. You can take some home for tomorrow, for you and Poppy.' She scooped up my plate, put it on top of the empty ones and got up to carry them into the kitchen.

'I'll load the dishwasher,' I offered, following her. Poppy had gone back to the toy she'd been playing with in the living room before lunch.

'OK,' Mum said as soon as we were in the kitchen. 'So what happened?'

'What do you mean?'

'Come on: you've been quiet and looking worried ever since you arrived, and you obviously didn't want to talk about the park. Or Crystal. Or was it this other mum, with the little boy?'

'Nicky. No, Mum, she seemed really nice.'

I crouched down to dishwasher level, hiding my face behind its top drawer as I pulled it out. But I should have known better than to try to hide anything from my mum.

'Seemed really nice but what?' she persisted.

I didn't want to say anything. I'd been telling my-self all day I was just imagining it, making something out of nothing. But on top of my annoyance with Crystal for telling Amanda my personal business, it had eaten away at me to the point where I couldn't hold it back any longer.

'She thought Crystal was Poppy's mum,' I said, still looking into the dishwasher rather than face my mother. 'It would be understandable. Except that...'

'You think Crystal's encouraged it? Or that she's actually *told* her she is?'

I sighed, stood up, and finally turned and looked Mum in the eyes.

'Yes,' I admitted – and I felt a little shiver run through me, just from saying it aloud. 'I think she might have done.'

34

CRYSTAL

I knew what Gemma was thinking – obviously: she thought I must have told Nicky I was Poppy's mum. I was sure I didn't say that – did I? No, Nicky must have just assumed it, and stupidly, it didn't occur to me that she would do that. Perhaps she recognised me, perhaps she'd seen me in the park years ago and made assumptions, assumed I'd now got a three-year-old little girl. And despite the awkwardness of it, the fact that Gemma was so obviously peeved, and Nicky was embarrassed, I couldn't help it... just for a few moments I felt a little thrill of excitement. *Poppy's mum.* Someone took me for Poppy's mum. Oh, if only!

But Gemma wasn't amused, and fair enough. I guessed she was beginning to feel a bit sidelined; after all, it was already becoming obvious that I was Poppy's favourite person. Poppy preferred me taking her to the park, making her tea and even putting her to bed. I didn't expect that, didn't set out for it to happen: it just did, naturally. But of course, it made me happy. How could it not?

As for the woman in the sweet shop: that was another storm in a teacup. I couldn't understand, to be honest, why Gemma was so upset about it. I didn't see her – Mandy – as being a gossip, or nosy. She was just concerned, just showing Poppy some love. I thought it was nice of her.

But I realised now that I was going to have to be more careful. I got carried away, sometimes, by the enjoyment of my times with Poppy. The last thing I wanted would be to give Gemma a bad impression – like I'd given both her mum and her dad already. I could imagine that they were talking to Gemma about me, trying to make her suspicious, perhaps trying to persuade her to stop me from seeing Poppy. I couldn't even bear to think about that. My mental health had improved massively since meeting Gemma and Poppy... apart from after the monthly visits that always set me back. And I knew I'd have a horrendous relapse if Poppy wasn't part of my life any more. No, I really couldn't afford to let that happen.

35

GEMMA

I wished, as soon as the words were out of my mouth, that I hadn't said anything to Mum about Crystal and the woman in the park.

'What have I been telling you?' she demanded. 'There's something not right about all this, Gemma. A single woman with no kids, wanting to spend all her time with Poppy? I'm sorry, but it just doesn't add up. And now she's been pretending to be Poppy's mother – well, I hate to say it, but I'm not surprised, I thought all along—'

'I know what you thought, Mum,' I said, wearily. 'But I just can't believe she's got any... malevolent intentions.'

'You're being too naïve. You were vulnerable when you met her – you still are, to be honest. Susceptible to... well, to someone being kind, helping you out, sympathising with your situation. Whereas your dad and I could see straight away that... well, there was something not quite right about it.' She paused, gave me a look and sighed. 'I'm sorry, I know you don't want to think the worst of her. I know you needed a friend; I do understand. But be honest – how well do you really know Crystal? What do you know about her? Have you ever been to her home? Met her family?'

'She hasn't got any family, apart from a brother who lives in London, and she hardly ever sees him.'

'Well, that's convenient, isn't it?' Mum said drily.

I was silent, thinking about the weekends when Crystal couldn't see me because she had to go somewhere else, somewhere mysterious that she never wanted to talk about. Were they a cover for something else? What exactly was she not telling me?

'So *have* you been to her home?' Mum persisted.

'No. She always comes to me, because the whole point is, she helps me out by looking after Poppy.'

'Yes. The *whole point*,' Mum said, nodding. 'That's exactly what I'm getting at. Why doesn't she invite you and Poppy to her place?'

'I suppose it's just easier...'

I tailed off, miserably. The more I tried to defend Crystal, the more Mum's arguments were ringing true. I didn't want her to be right. I didn't want to think badly of Crystal. But I had that shivering down my spine again, just from thinking, even for a minute: *What if Crystal really did want my daughter for herself?*

* * *

Inevitably, I had a phone call from Dad that evening, after Poppy was in bed. Mum hadn't wasted much time reporting back.

'Look, I'm not saying you ought to stop seeing her,' he said without any preamble. 'But please, Gemma, don't let that woman keep taking Poppy out on her own, will you? Not till you've sorted this out, at least.'

'Sorted what out, Dad?' I could hear the sulky tone in my own voice. I felt like I was about thirteen again, listening to my parents worrying behind my back about the suitability of one of my friends.

'Well, Mum seems to think you still don't really know enough about this Crystal. She thinks you rushed into the friendship – and don't get me wrong, love, we both understand why – but you didn't really know her. And you still don't. You don't know where she lives, you don't know why her own relationship broke up or why she doesn't have any kids of her own.'

'No, I haven't asked, because it's frankly a bit too personal, isn't it? She'd tell me if she wanted to, but I've just presumed her boyfriend left her before they'd even started trying for a baby, and now she doesn't want to have one as a single mother, and she hasn't met anyone she wants to—'

'I'd feel better if she'd told you, rather than you presuming. But this latest thing – pretending to be Poppy's mum – it makes me feel very uncomfortable, and your mum says you obviously weren't happy about it yourself.'

'Well, to be fair to Crystal, I don't *know* if she was pretending. It was just as likely the other woman assumed it.'

I could hear Dad sighing. 'Well, look, I won't say any more, but just think about it, will you? Your mum and I are both worried. Promise me you'll be careful. Don't let her have Poppy on her own until you're really sure about her.'

'I *was* really sure about her,' I said, 'until you and Mum started saying all this stuff.'

But of course, it wasn't true. Not any more. I *was* having doubts, however much I tried to deny it, and I didn't know how I was going to resolve them. Crystal was always around, always being her usual cheery, chatty self, and I couldn't find a way to suddenly start giving her the third degree about why exactly she hadn't had children, or why exactly she wanted to spend so much time with Poppy, having accepted the situation without question up till now.

I made up my mind; I'd have a serious talk with her as soon as possible, but when Crystal and I met for lunch on the Monday, she seemed quiet and preoccupied, barely able to give me a smile even when I started telling her about something funny Poppy had said.

'Are you OK?' I asked, concern now taking precedence over my worries. 'You seem... a bit down.'

She forced a smile. 'Oh, I'm all right. Just thinking about... well, about everything I've got to do before Christmas.'

'Tell me about it!' I laughed. 'I haven't even started my Christmas shopping yet. And Poppy's nagging me about putting the tree and the decorations up – they've had everything up at her nursery since the beginning of the month. I need to get on the case this weekend, really.'

I stopped, looking at Crystal, wondering. What did she do for Christmas? She'd never said. Surely she didn't just sit at home on her own on Christmas Day?

'Do you go to your brother's for Christmas?' I asked her. 'Or does he come to you?'

'Sometimes,' she said, not looking remotely pleased at the thought of it. 'But, well, it's just another day, really, isn't it? When there are no children to get excited about it.'

She's expecting me to invite her, I realised.

I felt my breath catch in my throat. How could I? Poppy and I would be going to Mum's; Dad would probably come down – unless he had a better offer. We'd stay over for Boxing Day – it was all planned already. There was no way I could ask to invite Crystal to join us, not the way Mum and Dad were feeling about her now.

'Why don't you come round on Christmas Eve?' I said quickly before I could change my mind. 'It'll just be you, me and Poppy – she'll be all excited about Father Christmas, you can help her do the milk and biscuits for him, and we'll do her stocking and tuck her into bed early, then we can have a special dinner, just the two of us—'

Her eyes had lit up. 'Oh, are you really sure? You really wouldn't mind? I mean, I know you'll be going to your mum's on Christmas Day, and, well, I might see my brother but I never know till the last minute – but it would be so lovely to spend Christmas Eve with you and Poppy. I can't tell you how happy that would make me. It'll make... everything else' – she paused and took a deep breath – 'everything else that goes on... feel easier to bear.'

I couldn't help feeling relieved that I'd cheered her up so much – that she seemed so pleased and enthusiastic about coming on Christmas Eve, even if she did have to spend Christmas on her own. I didn't care, right then, what Mum and Dad thought, I didn't care about my own uneasiness about her. The thought of her, alone and sad on the day when most of us would be enjoying ourselves with our loved ones, was almost unbearable and I couldn't believe I hadn't thought about it sooner. But that last, lingering comment she'd made about *everything else that goes on* was troubling me. Her smile had dropped as she'd said it, the frown lines coming back onto her face.

'What do you mean?' I asked her. 'What is *everything else that goes on*?'

'Oh, well,' she said vaguely, with a dismissive shrug. 'You know. All the hassle. Christmas shopping, like you say.'

I frowned. Christmas shopping? Who did she have to buy presents for? Just her brother, unless...

'Please don't start spending money on us – Poppy or me,' I said gently. 'There's no need, honestly—'

'It's fine. I'll only buy a little something. It's a pleasure to buy for Poppy, especially now I know I'll be able to give her present to her myself – if you don't mind her having it on Christmas Eve?'

'Of course I don't mind.'

I stared at her as she started to idly pick at her lunch. I couldn't make this out. There was something very strange about her mood: despite her excitement about the offer of Christmas Eve, she still wasn't really happy.

'Cheer up,' I said. 'How about we go shopping together on Saturday? Mum's offered to have Poppy for the day so I can buy my Christmas presents. I was going to get them all online, to be honest – I don't particularly like shopping in the crowds at this time of year – but if we go out together, it'll be more fun, won't it?'

'Your mum's having Poppy?' Crystal said, looking up at me. 'I suppose she doesn't trust me around her now.'

I stared at her. 'No, it isn't that, at all. I've just said, it's so that I can go shopping – if I want to. Poppy would hate it—'

She sighed and shook her head. 'I can't make it this weekend anyway. Sorry.'

'Oh.' I was taken aback by her tone. Was she sulking? Was she really so offended at my mum offering to have Poppy for the day? And this was before I'd even broached the subject of my concerns – or more specifically my parents' concerns – about her pretending to be Poppy's mum. I didn't feel able to even attempt to do that now.

'So are you busy all weekend?' I asked her. 'We could go on Sunday instead.'

'I'll be away. Sorry.'

'Oh – are you going to your brother's? That'll be nice for you—'

'No.' She put down her fork, looked at me across the table, seeming to hesitate for a moment, and at the same time I remembered that this had happened before. Several times.

'Is this – like the other weekends you couldn't make?' I prompted. 'Is it something horrible you have to do, something that upsets you? You never seem very happy about it. Why don't you tell me, love? Even if I can't help, it might just make you feel better to talk about it.'

'It won't,' she retorted. She pushed back her chair, got to her feet, trembling, on the point of tears. 'I *can't* talk about it, OK? It's private. Don't ask me to talk about it—'

'All right, I'm sorry, I won't – look, don't get upset, I didn't mean to... Oh, Crystal, don't just go!'

But she'd turned and walked away, out of the pub door, slamming it behind her, running down the road towards our work. I couldn't even run after her. We hadn't paid the bill.

36

CRYSTAL

I couldn't help it. I didn't want to completely break down in front of Gemma – in front of everyone in the pub – and if I'd let her continue with her so nice, so well-intentioned plea for me to open up and talk to her about what was upsetting me, I knew I would have done – I'd have broken down, and I'd have talked. I'd have told her everything. It was playing so heavily on my mind – the next visit, the crucial one we always made just before Christmas – knowing how it was going to turn out, how I was going to feel, how it would then affect me afterwards, all over Christmas, despite Gemma's lovely offer to let me spend Christmas Eve with her and darling Poppy. I was trying, really trying, not to dwell on it but I just couldn't stop, picturing the scene, picturing it all going wrong again, as it always did, however much I longed for a different outcome, however hard I tried.

I wondered, after I'd got back to work, tidied myself up and tried to calm down, whether she'd guessed. But how could she have done? OK, so she'd guessed that the weekends when I told her I couldn't see her were because of something that was difficult for me. Something upsetting. But she couldn't possibly have known what it was. It was nice of her, of course, to try to encourage me to talk about it. We were supposed to be friends – best friends, she always said – and it was what friends did, shared their worries with each other. I was so tempted, for a moment, to open my mouth and let it all pour out; so tempted, that I had to just get away, as fast as I could. And I really couldn't imagine how I'd be able to see her for lunch as usual the next day; it would have been impossible to carry on as if nothing had happened. I couldn't face it. I messaged her later to apologise, made an excuse about having a virus, and saying I'd see her after the weekend.

It was going to be a long, long week – not going to Gemma's house, not seeing my Poppy, not even hearing anything about her from Gemma. But I decided it was the only way I'd be able to get through it.

37

GEMMA

I was worried about Crystal now. I'd never seen her quite so upset before, and I wished, more than any-thing, that I hadn't broached the subject of those weekends that obviously caused her such a lot of stress – I was only trying to help, but I'd been well and truly warned off, now. It was weird, not seeing her for lunch the next day, not having her turn up any evening that week to see us and play with Poppy; weird, and a bit hurtful. I obviously wasn't buying the excuse about her having a virus. For one thing, I knew she was at work; I'd seen her car in the car park. Had I actually upset her so much that she didn't even want to see me? After spending a couple of days worrying about it, won-dering whether to call her, whether to apologise, check she was OK, I suddenly did a mental about-turn and started to feel aggrieved. I'd only been trying to help, hadn't I? Only tried to sympathise. It was hardly a crime. Hardly something to make her turn her back on me. All my worries about her started to flood back, then; I'd almost forgotten about them, in my concern for her, and my anxiety about whether I'd offended her. What *was* wrong with her? What was it that she was so determined to keep secret? Why *was* she so over the top in her attachment to my daughter that she was possibly pretending to be her mother?

Nevertheless, I had to admit that by the end of the week, I was missing her.

So was Poppy.

'When's Crystal coming?' she asked me that Thursday, and when I couldn't give her a definite answer, she started to work herself up into what threatened to be a full-blown tantrum. She was bored, that was the truth of it. I made a special effort, took time off from my work – which I couldn't really afford to do as I'd acquired a couple of new clients who were expecting their websites finalised before Christmas – to play with her; but I'd got out of the habit, because Crystal was normally with her at least a couple of times during the week.

'I want Crystal!' Poppy demanded. She threw one

of her crayons on the floor, followed by another one, watching me – daring me to get annoyed. I wanted to, but at the same time I felt, ridiculously, like throwing things around myself. It wasn't Poppy's fault I'd become so dependent on Crystal. It wasn't her fault that I'd taken advantage of Crystal's bond with her, to take on extra work that I normally wouldn't have been able to even consider doing. But I needed to do it. I needed the money, I was on my own now and that bastard Jack was never going to be found, never going to be forced to face his financial responsibilities.

'I know, darling,' I said. I pushed my laptop aside. 'I wish she was here, too, but she's not very well. Shall I help you with that drawing? Shall we draw a picture of Crystal, to give her when she feels better? Come on then – pick up those crayons off the floor first.'

Of course, Poppy's 'drawings' were still only at the stage of shapes, sometimes vaguely resembling that of what she was supposedly portraying. But with a bit of guidance and help, she produced a reasonable depiction of a head, body, stick arms and legs, all in bright colours, that could easily pass for Crystal in one of her crazy outfits. And after we'd played a couple of games together it was time for her tea. Another day with hardly any work done. How would I manage, now, if Crystal decided never to come back and help me again? I shuddered at the thought, and at the same time, I realised I'd become far too dependent, far too quickly. This really wasn't good. My child was my responsibility. If Mum and Dad were right in saying Crystal had got too attached to Poppy, I had to accept that it was my own fault. I'd let it happen.

* * *

'You seem a bit down,' Mum said when I delivered Poppy to her house the following day. 'Is everything all right?' She lowered her voice. 'Not more problems with Crystal, I hope?'

'No, Mum,' I snapped, immediately on the defensive. 'I still don't even know if there *is* a problem, OK? Only that she hasn't been free to come round at all this week.'

'Really?' Mum raised her eyebrows. 'That's unusual, isn't it?'

'Yes. Well, she says she's had a virus.' Even though I knew it wasn't true, it was a good enough excuse to stop Mum making an inquisition out of it. 'But it's made it difficult for me to get through all the extra work I've taken on.'

'For goodness' sake, why didn't you call me? I could have had Poppy for an extra day. What about tomorrow? Am I still going to look after her while you go Christmas shopping?'

'I don't know.' I sighed. I'd lost interest in the idea of a shopping trip since I'd invited Crystal to come with me – it had felt, for just those couple of minutes, like such a fun idea, and then, when she'd told me it was one of the weekends that she couldn't see me, it had all come crashing down. 'I'm not really in the mood for it. I think I'll just do it all online this year.'

'Well, let me have Poppy anyway. I can keep her tonight, and bring her back tomorrow evening. That'll give you another whole day to catch up on your work.'

'Oh. Are you sure, Mum? Two whole days – it's a lot to ask of you—'

'No it's not! I'll enjoy every minute of it. So will Poppy. I keep telling you how much I love having her – you really don't need to rely on Crystal so much. You know how I feel about that—'

'Yes, all right, let's not start on that again,' I said – and then immediately felt guilty for reacting so snappily, when she was being so good to me, and I was, definitely, very grateful. 'Thank you, Mum.' I gave her a kiss. 'I do appreciate it.'

* * *

The weekend seemed to drag. I'd worked on the new clients' websites all day Friday and all day Saturday, and by the time Mum brought Poppy home, tired but happy from an afternoon at Exeter's Christmas fair, I'd actually finished both projects, and started to catch up with some other outstanding work too. I was exhausted but pleased, and I was also more than ready to see my baby girl again, to grab hold of her, kiss her and hug her and tell her how much I'd missed her.

'Look! We bringed you chocolates!' she said, freeing herself from my arms and holding out a torn paper bag full of chocolate ginger – one of my favourites, even if a bit squashed.

'Wow, thank you, they look yummy,' I said, mouthing a silent *thank you* to Mum. 'Stay for dinner?' I asked her, but she said she wanted to get home, and I guessed she must be tired. She was still a young-looking sixty-six, but nevertheless I knew how exhausting it must be for her to have a full-on excited Poppy for two whole days.

'Your dad's coming down again tomorrow,' she said just as she was leaving, 'if you'd like to join us for dinner?'

I looked at her in surprise. Dad seemed to be coming down a lot more often recently. Wasn't he coming back yet again for Christmas Day? The thought went through my head, briefly, that they were getting together to discuss me, to share their gripes about Crystal – but I dismissed this quickly as paranoia.

'No. Thanks, Mum, but you've done enough for me this weekend. And I should spend some quality time with Poppy on our own, while...' I nearly said *while Crystal isn't here* – but I guessed it wouldn't be a good idea to invite any sarcastic comments. Or to start Poppy hankering after Crystal again.

* * *

Despite all my concerns about Crystal, she seemed to be completely back to normal on Monday lunchtime as if nothing had happened.

'Are you OK now?' I asked her gently over our lunch.

'Me? Yes, of course, why?' she asked, laughing as she tucked into her five-bean soup.

'From your virus,' I said pointedly – and she had the grace, at least, to look a bit shamefaced as she dropped her eyes and mumbled about it having cleared up suddenly within a few days.

I persisted. 'So how was your weekend?'

'Oh, fine, fine.' She gave me a beaming smile. 'Did you have a good one?'

I stared at her. All that melodrama, all the days the previous week that I'd spent worrying about her, wondering what on earth it could be about her mysterious weekends that caused her so much upset and suffering, and yet here she was, gulping back her soup with such a healthy appetite, smiling happily and saying everything was fine.

'No,' I said bluntly. 'I had to work flat-out, to get everything finished for my new clients, so Mum had to have Poppy overnight and for an extra day. And—'

I just managed to stop myself from saying: *And I missed you. So did Poppy.*

I didn't want to tell her that. I didn't want to emphasise how much I'd come to depend on her, or how upset Poppy had been without her all week. I'd already made up my mind – hadn't I? – that I needed to cut down on how much time Crystal spent with us; so Poppy and I both needed to get used to it.

'How is my little Poppy-Pops?' she asked eagerly. 'I've missed her so much.'

'She's fine,' I said rather more brusquely than I'd intended. 'It was good for her to spend a bit more time with me, and with Mum, for a change.'

Ouch. That had sounded cruel, even to my own ears, and I saw Crystal flinch slightly. But I needed to do this; I needed to make it clear there had to be some lines drawn.

'I think Poppy was beginning to wonder which of us was her real mummy,' I went on. 'And, well, if even other mums in the park think of you as—'

'Gemma, stop it. You know – you must know – I'd never want to take your place, I'd never deliberately take over from you in Poppy's affections.'

I looked back at her. She seemed genuinely hurt that I'd implied anything untoward. But could I believe her? I thought about my dad's warnings, my mum's insistence that something wasn't right. Even though I resented their interference, I did, reluctantly, respect their opinions. And the things they'd suggested about Crystal had eaten away at my own certainty.

'Well,' I said, 'all I'm saying is that I don't want Poppy to get too dependent on you. She was really upset about not seeing you this week, and that's not good; there are bound to be times when you can't come round, and I can't have her crying whenever that happens.'

'Please say you're not going to stop me coming round?' she said, her eyes wide with horror.

'Of course I'm not. But maybe you shouldn't come quite so often.'

'Oh. Well, OK,' she said quietly, looking down at the table, her previous jolly mood somewhat abated.

We changed the subject, talking about work, the weather, Christmas. Nothing more was said about the amount of time she spent with Poppy, and when, over lunch the following day, she asked if she could come over on the Wednesday evening, I said yes, that would be nice, and after that perhaps we'd leave it till the weekend. She looked hurt again, but didn't disagree.

Poppy, of course, was delighted when she arrived, and the pair of them were immediately back to their usual relationship – rolling around on the floor together like two puppies, playing silly games, chasing each other, singing their favourite songs, making me feel completely redundant as I was shooed upstairs to get on with my work.

Be grateful, I reminded myself, trying to quieten the protesting little voice in my head. *You need to earn a living.* We had dinner together, as usual, after Poppy was in bed, and everything began to feel like it was back to normal. Crystal was flushed and excited from playing with Poppy, and we chatted about Christmas Eve, what we could cook for our special meal together, and what she could buy Poppy as a present. She wanted to know what Mum, Dad and I were likely to buy her, so she could avoid duplicating. When it was finally time for her to leave, she started to suggest coming back the next evening.

'No,' I insisted, wishing I didn't have to sound so firm, so unfriendly, about it. 'Remember what I suggested. Let's leave it till Saturday now.'

'But... what about Friday evening? You could get some more work done.'

'I've caught up now, thanks. I'll be OK. Look, no offence, Crystal, you know how much I appreciate your help, but I need to spend a bit more time with Poppy myself. I'll see you Saturday.'

'OK,' she said, in a sulky tone. And then, brightening up, 'Perhaps I'll take her into town. Show her the Christmas lights!'

'I'll come too, then.'

'Oh. All right.' She glanced back at me, then, looking a bit guilty. 'I mean, yes, that'll be nice, Gem. OK, see you then.'

I watched her walking back to her car in the dark, and suddenly had a thought – remembering what Mum had said.

'Actually, Crys – why don't I bring Poppy to your place, and we can go from there? You live nearer the town centre.'

'Oh.' She stopped dead, her car key in her hand, staring at it as if she wasn't sure what to do with it. 'Um... well, that's, an idea, I suppose. Although it's really tricky to park outside my flat, especially at weekends. It's all resident parking only and well, it's easy for me to just drive over here—'

'It's no trouble. I'll pick you up, I'll drive, so I'll only need to park for a few minutes while you get in the car. And I've got the car seat, haven't I, for Poppy.'

'Oh. Yes, I suppose that's a point. OK, then.'

She didn't want us going to her place. And just as Mum had said, I couldn't help wondering why the hell not.

38

CRYSTAL

It was a confusing maelstrom of emotions I was feeling. I'd been so much happier – almost elated – since the weekend. For once, and for the very first time, the visit went a little better than usual. Of course, it was Christmas time – everyone feels better, don't they, around Christmas. There was a definite warming, a very slight thawing of the ice. It wasn't much, and it could just have been the general excitement, the deco-rations and the big tree in the room, the festive spirit in the air... but oh, I left feeling overjoyed, wanting to believe that we'd finally made a little bit of progress.

'Don't get carried away,' Donna warned me – and I felt annoyed that she'd found it necessary to burst my bubble. I wasn't getting *carried away* – I wasn't stupid, I knew it had to be baby steps, I knew we probably still had a long way to go and that the next meeting would probably be a step backwards again. I just wanted to enjoy my happiness and my little ray of hope, while it lasted.

But now I was back, and now Gemma was acting strange. She suddenly didn't want me to go round to her place so often. And it felt like she didn't want me to take Poppy out on my own – she was so quick to insist she'd come along too on the trip to see the lights – just because of a couple of people getting the wrong impression about my relationship with her. I knew it was all because of Gemma's parents – suggestions they'd been putting into her head. Her mum didn't like me, for whatever reason, and her dad was suspicious about me purely because he'd never met me. They seemed to have too much influence over Gemma, if you asked me. And why was she suddenly suggesting coming to my place? She'd never asked before. All that nonsense about me living closer to the town centre – there was hardly anything in it. Then she made the point about the car seat – well, surely she could take it out of her car and put it in mine? No, it was nothing to do with that, or the distance. She was starting to get suspicious. Well, I'd have to be more careful; I didn't want to give her parents any more ammunition against me. If Gemma was determined to come and have a nose around my place, I'd have to... sort everything out. Have a tidy-up. Yes – there were definitely things I'd have to hide.

39

GEMMA

I thought about it overnight. Was I being ridiculous? Should I just accept that Crystal was being kind by offering to drive, making my life easier, saving me the hassle of driving to her place and finding a parking space? But no matter how much I turned it over (and tossed and turned over myself in bed, worrying about it), I couldn't see anything other than the look on her face when I'd suggested going to her place. It was panic. There was definitely some reason she didn't want me there.

I felt so uneasy about the whole thing that I didn't even tell Mum I was going to see the Christmas lights, let alone that I was going with Crystal. As it was, she asked me, when I took Poppy round that Friday, whether I'd taken her – and Dad's – advice to stop Crystal going out with Poppy on her own.

'Yes. Just for now, till I've had time to think it all over,' I said.

'What is there to think over?' Mum insisted – but I changed the subject. I wasn't in the mood for another long drawn-out discussion of her suspicions about Crystal.

* * *

Saturday arrived – a bright but cold day – and I made up my mind to enjoy the day out, regardless of my worries. Poppy was looking forward to it too. Although she'd loved helping with our little Christmas tree at home, and putting up a few decorations, she had no idea what to expect from 'seeing the lights'. But when I explained that there would be a huge Christmas tree in the square in the town centre, and lights all the way along the seafront, she jumped up and down with excitement and started singing the few words she remembered of a song they'd been singing at nursery, about a Christmas tree with a fairy on it.

'Can we go now?' she was asking me every few

minutes, and I had to explain that we were going later at lunchtime, to have a bite to eat in town, before seeing the lights in the afternoon, when it started to get a bit darker.

Just before I was due to set off to pick Crystal up, I noticed an alert on my phone, warning that traffic into our town centre was tailing back, all the way to my own area and beyond. As well as the usual pre-Christmas shopping crowds, there were road works to contend with, and – oh joy – traffic lights out, at one of the main junctions. I gave Crystal a call.

'I'm beginning to wonder if we should actually go,' I said quietly. 'It's going to be a nightmare getting there, and just as bad coming back.'

'Oh, but we can't disappoint Poppy now,' she protested. She thought for a moment, and then added 'Look, why don't we just go on the bus?'

'Seriously?' I said, without any enthusiasm. I never went anywhere by bus.

'Yes! Look, there's a bus lane most of the way into town from where you live—'

'I know. It's really annoying.'

She laughed. 'Yes, when you're driving, it is, but not if you're a bus passenger. I used to use the bus all the time, a while back, when I... when I'd been ill for a while and I couldn't drive. I still use them occasionally. It's brilliant, much faster than driving when the roads are busy, and no worrying about parking. It made me wonder at times why I ever bothered driving. I've got the app on my phone. I'll have a look at the times and message you back.'

Within minutes she'd texted me the times of the next couple of buses.

'Text me which time bus you're getting,' she added, 'and I'll go out and get the same one when it arrives here. The stop's just around the corner from me.'

It did seem a sensible idea.

'Come on, Poppy,' I called her. 'Let's get your coat and shoes on, we're going on the bus.'

'The *bus*?' she repeated, looking at me as if I'd spoken in a foreign language. '*All Day Long*?'

'Yes, just like in the song!' I agreed.

And we walked to the bus stop, singing 'The Wheels on the Bus' at the tops of our voices. She'd apparently forgotten, in the excitement, to ask if Crystal was still coming. And I'd forgotten completely to worry about the fact I'd wanted to go to Crystal's home. I'd forgotten to worry about any of it. It was nearly Christmas, I was with my little girl and we were going on an outing. I was happy.

Of course, when we eventually pulled up at the stop nearest to Crystal's road and she got on the bus, Poppy jumped to her feet, amazed.

'Crystal's here!' she shouted.

'Yes! She's coming on the bus too,' I laughed. Crystal had been right. It was more like an adventure, a proper day out. The bus wasn't too crowded at first, but quite a lot of people got on at the next stop so I put Poppy on my lap, and Crystal came to sit next to us to allow someone else to sit down. We moved on again, and Poppy, who'd knelt up on my lap to look through the gap in the seats, said a shy little *hello* to whoever was sitting behind. I turned, to see it was an elderly lady wearing a bright red woolly hat, who'd got at the stop after Crystal, and she was smiling back at Poppy.

'Hello again, dear!' she said. And then, turning to Crystal, she added, 'Are you taking her into town to see the lights, Mummy?'

Crystal and I both froze. I stared at Crystal, but she – wide-eyed, with a look of panic on her face – just looked back at the older woman, stammering something about having lunch and yes, seeing the lights.

'Excuse me,' I said, appalled by the icy tone to my voice, even as I spoke. 'But *I'm* Poppy's mother.'

'Oh.' The poor woman looked as if she was crumpling into her own hat. She stared from me to Crystal and back again. 'I'm so sorry. I thought... I thought I'd seen you around here together before, so I just assumed...' She stuttered to a stop, shook her head, apologised again and turned away, mumbling that her stop was coming up now. It was ours, too, and I took Poppy's hand, pulling her away from the hand Crystal was offering, and followed the other passengers off the bus. As soon as we were safely off, Crystal tapped me on the shoulder. I had to struggle with myself to even look round at her, but when I did, her eyes were full of pain.

'I'm so sorry,' she whispered.

'Another *presumption*?' I hissed back at her.

'No,' she admitted, and closed her eyes, swallowing. 'No, I'm... I'm...'

'You're sorry,' I finished for her.

Well, at least she was being honest, this time. But – what the hell? How many people around here had she pretended to be Poppy's mother to? And *why*? I couldn't ask her, couldn't have a proper conversation with her about it, with Poppy skipping along beside me, still singing about the wheels on the bus, excitement glowing in her eyes, her little cheeks red from the cold wind outside after the heat of the crowded bus. But for me, the day was spoilt, the excitement abruptly gone. I'd tried to think the best of Crystal, to ignore Mum's and Dad's worries, as well as my own, to give her the benefit of the doubt and try to convince myself that it really was just an accident that people were assuming she was Poppy's mum. But now she'd really been rumbled. And she'd admitted it. Did she think I wouldn't care? That I wouldn't think it was strange, or, frankly, suspicious?

Luckily Poppy was too excited to notice the tension – and the silence – between Crystal and me. When we arrived at the square and Poppy looked up at the huge, glittering, tree, her eyes lit up, and her mouth dropped open in awe.

'It's big!' she said, staring up at the star on the top. Despite how cross I was feeling, I couldn't help smiling at her innocent ability to be so impressed. A local choir was stationed beneath the tree, singing popular Christmas carols and songs – and when they announced that it was time for a couple of songs for the children, and launched into 'When Santa Got Stuck Up the Chimney', Poppy turned to me, almost beside herself with joy. I'd been singing this one to her at home, to make her laugh while she watched me putting our decorations up.

'Santa up the chimney!' she shouted gleefully. 'Sing it, Mummy!'

It was all too easy to put aside my bad mood while my little girl was so happy and excited. We sang along together with enthusiasm, Poppy joining in where she remembered the words. Following this song was 'Rudolph the Red-Nosed Reindeer', another of her favourites, so it was some time before Poppy had had enough of the singing, and we all began to feel the cold from standing still in the crowd for so long.

'Come on,' I suggested, 'let's go and get some lunch.'

Over soup and a sandwich in a café just off the square, the silence between Crystal and me became more obvious, but I still couldn't say what I needed to, with Poppy sitting at the table with us, her ears flapping. Crystal picked at her sandwich while doing something on her phone, and after a few minutes my own phone pinged with a message.

> Are you still angry with me? I'm so sorry. It wasn't deliberate. I just didn't bother to correct her when she assumed. C. xx

I looked up at her. She was watching me, waiting for a reaction, her eyes heavy with unshed tears. I sighed and tapped a message back to her.

I don't understand why you wouldn't correct people who 'assume'. It feels like you've been passing yourself off as P's mum, and I don't like it. You've obviously been bringing her all the way over here, near your own place, which I didn't know about and I don't like. I think this had better stop.

Please don't stop me from seeing her.

I'm not saying that. But I'm starting to feel uncomfortable about you taking her out on your own.

She read the message, looked back at me and nodded. She looked pale and sad and had hardly eaten anything. I felt a flash of regret. I didn't like being like this. But even for a best friend, she'd overstepped the mark, made me feel very uncomfortable, and I really didn't know if I could trust her now. Why was she so obsessed with Poppy that she had to pretend to be her mum? I'd tried my best, hadn't I, to understand and sympathise with her about having no children of her own. I'd shared my daughter with her so freely that I'd felt, at times, like Poppy preferred being with her – and still I hadn't taken offence. But now it seemed like she'd been taking my place, behind my back. Pretending to be me. Pretending Poppy was hers. It was no good – however much it hurt her, I had to stand firm. She had to stop doing that.

I bought Poppy a cake after she'd finished her sandwich, and by the time we left the café and had started to head for the seafront, the sunshine had disappeared, replaced with dark, forbidding looking clouds.

'All the better for seeing the lights!' I said, making an attempt at being cheerful. It sounded forced. 'Let's walk all the way along the seafront to the pier. Look, Poppy, the pier looks amazing!'

'It looks pretty,' she said. 'Twinkle, twinkle!'

'Yes, the lights twinkle like stars, don't they, Poppy?' Crystal agreed. It seemed she'd decided to try for a pretence of normality too. 'Oh, look! Can you see what shape those lights up there are?'

'Father Kissmas!' Poppy squealed.

'And over there?' I added, pointing.

'Wudolph!' Poppy did a little hop and skip in her excitement. 'Wudolph the Weindeer!'

'Yes!' Crystal and I both laughed, enjoying her exuberance as she ran ahead of us a few paces to see what the next part of the display was. We glanced at each other – both smiling – and for just a moment, everything almost felt normal.

But it wasn't. And I wasn't sure if I'd be able to let it be, now. Not any more.

40

CRYSTAL

How the hell had I let that happen? It wasn't what Gemma thought. I'd never set out to pretend to be Poppy's mother – although I couldn't deny not bothering to correct Nicky in the park, who had just assumed that was the case, or the woman in the post office who – just as innocently – thought I was her auntie. But as for the woman on the bus, I suppose it was inevitable really that she'd make the assumption she did. I should have known that this would happen one day. Now Gemma was angry and upset with me, and she'd hinted that I wasn't going to be allowed out with Poppy on my own any more, and I had no excuse to offer her this time. I knew I couldn't argue or make a fuss about it – that would have only made things worse, made her even more convinced I was not to be trusted with Poppy at all.

And it was all her parents' doing. Gemma had never had any doubts or suspicions about me until her mum had started getting involved, and then told her dad about it. They'd been drip-feeding her their own jealousy and resentment until she started believing them. I didn't know what I could do to counter it – after all, I was just the new friend, while they were her parents, the main guiding forces in her life, especially since Jack had deserted her. He'd left her weakened and defenceless, and I liked to think I'd tried to rescue her, to give her back some stability and support.

I loved Gemma, she was my best friend, I wasn't faking it. But... of course, I knew perfectly well, right from the start that she wasn't the main attraction. Poppy was.

41

GEMMA

A couple of days later was Christmas Eve. Crystal had asked me, quietly, before we parted company on the Saturday, whether I still wanted her to come round, and despite how I felt right then, I didn't want to let her down. The thought of her sitting at home in her flat on her own on Christmas Eve, as well as all over Christmas, was just too much. I was annoyed with her, I felt let down and unsure of her now, but I couldn't go as far as to cancel the day together that I'd promised. What made it worse was that Dad had called me the previous day to say he'd already arrived at Mum's for the Christmas celebrations, and suggested coming over to see me and Poppy for Christmas Eve.

'I've got Crystal coming round, Dad,' I said. 'I've promised her.'

'Oh.' I could tell from his voice that he was disappointed. Then he brightened up. 'Well, how about I come round anyway, just to finally meet her? I won't stay long.'

It had put me on the spot. I didn't really want Dad and Crystal getting together, not while I was still feeling so conflicted about her myself. I'd be on edge, it would feel awkward and he'd go back to Mum's and tell her something wasn't right.

'Um... look, can we just do it another time?' I said. 'And Poppy and I will be seeing you on Christmas Day, and Boxing Day, won't we?' I paused, thinking about this. 'When did you come down from Manchester, anyway? You were only down last weekend, weren't you?'

'I drove down again on Saturday. I'm staying for a week this time.'

'Oh. You've got a whole week off work? That's great.'

It was unusual, though. In the past, however much he'd enjoyed coming down to see Mum, me, and Poppy (and Jack, before he did his disappearing act), Dad would always be keen to get back to his own place, his new life with his work and his social circle up north. I'd already noticed how much more frequently he'd been coming down recently. All I could think was that he was checking up on me. Or, I supposed he'd just say he was worried about me.

'Well, I'm winding down slightly now,' he said casually. 'Working less hours. Thinking about retiring, to be honest. I think I've earned a break.'

I felt my jaw drop. Was this really my workaholic father, talking about actually *retiring*? No, I couldn't believe it.

'Is anything wrong?' I asked, a sudden feeling of panic starting to overwhelm me. 'You're not... ill, or anything?'

He laughed. 'No, of course not. But I'm nearly seventy, Gemma. Don't you think I should retire at some point?'

'Well, yes, of course. Absolutely.' *Nearly seventy*? How had that happened? 'Of course – you should be retired, Dad! You shouldn't still be working at all—'

'All right, hang on, don't put me out to grass straight away!' He was still laughing. 'For now I'm just doing less hours, working from home – like everyone else seems to do these days – but I'm definitely going to retire before too much longer.'

'Well, good for you. Look, I'm sorry about tomorrow, Dad. But I'll see you on Christmas Day, OK? Looking forward to it.'

* * *

Poppy was excited to hear that Crystal was coming round for Christmas Eve, and she kept climbing on the sofa to look out of the window for her car.

'Yay! Crystal's here!' she shouted as soon as the car pulled onto the drive. 'She's here, Mummy!' She ran to the front door. 'Quick! She's here!'

'OK, OK!' I had to laugh, despite the mixed feelings I had about it, and when I opened the door to let her in, Crystal – dressed in a sparkly rainbow-patterned jacket that I hadn't seen before, and a pair of blue, patchwork dungarees – enveloped me in a hug and whispered that she couldn't possibly ever be able to tell me how grateful she was for the invitation.

'You're welcome,' I said, the chill in my heart thawing a little. 'Come on in. You look great!' I added, although if I'd been truthful, I'd have said the designs of her clothes clashed so much they were threatening to give me a headache.

And within a few minutes, everything was back to how it always was. Crystal and Poppy ran off to play, as if they were both kids and I – left alone in the kitchen to make lunch – was Mummy to them both. But it was hard to keep up the resentment, seeing how happy it made Poppy. We ate a cheerfully unhealthy lunch of sausage rolls and mince pies, and afterwards – as it was cold and raining outside – settled down to watch *The Gruffalo*, one of Poppy's favourite films, and drink hot chocolate.

'It feels like a proper Christmas.' Crystal sighed when the film finished. 'I haven't had one of those since...' She shook her head, and then finished, quietly, 'For a long time.'

'So will you see your brother tomorrow?' I asked her.

'No. Apparently he's going to his latest girlfriend's parents.'

'Oh. I'm sorry you're going to be on your own,' I said, wishing that – despite my recent uncertainty about her – I didn't still feel guilty just imagining her sitting in her flat with nobody to celebrate with.

She shrugged. 'I'm thinking of today as my Christmas. And – on that note – I've got a P – R – E – S – E – N – T in the car for a certain person here. Are you still happy for me to give it to her today?'

'Yes, that'll be lovely,' I agreed. 'Probably best to do it now; she'll be tired tonight from all the excitement, especially after we've reminded her about S – A – N – T – A coming!'

Crystal went out to her car and returned with a large shopping bag.

'What's *that*?' Poppy asked, looking at it with interest.

'Well, it's Christmas Day tomorrow, isn't it – but as I won't see you tomorrow, I thought you might like a present today. What do you think?'

'YES!' Poppy squealed.

'Yes *please*,' I corrected her gently. 'And we've got one for Crystal, too, haven't we, Poppy?'

'Yes, we got you earrings!' she said, and Crystal and I both laughed.

'You're not supposed to tell people what their present is!' I said. 'But here you are, Crystal – no need to guess what it is, now.'

'And here's yours,' she said, handing me a similarly small package. I unwrapped it to find a beautiful silver friendship-knot necklace inside, with the inscription *best friends forever*. I gave her a hug and put it on immediately, feeling a lump come to my throat as I thought of how I'd been feeling about her recently. She looked equally moved by the dangly silver earrings I'd bought her.

And meanwhile, Poppy was tearing the wrapping off her own present.

'Oh!' She gasped, looking up at me, wide-eyed in surprise. 'Look, Mummy! Same as Crystal!'

It was a child's size version of exactly the same sparkly jacket, and exactly the same blue dungarees that Crystal was wearing. Poppy was already pulling the jacket on, over her jumper. She held up the dungarees.

'Boo! My favrit!' she said, stroking them lovingly. She looked from herself to Crystal and back again. 'We're the same!'

'I thought you'd like that, sweetheart,' Crystal said, pulling Poppy towards her for a cuddle.

I watched, feeling my face slowly turning to stone.

'How...?' I spluttered. 'I mean, where did you get them...?'

'There's a lovely website I know about,' she said, the excitement almost steaming off her. 'It's called *Like Mother Like Daughter*. Isn't that adorable? I just couldn't resist.'

'*Like Mother Like Daughter*,' I repeated. My voice sounded hollow. 'I see.'

She looked up at me, finally noticing my tone, seeing my expression.

'Oh! I mean... look, it's just the name of the website,' she said quickly, going a bit red. 'It doesn't mean...'

'Doesn't it?' I retorted. I glanced at Poppy, who had also now picked up on my tone. She looked puzzled.

'I look pretty?' she asked me, doing a twirl so that the jacket shimmered in the light. 'I look like Crystal?'

'Yes, darling. You always look pretty,' I said, forcing a smile.

I turned back to look at Crystal, just in time to see she had her phone raised to take a picture. I automatically forced another smile while the camera flashed – wondering if my smile would look more like a grimace in the photo. My mind was racing. What in the world had possessed her to buy Poppy identical clothes to hers – from a website with a name that was frankly guaranteed to infuriate me? Unless infuriating me, taunting me, was the whole idea? She *knew* she'd already overstepped the mark by pretending to be Poppy's mum when she was out with her. Did she secretly *want* me to stop her seeing Poppy? No – look how upset she'd been the other day, just at the idea of it. And she'd seemed oblivious right up until the moment she saw the look on my face just now. It was unbelievable! Was she really this stupid, this insensitive, or... was she so obsessed with my daughter that it blinded her, completely, to what would have been absolutely fucking obvious to anyone else?

I sat in silence, steaming, trying to make myself behave normally for Poppy's sake while Crystal helped her change into the new dungarees, telling her to keep the jacket for going out – perhaps to wear to her nanny and grandad's house the next day? – as it was too warm for indoors. She took photo after photo of Poppy posing in the dungarees; she took selfie after selfie of herself, with Poppy on her lap, their blue patchwork dungarees merging before my eyes into something sinister, hateful and suspicious.

'Right!' I said eventually, having had enough. 'Time for you to have some dinner, Poppy-Pops, and an early night. Remember who's coming tonight!'

'Father Kissmas!' she yelled. 'Put my stocking up now?'

'After dinner,' I said firmly.

'Let me do her dinner,' Crystal suggested.

'It's OK. It'll be a quick one. Pasta, I think.'

I went into the kitchen and worked off some of my annoyance making a cheese sauce while the pasta cooked. When it was all ready and I called Poppy in to eat, Crystal came in too and put on the kettle, suggesting we could have a cup of tea while Poppy was eating.

'I've brought a bottle of fizz for us to share with our dinner later,' she said cheerfully. Then she stopped, looked at me uncertainly and added, 'That's if you're sure you're still OK about me staying the night?'

I'd almost forgotten I'd made the offer.

'Yes, of course,' I said automatically, thinking even as I said it that I wished I hadn't been brought up to be so endlessly polite. So civilised that even when I felt like nothing less than showing her the door, I couldn't go back on a promise. I'd felt sorry for her, being on her own – and now all I was wishing was to be rid of her, but somehow, I couldn't do a thing about it.

'OK,' she said, getting to her feet. 'Finished, Pops? How about I take you up to bed and get your stocking hung up?'

'She needs a little while for her dinner to go down,' I said. 'And we have to put milk and biscuits out for Father Christmas.'

'And a carrot for the weindeer!' Poppy said, jumping down from her chair. 'Where's a carrot, Mummy?'

'I'll get you one in a minute. Pass me your plate, please.'

'Shall I read you a story?' Crystal suggested. 'While we're waiting for Mummy to get the things for Father Christmas?'

I turned, closing my eyes for a moment, counting to ten. Everything Crystal offered to do was beginning to irritate me. I had to try to calm down.

'We do something special for her Christmas Eve story,' I said. 'It's... a family tradition.'

'Oh.' Crystal was obviously expecting me to enlighten her, but I didn't. 'Well... um, she could have two stories tonight, couldn't she? As it's a special day.'

'OK. Sure,' I said. Again, I somehow just couldn't say what I really wanted to, which was: *No, she can't have two stories, she'll want two every night now, can't you just take the hint and sit down and be quiet?*

I heard – while I kept my back to the room – Crystal chasing Poppy upstairs to choose a book, both of them giggling. I heard her suggest Poppy could get into her pyjamas while she was up there, so that she'd be all ready for bed in plenty of time for Father Christmas. And I gave myself a shake, telling myself to get over it. These were exactly the kind of things I'd had in mind – suggested to her – when I'd invited Crystal to share this special day with us. They were exactly the kind of things she'd been doing with Poppy for months now, and I'd been grateful. It had been helpful, I'd thought it kind, and it was no good regretting allowing it now. I needed to get through the rest of the evening with good grace. And then decide how to...

yes, how to extricate myself from this relationship. Without causing too much damage to my daughter.

So we read Poppy the two stories, and between us we assembled the treats to leave out for Father Christmas and Rudolph. We both put Poppy to bed, and hung up her stocking, warning her that she'd better go to sleep early so Father Christmas wouldn't have to go away again if he arrived to find her still awake. She closed her eyes so tightly, pretending to be asleep, that we both laughed, then we kissed her good-night and tiptoed downstairs.

'She'll probably take ages to get to sleep,' Crystal said. 'She's so excited.'

'Yes. And she'll wake up ridiculously early to see what Santa's left her.'

Crystal smiled, wistfully. 'She's at a lovely age,' she said. 'So innocent and trusting.'

I wanted to agree, to smile and bask in my friend's enjoyment of my daughter. But I couldn't. All I could think about was that outfit, that ridiculous outfit from *Like Mother Like Daughter*. The expression on Crystal's face when she'd looked at Poppy dressed like her mini-me.

We cooked dinner together, the way we normally did, trying to make conversation, both of us obviously aware of how stilted it was. Now Poppy wasn't with us, it was harder to keep up the pretence, harder not to show how I felt.

'You're annoyed with me, aren't you?' she said, finally, as we sat down with a drink after dinner. 'I'm really sorry – I honestly didn't mean anything by giving Poppy something from that website.'

'Didn't you? It seemed an odd thing to do: the exact same clothes as you're wearing.'

'I thought they'd suit her,' she said quietly, looking down at her glass.

'Right.'

I really couldn't be bothered to discuss it with her. There was no possible excuse for it. She finished her drink, looked at her watch and said perhaps she'd have an early night. I couldn't let her drive home – she'd had two large glasses of wine now – so I agreed, pretending to be tired myself. But I tossed and turned all night, unable to sleep, unable to look forward to Christmas Day with my daughter and my parents, because all I could see was that image of Poppy dressed the same as Crystal. It felt like the image would never fade.

42

CRYSTAL

I was awake nearly all night. I knew – knew as soon as the wrapping paper was off and I saw the expression on Gemma's face – that my present to Poppy was a terrible mistake. How had I not even realised she'd be offended? How had I made such a bad miscalculation?

The truth was, I'd forgotten what the name of the website was, until Gemma asked me where I'd bought the matching outfits from. I hadn't only just bought them; I'd had them hanging in my wardrobe for years – my own outfit, and the one for a child. I'd never even worn mine – and the child's one had never been worn either; I'd had covers over them ever since I'd bought them. I found them there a couple of weeks ago and... I suppose I just got carried away. Perhaps I should have wrapped up the adult clothes and given them to Gemma – that would have been a lot more thoughtful, and more sensible. But then again, they probably weren't really her style, and they might have been a bit big for her, she was so slim.

Yes, I'd been carried away with the thought of how cute Poppy would look in those clothes, so carried away that I'd forgotten how insensitive the whole idea really was. Gemma had already been angry with me and instead of trying to regain her trust, I'd probably lost it completely.

How had I allowed myself to make such a stupid mistake? I tossed and turned until the early hours of Christmas morning, but even when I heard Poppy's little feet pattering along the landing, and heard her squeals of excitement as she showed Gemma the contents of her stocking – the little toys and treats 'Father Christmas' had left her in the night – I stayed put on the sofa, under Gemma's spare duvet, my eyes closed. I couldn't just get up and pretend to act normally; I felt like everything had been spoilt. Gemma was barely even being polite to me; I knew she'd be glad to see the back of me now, as soon as possible. She'd be taking Poppy off to her Mum's for Christmas Day, for a lovely family day together – even the dad, was joining in – and I'd have to go home, my tail between my legs, to

spend a miserable day all on my own with just my regrets and my self-recrimination.

What an idiot I'd been. I'd messed everything up.
I'd just given Gemma another reason not to trust me. I
felt sick with disappointment and anxiety. Would
Gemma get over it? Would she forgive me? Or had I
actually gone too far this time? Was she going to stop
me from seeing Poppy at all? I had no idea how to
make everything all right again.

43

GEMMA

Poppy and I were downstairs early on Christmas morning. Poppy was jumping around excitedly, wanting to show Crystal the contents of her stocking. I opened the living room door very quietly and looked in, but to my surprise Crystal was still huddled under the duvet, fast asleep. I wondered how on earth she'd slept through Poppy's shouts of excitement – perhaps, like me, she'd had a bad night.

'Ssh!' I told Poppy, closing the door again. 'Let's leave her to sleep for a little while.'

I wasn't in a hurry to see her, the way I was still feeling.

'Owh, but I want to show her—'

'Yes, and you can, in a little while. But let's see about breakfast first, shall we? We don't want to be too late going to Nanny's.'

'Going to Nanny's!' Poppy repeated, her eyes shining. ''Cos it's Kissmas!'

'Yes!' I smiled at her. 'And I thought you might like crumpets for breakfast as a special treat. With jam?'

'Crumpets and jam!' she squealed, following me into the kitchen. 'Yum yum!'

While I started getting everything ready, Poppy laid out all the contents of her stocking across one side of the kitchen table 'ready to show Crystal'. After a minute or two, I heard Crystal get up and go upstairs to the bathroom.

'Wait till she comes down,' I warned Poppy. 'She probably wants to have a shower.'

In fact, she came back down almost immediately, popped into the kitchen quickly, as if remembering her manners, said 'Happy Christmas' and asked if it was OK to take a shower.

'Of course,' I said – but Poppy was already swallowing her mouthful of crumpet to shout out that Father Christmas had come, and *look! Look what he brought.*

Crystal just gave her a little smile, and promised to look as soon as she'd had her shower. As she left the room she picked up her phone, which had been lying on the corner of the kitchen worktop, near the fridge. She took it out into the hallway with her and, out of the open doorway I saw her open it, glance at, presumably, a few messages, and then put it down on the hall table and head up the stairs.

I don't know what made me do it; it was contrary to everything I believed in: respecting people's privacy, not taking liberties or crossing lines. But there was just a split second when I managed to convince myself it was the right thing to do. Not only that, but I *needed* to do it, and couldn't be blamed for it. As she turned the corner on the stairs I nipped out into the hall and picked up the phone before it could automatically lock again. And I looked at her photo gallery.

What was I looking for? I don't know; I'd like to say I just wanted to see the pictures she'd taken the previous day, all those selfies of her with Poppy, those infuriating pictures of them in their matching outfits. And yes, I did look at them, and I did feel another wave of irritation, and a powerful urge – which I managed to resist – to delete them all. But when I scrolled further back, I nearly dropped the phone in shock. I actually had to put a hand out to lean against the fridge, to steady myself. There were *dozens* of pictures of Poppy, and dozens of selfies of Crystal with Poppy, not just from Christmas Eve but from longer ago. Pictures of Poppy playing in the park, smiling happily on the beach, posing with a cake in her hand, with an ice cream, with a cup of something that looked like hot chocolate. Selfies of the two of them sitting together in cafés, grinning from a bench on the seafront, hugging in their winter coats and hats. There were so many pictures, I was surprised her phone hadn't run out of storage. I put the phone down, without bothering to exit the gallery. *Let her find out what I've seen*, I thought. I went back into the kitchen, where Poppy had finished eating and was looking a little bit downcast.

'Crystal looked sad,' Poppy said when I went back into the kitchen. 'We mustn't be sad on Kissmas, must we, Mummy?'

'No,' I agreed with a smile. 'Perhaps she didn't sleep very well.' Poppy stayed sitting at the table, rearranging her display of presents, while I toasted myself a crumpet that I didn't feel like eating. After a while we heard Crystal coming back down the stairs.

'Morning!' she said from the kitchen door, and repeated her 'Happy Christmas!'

She still sounded a little strained, and she wasn't wearing the blue dungarees any more. Poppy ran over to her for a hug, yelling 'Happy Kissmas!' and pulling her towards the table to show her the presents from Father Christmas.

'Wow, aren't you a lucky girl!' Crystal said, giving me a cautious smile, probably wondering whether I'd forgiven her yet for the present. I almost strained my face in trying to return the smile, but I suspected it looked more like a grimace.

'Yes, *and* we've had crumpets!' Poppy said. 'And jam.'

'Well, that sounds lovely.'

'You want crumpets too?'

'Um... well, actually,' Crystal said, glancing at me again. 'I think I might just have a quick cup of coffee, and then I'll get on my way. You'll be rushing to get to your nanny's house—'

'Owh, I don't want you to go.' Poppy held onto her arm. 'Stay!'

'Not today, sweetheart. Maybe another time, OK?' she said quietly.

'All right.' Poppy shrugged, far too excited about everything to be too disappointed.

Crystal went to get a mug to make herself a coffee, but I beat her to it, taking the opportunity to lean close to her and say, very quietly, 'I hope you never put photos of Poppy on social media.'

'What?' She looked back at me, alarm in her eyes,

and then looked out of the door at her phone lying on the hall table. I saw the realisation dawn, and a flicker of annoyance in her eyes.

I wanted to say that I had the right to look at her phone because of the way she'd been behaving. But I didn't. I just returned her gaze, holding it until she looked away.

'Of course I don't,' she said. 'I'm not even on any social media anyway.'

'Good.' It was hard to believe, frankly – who, at our age, wasn't on social media? It seemed unlikely but to be fair, earlier in our friendship, I'd looked for her, and hadn't found her.

'I closed down all my social media years ago,' she went on quietly. 'I was fed up with it. I wanted to re-embrace the *real world*.'

'I see.' I filled her cup with coffee, handed it to her and watched her sit at the table opposite Poppy.

'I'll go when I've had this,' she said quietly.

'OK.'

Despite myself, I struggled against a wave of pity, once again thinking of her sitting in her flat on her own today. I pushed the image of it out of my mind, concentrated on eating my cold crumpet, trying to think happy thoughts of Christmas with Poppy and my parents. I needed time away from her, time to digest it all, and to plan the conversation we needed to have if we were going to move forward, to keep up with our friendship. I couldn't even think about it yet.

* * *

After we'd said goodbye to Crystal, I packed an overnight bag for Poppy and me, another bag full of presents for Mum and Dad, and one with some chocolates, mince pies and other treats to contribute to the Christmas goodies.

'I can't wait!' Poppy said, hopping from one foot to the other as I finished getting everything ready. It was a new favourite phrase for her, one she'd picked up from nursery during the past week when all the children had been getting overexcited about Christmas.

I smiled. 'There's no more waiting, Pops! Come on – get your shoes on, we're on our way.'

* * *

'Hello, darlings, come in, come in, Happy Christmas, both of you!' Mum gushed when she opened the door to us. 'Come in and get warm – what on earth have you got in those bags? I told you there was no need to bring anything!'

'Oh, it's only a few little things,' I said, laughing. 'Oh, hello, Dad! Happy Christmas to you, too. You look very festive!'

He was wearing a particularly garish bright green Christmas jumper with a red Father Christmas on the front – much to Poppy's delight.

'Father Kissmas!' she shouted excitedly, running to stroke Dad's jumper. 'He came down my chimney.'

'And what's this *you're* wearing, my Poppy-Pops?' Dad said, holding her at arm's length and looking down at her. 'What a very special, shiny new jacket. Was this from Father Christmas too?'

'No!' Poppy squealed. 'Crystal gived it to me.'

Dad raised his eyebrows at me and, from behind Poppy's head, I pulled a face. I'd tried to dissuade her from wearing the new clothes today, and had won the battle over the dungarees by reminding her she'd wanted to wear her best party dress. But when I tried to talk her out of the shiny jacket, she'd looked so close to having a full-blown tantrum that I gave in, for the sake of a peaceful Christmas.

'I see,' Dad said calmly. 'Well, that's nice, but let's hang it up now that you're indoors in the warm – so that we can see your pretty new dress properly.'

'Sore point?' Mum whispered to me as she followed me into the living room.

'Yes. But I don't want to talk about it today.'

'Understood.'

I was glad she didn't push the point.

As usual, Mum had decorated the house beautifully; there was a huge Christmas tree, with twinkling fairy lights and presents piled underneath, home-made holly-wreaths hanging on the walls, tasteful gold and silver garlands over the mantelpiece and windowsill, and elegant slender candles on the shelves. All I'd bothered to put up at home, apart from a small artificial Christmas tree, were the plush snowman and Father Christmas ornaments we'd bought the previous year that danced and sung 'Rocking Around the Christmas Tree' when their hands were pressed. Of course, Poppy had pressed them so often that the batteries had run out already and I'd pretended they couldn't be renewed until next year. It had been hard, at home on my own with her during the lead-up this year – the first year without Jack – to pretend to be excited, but I'd had to try, for Poppy's sake. Now I was at Mum's, the pressure to be Cheerful Mummy was finally off me and I immediately felt more relaxed, determined not to think about Crystal until I went home.

'A glass of fizz, darling?' Mum asked. 'And I've got some of your favourite blackcurrant squash, Poppy.'

By the time the drinks were poured, we'd toasted

each other and sat down to enjoy them. Poppy was almost delirious with excitement to exchange Christmas presents, resulting in the usual mountain of wrapping paper to be tidied up before I went into the kitchen to help Mum with the dinner, leaving Poppy playing with her new toys under the loving watchful eye of her grandad.

'I know it must be difficult for you this year,' Mum said, enveloping me in her arms as soon as the kitchen door was closed behind us. 'It must feel so horrible, remembering the Christmases when you and Jack were together.'

'I'm trying to put all that behind me,' I said.

'I know. And your dad and I think you're doing brilliantly. We just wanted you to know that.'

'Oh. Well, thank you, Mum. I don't always feel like I am, though.'

'It'll take time.' She hesitated, turning away, opening the oven door to a cloud of steam and the scent of roast turkey. 'Anyway...' She dropped her voice, sounding more serious as she went on. 'I won't say anything yet, while Poppy's around, but Dad's got something to tell you later.'

'Oh.' I felt a frisson of alarm. 'What kind of *something*?'

'He's going to tell you later. After Poppy's in bed.'

She shook her head, as if she was cross with herself. 'I shouldn't have even mentioned it yet.'

But she had. And now I was going to spend the rest of the day wondering what it could be, what could be so sensitive that Poppy mustn't hear it. All through Christmas dinner, I kept looking at Dad, worrying. Mum had sounded like it was something pretty serious. I thought about how often Dad had been coming down from Manchester recently. I'd thought, at first, that it was because he was worried about my situation, and the reports he'd had from Mum about Crystal – but I'd recently found out he'd been staying here at Mum's over several weekends when I didn't see him at all, didn't even know he'd been there until afterwards. Why? Was he worried about *Mum*? Keeping an eye on her? Was there something wrong with her – something they hadn't told me about? I started to feel panic building in me, so much that I couldn't even finish my Christmas pudding. I wanted to know what it was… but at the same time, was dreading finding out. But of course, Poppy wanted us to play with her, with every one of her new toys, keeping up the frantic Christmas excitement right until she was falling asleep on the sofa, worn out from her long day of presents and fun, and I was finally able to settle her down for the night.

'Are you going to tell me what the big secret is,

now, then?' I demanded as soon as I came back downstairs.

'Big secret?' Dad said, looking from me to Mum in surprise.

'I told Gemma there was something you wanted to talk to her about,' Mum said.

'Oh. Right.' He glanced at me and back at Mum. 'Shall we all get a glass of wine or something in front of us first, then?'

Of course, this just added to my anxiety. What was so bad that he thought I'd need to down a glass of wine to recover from hearing about it?

'Well,' Dad said when, finally, he'd finished pouring drinks, and Mum had finished scurrying around in the kitchen getting out crisps, nuts, chocolates and more mince pies, for all the world as if we hadn't already eaten more than enough, 'I didn't mention this before, Gem, because I thought you'd be cross.'

'What?' I stared at him, waiting. 'Why would I be cross?'

'I hired a private detective,' he said.

'A private—'

'Your dad thought you'd say he was interfering,' Mum put in quickly. 'But Gemma, we had to do something. You'll do the same, believe me, if ever Poppy needs help one day, when she's grown up.'

'Oh.' I looked from one of them to the other. They both looked tense – waiting, no doubt, for me to explode. 'I see. You hired someone to look into her. Her background. Instead of trusting me to find out for myself...'

'*Her*?' Dad repeated, looking puzzled now.

'Crystal. I presume that's...' I stopped. 'That's not what you meant?'

'No! No, of course not.' Dad gave a little laugh. 'I meant that I hired him to try to find *Jack*, obviously.'

'Oh!' It took me a moment to refocus. I'd got myself so worked up about Crystal, and had so totally given up hope by now of ever tracking Jack down, that this was the last thing on my mind. 'You hired someone to look for Jack? Really?'

'Really,' Dad confirmed, and he gave me a smile, probably relieved that I hadn't bitten his head off. 'And... he's been found.'

'Oh!' It was all I seemed to be capable of saying. Then the reality of it suddenly hit me, full-blast. Jack had been found! I knew I should be jumping for joy – presumably this meant he'd be taken to court, forced to pay some maintenance for Poppy. Forced to comply, to act like a decent human being, like a responsible father. But instead, and inexplicably, I just burst into tears.

'Oh, darling!' Poor Mum almost spilt her wine in her hurry to be by my side, comforting me. 'Oh, don't cry, it's OK, it's all going to be better now, he's going to have to pay for Poppy, it'll make your life so much easier.'

'I know! I know, and thank you, Dad, I'm not cross, it was good of you. I don't know why I'm crying. It's just... I've tried so hard not to think about him. I put him – his memory – in, well, kind of in a box, a locked box, and refused to look into it any more. He'd disappeared, and I didn't know where he was so I couldn't picture him anywhere. He'd just *gone*. And now, well, now he's been found, it's like—'

'Like the box is open again?' Mum said gently.

'Yes! Exactly. Like suddenly I'm going to have to see him again – well, imagine him – somewhere out there in the world, and...' I gave a little sob. 'And *not with me*. With someone else. Not caring, not giving a *stuff* about me or Poppy.'

Mum looked at me sadly, stroking my hand. 'I'm sorry it's such a shock,' she said. 'We were hoping you'd be pleased.'

'I am. I mean, I will be. I just wasn't expecting... I

really didn't think he'd ever be found. Where is he, anyway? Still in Australia?'

'Yes.' Dad nodded. 'Somewhere in the *bush*, as they call it, right in the centre of the country, in the back of beyond. The whole family is there, apparently, living in some kind of commune, like hippies or whatever. According to the report the detective gave me, Jack is saying he always intended to pay you maintenance for Poppy—'

'Yeah, right,' I muttered.

'Exactly.' Dad glanced from me to Mum and back again, looking uncertain, before continuing quietly, 'I don't know if you'll want to hear this...'

'Tell me anyway,' I said. 'I might as well hear it all, now.'

'He – and the woman he's living with now – have got a baby. A little boy. He's using that as his excuse for being too busy to sort out maintenance payments for Poppy.'

'I see.' I was too angry now to cry any more. 'Great. So how the hell is he looking after a new baby son while he and this woman – and all his family – are living like, like *dropouts* in the middle of nowhere, presumably unemployed, bumming around in the desert—'

'That's his problem, frankly,' Mum said icily. 'Certainly not ours.'

'Except that he's hardly likely to have any money to spare, to pay for Poppy...'

'Well, if there's a court order to make him pay, he'll have to!' Dad said. 'He'll... well, he'll just have to get a job.'

'Or they'll take the money out of his benefits, if that's what he's living on,' Mum said. 'I've heard that's what our government does here, anyway. Although I don't know how it works in Australia, obviously,' she added a little uncertainly.

'That's what my detective's looking into,' Dad said, nodding. 'Don't worry, Gemma, we'll keep on the case. He's going to pay you what's due to you, whether he likes it or not.'

Finally, I started to feel a little spark of relief. Accompanied by a definite streak of something I thought must be what people called *schadenfreude*. Jack had tried to hide – from me, from Poppy, from the law – and he'd been caught. He'd be made to pay. It served him right – the coward, the pathetic, cowardly creep, hiding away with his despicable family in the Australian bush – I hoped he'd get bitten by snakes and catch some horrible disease.

I didn't feel proud of these thoughts, but they

helped. They stopped me from crying again – crying on Christmas Day was never a good look – and... more, much more than that... they stopped me from picturing that baby son, the baby son held in the arms of some unknown, presumably beautiful, Australian woman. The woman and baby son he loved more than he'd ever loved me or Poppy. Those were definitely not pictures I wanted in my head, not on Christmas Day and not on any other day, either.

44

CRYSTAL

Spending Christmas Day on my own wasn't exactly a new experience for me, but I supposed I'd hoped this year might have been different. That I might, by now, have been accepted into Gemma's family as a special friend – that I might have been invited to share at least an hour or so of the day with them. Whenever I thought back over the months that I'd known Gemma, I'd always felt that it had all been perfect until her mother had got involved, spreading her suspicions and antipathy to her daughter and putting doubts into her mind. But now, I knew I had to accept some responsibility for those doubts. I'd gone too far, messed things up, and there was nobody I could blame for that but myself.

I spent much of the day in front of the TV, trying to tell myself that it was just another day, that there was no more reason to feel miserable on that day than on any other I spent on my own, without Poppy, without Gemma. By dinner time, when I sat down with my turkey meal for one, I'd made up my mind what I had to do. I had to come clean with Gemma – not about everything, obviously, but at least about the aspect of my life that was the most relevant. I was dreading it; it could go either way – either make her understand me and forgive me, or make her feel even more suspicious about my attachment to Poppy. But I had to take the risk, because Gemma had already been talking about cutting down my involvement with her, and what I'd done – with that present – had surely added fuel to the fire.

Then – just as I was warming up my Tesco mini Christmas pudding, pretending to feel festive and wondering what was happening at Gemma's mum's place, picturing Poppy laughing and happy with all her new toys – I had a phone call. It was the phone call I'd longed for, dreamed of, tried to imagine, for so long that the very idea of it had pretty much taken on the aspect of a miracle – something that was never going to become a reality. But that afternoon, on Christmas Day, my dream came true, albeit for just the tiniest, briefest moment. From all those miles away, I heard the voice I heard every night in my dreams.

'Hello. Thank you for my Christmas present,' she said. 'I love it.'

'Oh!' was all I could manage at first. I had to sit down. I was stuttering, like an idiot, my smile fighting with the tears that had sprung to my eyes. 'Oh, you're very welcome, darling. I'm so glad you like it—'

'I do. I hope you had a nice Christmas. See you soon. Bye...'

There was a moment of hesitation. And then, a little cough, as if she was embarrassed at herself, before the muttered final words that broke my heart and yet mended it at the same time:

'Bye, Mummy.'

45

GEMMA

I slept badly again, flitting erratically between dreaming about Jack being bitten by snakes while a newborn baby screamed in the background, and worrying all over again about Crystal and what I should do about her. Boxing Day morning was bright but cold, and over breakfast, Mum suggested it might be nice for us all to go out for a little walk, to give us an appetite for the hearty dinner she had planned.

'Actually, Mum,' I said while I helped her load the dishwasher. 'If you and Dad don't mind taking Poppy out for a while—'

'You just want to stay here and rest? Of course, that's absolutely fine, I must admit you do look tired, darling – your dad and I are both quite concerned about you—'

'Well, in fact I need to do something. See someone. It won't take long, but... well, if I don't do it today, I'm worried that I'm going to... lose the momentum.' I sighed, looked Mum in the eyes and admitted, 'Or change my mind.'

'Crystal?' Mum guessed, pushing the kitchen door closed and lowering her voice. 'I could tell you were upset about the jacket – the Christmas present.'

'It's not just that. I... think you and Dad might have been right all along. I should have been more worried about the amount of time she wants to spend with Poppy.'

And before I could stop myself, I was spilling it all out: how Crystal had been pretending to be Poppy's mum, how she'd bought Poppy the matching dunga-rees and clothes from *Like Mother Like Daughter*, and how I'd found dozens and dozens of photos of Poppy on her phone.

'I know I shouldn't have been looking,' I added, but Mum shook her head.

'I don't blame you. I would have done the same. Poppy's your child – you needed to know; I mean, she could be sharing those pictures on Instagram or what-ever, and saying she was *her* daughter—'

'She said she doesn't do that. She's told me she doesn't use social media at all – I'd already looked for her, but I've tried again, and it's true, there's no sign of her on any platform that I can find. But I don't feel comfortable with what she's doing any more – any of it.'

'You need to set boundaries. That's if you even want to stay friends with Crystal—'

'It's not even her real name,' I said. 'I never told you that, did I?'

'*What?* Well, that rings alarm bells right away, Gem. How did you find out?'

'She told me.' I shrugged. 'Soon after I met her, actually. Apparently she just prefers Crystal to her real name. It's what they call her at the self-help group she belongs to. Her real name's Suzanne. Suzie. It never bothered me, to be fair – I mean, lots of people call themselves by different names if they don't like their own.'

'Well, it sounds to me like you're talking yourself round, trying to sympathise with her, when you really need to challenge her. *Like Mother Like Daughter* in-deed! It's insulting, that's what it is – insulting to Pop-py's real mother – *you.*'

'I know. I was furious about it. So – yes – I need to talk to her, on my own, and the sooner the better. So...'

'We'll take Poppy out for a walk. Tell her you need to go somewhere – get a bit of shopping, whatever.'

'On Boxing Day?'

'She's too young to wonder about it. Pick up something from the Co-op as you go past. A loaf of bread, maybe – I could do with some more.'

'OK.' I opened the kitchen door and called out to Poppy, giving her my excuse, and before I could change my mind, I was in the car. Heading to Crystal's place.

It was the first time I'd been there, but I knew the address. I wondered, too late, whether she was likely to be out, but I was pretty sure she'd said she was going to be at home on her own for the whole holiday. I pressed the buzzer for flat 14 and it only took a few seconds for her to respond.

'Crystal, it's me – Gemma.'

I could hear her gasp with surprise. Well, she probably hadn't expected to hear from me again until we were back at work.

'Come in,' she said, buzzing the main entrance door open. 'I'm on the second floor.'

I ignored the lift, climbing the stairs instead to give me a few extra minutes to compose myself. I needed to be calm, to say what I had to say.

Crystal met me at the door of her flat.

'I didn't expect to see you today,' she said. She sounded wary – unsurprisingly – but at the same time, there was a light in her eyes, as if she was... what? Excited? Pleased?

'Is Poppy not with you?' she asked, looking behind me. I shook my head, presuming the pleasure in her eyes would quickly disappear once she realised I was on my own... but to my surprise, she nodded and said it was just as well, as we needed to talk.

'Yes, we do,' I agreed.

She held the door open for me and showed me into a comfortable-looking living room. There were fabric prints on the walls, brightly coloured throws on the sofa, a huge patchwork floor cushion on the rug in front of the fireplace. Somehow it all looked very *Crystal* – and at the same time, somehow quite sad, quite... lonely. I shook myself, remembering why I was here.

'Would you like a tea or coffee?' she asked. 'Sorry, I've only got decaf.'

She marched off into the kitchen, leaving me feeling slightly perplexed. She must have known why I wanted to talk – she'd said herself that we needed to. When she'd left my place the previous morning, she'd seemed so distressed and regretful, I was sure she knew I was upset with her, that I was going to demand

answers, or stop her from seeing Poppy – and yet today, she didn't seem overly concerned.

'I won't be a minute,' she called over the sound of
the kettle boiling.

But I didn't answer. Because I'd walked over to the
fireplace and was looking at the picture she had in a
frame on there. It was of Poppy, wide-eyed and smiling, her lovely red hair tied in a tiny ponytail on top of
her head. She was wearing a blue jumper that I'd
never seen and certainly hadn't bought her, and... I
glanced down at the rug I was standing on and felt my
mouth drop open in shock. She was sitting *here*. On
this rug. In this room. What the...?

Before I could look back at the picture for closer
scrutiny, it was suddenly whipped from off the shelf
and I turned to see Crystal behind me, red in the face
but not meeting my eyes.

'I'll put it away,' she said. 'I know what you think,
and you're right, I've done some serious soul-
searching and I know I take too many pictures of
Poppy and it's not fair. You're her mum and I realise
I've been making you feel sidelined by me spending so
much time with her.' She paused, and went on, more
quietly, 'I know you think I've been playing games,
pretending to be her mum, but I haven't, not really,
people just seemed to *think* I was. I never meant to

hurt you, Gemma, this was what I was going to talk to you about, but—'

'Show me the photo,' I said. 'It was taken *here*, Crystal, wasn't it? Here in this room! Have you been bringing Poppy here, to your flat, when you were supposedly just taking her out for walks, to the shops, or the park?' I held my hand out for the picture, but Crystal was already backing away from me, holding it behind her.

'What?' She was laughing now. 'Of course it wasn't taken here – I've never brought Poppy here. I promise you I haven't. Ask her! Why would I bring her here?'

'Show me!' I repeated.

'No, I'm going to put it away, like I'd already promised myself I would. I'm not even going to look at it again, OK? But you're wrong, I might have taken some liberties, I might have got too close to Poppy, but I've never once brought her home with me. You do believe me, don't you?'

She'd backed all the way to the door out to her lobby now, and immediately turned and headed – I presumed – to the bedroom beyond. I stood, staring after her, wondering if I should go after her, whether I should have insisted on a proper look at the picture – but how, exactly? Should I have wrestled her to the floor to grab it from her? Already I was starting to

doubt myself. She was admitting to everything I'd suspected her of – taking too many photos of my daughter, and – although she was trying to persuade me she
hadn't deliberately pretended to be her mum – admitting letting people think it. Why would she admit to all
of that, but categorically deny ever bringing her home
with her, unless it was true that she hadn't? Perhaps I
was imagining things. It certainly didn't look like my
home in the background but I supposed my living
room carpet was a similar colour to the rug here. And
to be fair, Poppy had a couple of blue jumpers and
maybe it could have been the one she didn't wear very
often because she'd almost outgrown it. Perhaps I had
jumped to conclusions, perhaps I was so wound up
about Crystal now that I automatically assumed the
worst – that she'd been buying Poppy new clothes
without telling me, bringing her home here...

'I've never seen Poppy with her hair in a little
ponytail like that, before,' I said when Crystal –
smiling broadly again now – came back into the room.
I heard the icy tone of my voice but she didn't even
flinch.

'She's sometimes asked me to do it for her when
I've been looking after her while you're working,' she
said. 'I won't do it again if you don't like it – she always
asks me to take it out again straight away, anyway.'

There was something about her tone, her avoidance of my eyes, that told me she was lying. Poppy had never asked to have her hair in a ponytail. She'd never expressed any interest in how her hair was done! But all the same, I was beginning to wonder if I was just making something out of nothing.

I sighed. 'It's OK.'

I sat on the sofa, waiting while she brought in the tea, trying to calm myself down and get my thoughts back on track.

'Did you have a lovely Christmas with your parents?' she asked, sitting down next to me.

'Yes, I did, thank you. Look, I can't stay long but you've already guessed what I wanted to talk to you about. You're right: it has to stop, all this pretending to be Poppy's mother, all these photos, and frankly the last straw was the present – the *mini-me* outfit – if it wasn't for the fact that it would upset Poppy so much, I'd ask you to send it straight back. It's just—'

'Too much. I know.' She dropped her head. 'I'm really sorry. I got carried away.'

Despite everything, I felt... not only a sense of relief just from knowing that she wasn't going to argue, but I suppose, a little frisson of sadness for her. Perhaps I'd been too harsh in my judgement. She loved Poppy, that much was clear, and whilst it had without a doubt been right to tell her enough was enough, that I couldn't let her keep pretending to be me, or buying such inappropriate gifts, nevertheless she had no kids herself, she was completely alone in the world and she'd been a lot of help to me.

'OK,' I said, taking a sip of my tea. 'Look, I really still think I need to insist on a bit of space between us for a while. I mean, not so much between *us*, as be-tween you and Poppy. It's not fair to let her to get so attached to you.'

She nodded. 'I know.'

'But I do understand – well, I'm trying to. I mean, I know you haven't got any children of your own, so...' I paused, looking at her in surprise. She was giving me a secretive little smile. 'What?'

'Gemma, like I've said, you're absolutely right and I'm... absolutely sorry. But I've got something *I* need to say, too. I told you a little lie when we first met.'

'A lie? Oh – about your name? I know, and really that's irrelevant, you can call yourself whatever you like, why does it matter?'

'It doesn't. It's something else.'

I felt a little shiver of anxiety. 'Well, come on then – what is it?'

'You're going to be cross. You're going to wonder why I didn't tell you.' She was looking nervous now.

'Why would I be cross? What is it? It can't be so very bad, can it? Well, come on, just tell me!'

There was a long pause. She looked down at her lap. I could almost hear her heart beating in the silence, her anxiety was so palpable, and mine was increasing in sympathy. What on earth could be so earth-shattering that she was this nervous to tell me? Then she looked up, suddenly, and spoke in a tumbling rush of words:

'I lied when I told you I haven't got any children. I have. I've got a daughter – but she doesn't live with me.'

I stared back at her, a feeling of horror coming over me.

Please don't tell me she's having some kind of psychotic episode – referring to Poppy now as her actual daughter? I have no idea how to handle this.

'My daughter lives with foster parents,' she went on smoothly, 'on the Isle of Wight.'

'What?' I gasped. 'No! Really?' I stared at her, trying to make sense of this. 'Are you joking? I can't believe you'd actually lie to me about something like that.'

'I didn't tell you because I was worried what you'd think – that you'd think the worst, because I'm sure people think children are only put in care for the worst possible reasons. But it's not my fault,' she said, emphatically. 'I was a good mother – I mean, I *am* a good mother. But my daughter was taken away from me, and she's been – she can't help it, she doesn't understand – she's been punishing me for it, refusing to talk to me, not wanting to even see me. But finally, now, *finally,* after three and a half years, she actually called me yesterday. And she called me *Mummy.* I...' She gave that little smile again. 'Finally, I have some hope.'

'Hang on, hang on. I can't get my head around this. Why was she taken away from you?' I asked, my mind whirling. I wasn't even sure yet whether I believed her. It all sounded so far-fetched, and so – sudden, out of nowhere.

'That's what I can't tell you. Sorry. I just can't.'

'But...' I was staring at her, completely stunned, suddenly feeling that despite all the hours and days we'd spent together, I didn't know Crystal at all. I didn't know who she was. She'd told me a pack of lies. 'You can't just – it doesn't make sense – you can't suddenly have a child, a daughter, that you've never told me about. Why are you suddenly telling me now?'

'Because I know you've been having doubts about me. I know I've been a bit over the top with Poppy and I just wanted you to know I'm not... *dangerous* or anything, I'm not about to abduct her. I love her, I do, but I'm not some crazy woman, I know she's not really my daughter. I *have* a daughter, it's just that I'm only allowed to see her once a month.'

I stared at her, the truth slowly dawning. 'So that's where you go – on your mysterious weekend trips?'

'Yes. And it's only once a month because Evie always gets so upset, and then... I do, too.'

'Her name's Evie? Your daughter?' I was still having trouble actually taking this on board. 'How old is she?'

'She's six now.' Crystal's smile had dropped. She had tears in her eyes. I wanted, instinctively, to comfort her, but I couldn't: I was still totally immobilised by shock. 'Every time I go to see her, I always promise myself I won't get upset... I try to be calm, and sensible, and rational. She's only little, she still doesn't understand, I always knew it would take time. But it hurts so much when she rejects me, every time – like I'm some kind of ogre, like I terrify the life out of her.' She wiped her eyes, shook her head. 'I make matters worse – I know I do; it probably scares her even more, seeing me cry, but it's *so hard.*'

I swallowed. It was hard enough just to imagine it: only seeing your daughter once a month and having her reject you – I couldn't even begin to understand how that must feel. But why? Why was Evie in foster

care, why didn't Crystal tell me, why wouldn't she explain now?

'But you said she's phoned you, now?'

'Yes. Just to thank me for her Christmas present –
but, you can't believe how much that has meant to me.
To hear her voice, talking to me nicely, calling me
Mummy, instead of screaming at me like she normally
does: *Get out, go away, you're not my mummy, I hate
you—*'

'Oh, Crystal.' Finally, I reached out and put my
arms round her. Whatever was behind all this, it didn't
matter. She was a mum, like me, and for whatever
reason that she couldn't tell me about, she'd been separated from her child, only allowed to visit her as a
stranger, a frightening and unwelcome stranger. How
awful it must have been for her. I felt like my own
heart was breaking just at the thought of it. No wonder
she'd allowed herself to get so attached to Poppy, no
wonder she'd daydreamed about her being her own
daughter. How could I resent that, now?

'I'm so glad she called you. Perhaps there's finally
been a breakthrough and she's going to accept you
now,' I said.

'I daren't get my hopes up too much.'

'No. I can imagine.'

Crystal looked up at me through her tears. 'Thanks

for being so understanding, Gemma. I'm really sorry I didn't tell you before. I was so scared you'd think the worst about me – like I said, people tend to assume children only get taken into care because they've been ill-treated.'

'I wouldn't have assumed that,' I said.

But as I drove back to Mum's house a little later, I had to ask myself whether that was really true. What *would* I have thought, if she'd told me about this when we first met, before I got to know her properly? And, come to that, *did* I still know her really, even now? There were still gaps in her story, still things she wasn't telling me. However much I sympathised with her now, it all felt odd. I knew, instinctively, that if I told Mum what had happened she'd give me that look of disbelief, she'd tell me I was being naïve again and suggest that Crystal was giving me a sob story to stop me being angry with her. To stop me keeping her away from Poppy.

Luckily, I got back before Mum and Dad returned from their walk with Poppy. So I pretended Crystal hadn't even been at home.

46

CRYSTAL

I felt so relieved after I told Gemma about Evie. She was shocked, of course, but once she'd listened to me describing how hard it'd been, she seemed so sympathetic that I ended up wishing I'd told her sooner. Of course, she still couldn't understand why I hadn't told her the reason for Evie being in care, but that would have opened up a huge new can of worms – she really would have been suspicious if she'd known the rest of my story. I just hoped that by baring my soul about Evie, I'd managed to convince her that I didn't have any nefarious intentions regarding Poppy. Darling Poppy. As if I'd ever have done anything to hurt her. I knew she loved me, but I also knew, even while I was playing the silly game in my mind, imagining her as my own child, that she loved her real mummy best. It just... helped. It helped me to be able to play pretend like that, because it stopped me from constantly crying over Evie.

Had Gemma properly forgiven me now for the stupid mistake with the clothes? Was she still going to let me see Poppy? Take her out? I didn't know, but at least she did seem a lot less hostile. The photo on the mantelpiece was a problem, of course – I'd have taken it down right away if I'd known she was coming, but I was pretty sure that when I told her about Evie, she was so shocked that she forgot all about that. I realised I'd just have to wait, give her time to absorb what I'd told her, and decide if she could trust me, despite me having kept Evie a secret.

I spent the rest of Boxing Day watching films on Netflix and dreaming of when I might next be able to see Poppy. Needless to say, I thought about Evie, too – she was never out of my thoughts – but despite the thrill of happiness I'd felt when she'd called to talk to me, despite the absolute joy and amazement when she'd finally called me *Mummy*, I'd had so many set-backs during the past three and a half years that I'd schooled myself against hoping for too much. I knew that, next time I visited, it was entirely possible that Evie would reject me just as bitterly as usual. It might,

I knew, only have been the Christmas present that prompted the phone call. I'd bought her a kids' smart watch and headphone set in purple, her favourite colour according to Donna, her foster mum. How sad I didn't even know such basic things about my daughter as her favourite colour, but Donna was always really helpful with suggestions for presents, always warning me against 'overdoing it' and 'trying to buy her affections'. Well, it certainly hadn't worked up until then, anyway. But perhaps I couldn't be blamed for hoping things might finally be changing.

47

GEMMA

I'd taken the post-Christmas week off work as holiday, and I was up to date with all my self-employed work too, so I was able to spend plenty of extra time with Poppy. I decided against contacting Crystal until I went back to work, but as New Year's Eve approached, I felt a stab of conscience. She'd be on her own again. And, once Poppy was in bed, I would be, too. Once we had Poppy, Jack and I hadn't been in the habit of celebrating New Year. Like most parents of young kids, we were too exhausted to stay up until midnight. But it was going to feel strange and lonely this time. Even though Mum usually went to a New Year party at one of her friends' houses, she'd offered to be with me instead this year. But I'd said no. There was no way I was going to let Mum give up her own social life just to keep me company. I should have made more effort to keep in touch with my own friends, and I knew I needed to try to put that right.

But... I did have Crystal.

I called her on the thirtieth.

'Would you like to come over tomorrow evening? Or are you doing something?'

She gave a snort of laughter. 'Me, doing something? Of course not. I'd love to come over, Gem, if you're sure—'

'Good. We can just celebrate... quietly. Watch a film, or one of those ridiculous countdown-to-midnight programmes or whatever. I'll make a curry.'

'I'll help. And I'll bring wine.' She paused. 'If you don't mind me staying the night.'

'Of course,' I agreed. Perhaps we'd have the talk about how involved she should be with Poppy, the talk I hadn't even had the heart to attempt on Boxing Day after hearing about her daughter. *Her daughter*! I still couldn't quite get my head around it. How had she kept such a massive piece of information from me, when we'd shared so much else? It didn't make sense, although I'd realised, as I'd been thinking about it during the week, that it did explain how she'd always seemed so experienced with young kids. In a way, I

was glad that was the reason, that it wasn't just because she and Poppy seemed to have a special bond.
But she'd told me a whole network of lies, just to
make sure I didn't know about her daughter – and
why? I wasn't sure, even now, how much I could
trust her.

Crystal seemed particularly happy and excited
when she arrived for New Year's Eve. Dressed as flam-
boyantly as ever, in a purple flowery smock worn over
a yellow shirt and pale blue leggings, with her hair
tied in a yellow scarf, I almost felt like I needed sun-
glasses just to look at her. Poppy was beside herself
with excitement to have her 'friend' back to play with
her again, and within minutes they were chasing each
other around the house. I wondered if this was how it
felt to have two children, albeit one much bigger than
the other, and although it still irritated me, and I still
wasn't particularly happy about it, I knew Poppy loved
her and I worried about how long it would take her to
get over it if I did have to stop Crystal from seeing her.

It wasn't until Poppy was finally in bed an hour or
so later, tired out by all the fun she'd had with Crystal,
that we could talk properly.

'I've been desperate to tell you,' she said as we
chopped onions and garlic, 'after you called me yesterday, I had another call.'

I looked at her expectantly. 'From your daughter again?'

'No, *but...* it was from Sarah, the social worker, the one who always takes me to visit Evie. We've got quite close, over the years; she always does her best to try to help me. She said she's been talking to the foster mum, who's told her that Evie is definitely coming round to the idea of seeing me now, and she thinks it would be worth trying to increase my visits to twice a month.'

However I felt about Crystal, whatever my reservations about her spending time with Poppy... I was a mother too and I couldn't help feeling a massive surge of sympathy.

'Oh, Crystal, I'm so happy for you—'

'It doesn't necessarily mean it's going to work. She's warned me that, if increasing the visits ends up making Evie unhappy or uncomfortable in any way, we might have to go straight back to only once a month. But—'

'But it's a good sign, surely. It sounds like she's beginning to accept you, doesn't it?'

'I'd really like to think so, obviously.' There was such a light of hope in Crystal's eyes – how could I not feel for her? 'But I still need to tread carefully.' She dropped her eyes, her voice faltering slightly. 'It would feel worse than ever if I started to see her more often and it didn't work out.'

'Don't think like that. I'm sure it'll work out.'

Crystal smiled, looking grateful for the encouragement, and we carried on preparing the curry in silence. I didn't know how I was going to broach the things I wanted to say, now. I still felt uncomfortable with the idea of her taking Poppy out on her own, but now she'd told me about her hopes for a reconciliation with her own daughter, I hated having to burst her bubble. I had to do something, say something, though – I couldn't let things go on the way they had been.

'Anyway,' she said, throwing onions into the hot oil in the pot, 'I'm sorry, love, I haven't even asked you very much about your Christmas, at your mum's?'

'It was really nice, thank you. How was yours—?' I stopped, shaking my head. How did I think it was? It must have been awful, sitting on her own all day, knowing I was annoyed with her about the present she'd bought Poppy.

She shrugged, shook her head. 'No, tell me about yours. Did Poppy enjoy spending it with her grandparents?'

'Yes, she did. And – oh, there *is* something I haven't told you. I've got some news. About Jack.'

Crystal looked up at me in surprise. 'Really? You've heard from the child support people?'

'No. My dad hired a private detective.'

'*Did* he? Well, good for him. And has he had any luck?'

'Yes! Can you believe it – Jack's been found, with his whole family, living in what Dad described as a commune, somewhere deep in the Australian bush.'

'Well, that's great news, isn't it?' She sounded almost more pleased than I was. 'They'll make him pay you maintenance for Poppy.'

'Yes.' I sighed. 'Oh, of course I'm pleased about that, yes. But—'

'He *should* pay. It's disgusting the way he's just gone off, living his own life, hiding away and not caring, not giving a stuff about how you're supposed to manage with his daughter on your own!'

I looked at her in surprise. She'd dropped her knife in the vehemence of this speech and was grabbing a cloth now to wipe garlic from the worktop.

'Yes, you're right,' I said quietly. 'But it was the rest of what the detective found out that really upset me. Apparently he's got another child – a baby boy – with some new woman. No wonder he doesn't care about Poppy any more. Or me.'

'Oh, he has, has he?' Crystal said. 'Well, I wonder

how long he'll stay with *that* poor woman before abandoning her for someone else without a backward glance?'

'It's weird, though,' I said, thinking back on my time with Jack. 'He was never a flirt or a womaniser. I mean, when we were together. He just wasn't like that at all, he never looked at anyone else, never made me feel like I couldn't trust him. He really loved us – me and Poppy. He said we were his world.'

'And you think he just happened to fall wildly in love with this woman in Australia, so much so that it made him forget all about you? All about his little girl? You think it was the woman's fault? No, I bet she doesn't even know he has a partner and child back in England.'

'Perhaps I never really knew him at all,' I said, miserably. Crystal's reaction was making the whole thing hurt desperately, all over again. But I knew she was right. Jack couldn't have been the man I thought he was, could he? The Jack I thought I'd fallen in love with wouldn't have behaved like this. It was time I accepted that. 'Perhaps everything he ever said was a lie.'

'Men like that never change,' she agreed. 'I bet he'll treat the new woman just the same sooner or later, leave her in their commune with her baby and head off somewhere else, with someone else.'

'It's so depressing. Aren't there any decent men around? Not that I'm interested in finding one,' I added, and then bizarrely, started laughing at myself.

'Who cares?' she agreed, laughing too. 'Who needs them? Where's that bottle of wine I brought with me – shall we have a little glass while we finish cooking? I know you don't normally drink unless Poppy's with your mum, but—'

'But it's New Year, and I'll only have a little one, and—'

'And we're both celebrating,' she finished for me, removing the cork from the bottle with an impressive pop.

'Are we?' I didn't feel at all like celebrating, to be honest. I felt pretty depressed, having just forced myself to admit my boyfriend might never have loved me the way I thought he did.

'Yes,' she said firmly. 'I'm celebrating my daughter calling me Mummy – even if it was only once, even if it never happens again.'

'Oh, don't say that!' I paused. 'And what am I celebrating?'

'Obviously, you're celebrating finally looking forward to getting some dosh out of that love-rat.'

'Fair enough.' She handed me a full glass and I

raised it to hers. 'Cheers. Here's to the end of a rotten year.'

'And the start of a better one,' she added.

I wasn't sure how it had happened, but suddenly I seemed to have forgiven her. By the time we'd finished cooking and sat down to enjoy our dinner, I'd almost forgotten why I'd been on the point of talking to her about her involvement in Poppy's life. She was a good friend. We laughed a lot together. She loved my daughter – what was so terrible about that? So she'd made some mistakes, but I understood why, now, and I sympathised with her so much about her daughter that, for that one night, as we celebrated together at midnight, I forgot to wonder – as I had been doing constantly during the previous few days – *why* her daughter might be in foster care. And why she was so reluctant to tell me.

We went to bed late, and when I woke up on New Year's Day, the house was in silence. I almost turned over and went back to sleep, but then I glanced at the clock: it was after nine o'clock, but Poppy hadn't come in yet from her bedroom, as she always did. She never slept this late.

I jumped out of bed and ran into her room, to find her bed empty, the princess-themed duvet thrown back, her pyjamas in a heap on the floor.

'Poppy?' I called as I ran down the stairs. She knew never to go downstairs on her own until she'd seen that I was up. Crystal must have come upstairs to see her and got her up. Well, I guessed she would have been hungry for breakfast by now – thank goodness Crystal had woken up, at least.

But the kitchen was silent and empty. I went into the living room, half-expecting them both to jump out at me shouting, *Surprise!* It was just the sort of game Crystal would play with Poppy. But no, there was no sign of life in there either; Crystal's duvet and pillow from the night before were neatly folded on one side, but there was no pile of clothes, nothing else to show that she'd even been here.

My heart beating faster now, I ran back to look in the kitchen again. There were no plates or dishes on the table, no crumbs, no sticky knives or spoons... nothing. I dashed back out into the hall, where Crystal had hung her coat the night before. It wasn't there, nor were her shoes. And... nor were Poppy's little boots, or her warm winter coat, her hat, her mittens...

I opened the front door, the cold wind whipping my hair across my face, making me shiver in my thin pyjamas. But it wasn't just the cold that now had me shaking from head to foot. It was the realisation that Crystal's car had gone. She'd put my daughter in her car – presumably without even the benefit of a child-seat – and had disappeared with her.

I'd had a glass of wine – just one – and stayed up so late that I'd slept in, for the first time since Poppy was born. And without me hearing a thing, Crystal had taken Poppy. She'd done what, in a corner of my heart, I'd always feared she'd do one day. She'd let me drop my guard, she'd talked me into trusting her again, and she'd used the opportunity to steal my daughter.

48

GEMMA

I almost fell back inside the house, tears spurting from my eyes, letting out a scream of protest as I flew around the house one more time, opening and slamming doors and cupboards, not knowing what I was doing it for. It was a waste of time, I knew Poppy wasn't here. I knew Crystal had taken her. Where? Why? How long had they been gone?

Calm down, Gemma, calm down, this isn't helping. You need to think.

I grabbed my phone, hit Crystal's number and pressed call, letting it ring until it stopped ringing out, then starting again, with the same result.

Shit, I thought, my panic increasing. *If she's not answering, it can only be because she's guilty – she really has taken Poppy against her will, she's kidnapped her, she's going to take her abroad and I'll never get her back...*

I sat down for a moment, trying to slow my breathing, trying to make myself think logically. But I kept coming back to the fact that she'd taken her in her car, with no car seat. How could she *do* that – she was a mother herself; it was unforgiveable! When did she set off? It was impossible to know. Perhaps she went in the early hours of the morning – waited for me to go to sleep and then got Poppy out of bed, dressed her and slipped out of the house under the cover of darkness.

She could have been anywhere by now. She could have been on her way to London, or... to an airport. I felt sick, just at the thought of it.

I ran upstairs to Poppy's room again, flung open her wardrobe and searched amongst her clothes. Her warmest jumper, a favourite purple one, was missing and so were the hated blue patchwork dungarees.

Nobody but Crystal would pair purple with blue, I thought, as if it even mattered. I wondered why I'd automatically checked to see what she'd dressed Poppy in – and then I realised: if I needed to call the police, they'd want to know what she was wearing. That thought made me sob aloud with fear. *Did* I need to call the police? What would I say? *I think my best friend has abducted my child*?

I sat down on Poppy's bed, my head in my hands. I needed my mum. She'd help me; she'd know what to do. I ran back downstairs to get my phone, to call her, to beg her to come round right away – but when I picked it up from where I'd stupidly left it on the kitchen table, I saw I'd had a missed call. How had I not heard it? I must have been sobbing too loudly while I crashed around in Poppy's bedroom searching through her clothes. And it was Crystal's number. I had to lean against the wall to stop myself from collapsing while I hit her number to call her back.

'You called me,' she said, cheerfully. 'Sorry I missed—'

'Where are you?' I shouted. 'Where the *fuck* have you taken my daughter?'

There was silence. Had she hung up? I felt the room spin – I was close to losing control. Then I became aware that not only was I still connected, but there was background noise on the line: people chatting, music playing, a child's voice.

'Poppy!' I said, clutching the phone closer as if I were actually holding onto her. 'Are you there? Can you hear me?'

'Gemma, it's me,' came Crystal's voice again. 'Are you all right? What's the matter? Has something happened?'

'*What's the matter*?' I repeated. 'Are you joking? You've got Poppy. Where have you taken her?'

Another pause. Heavy breathing. I was just about to shout again when she replied, quietly, 'Did you not read my note?'

'Note?' I couldn't help it – I was repeating everything she said, like an echo. 'What note?'

'The one I left, this morning, to tell you I was taking Poppy out for breakfast. To give you a break.'

'You...?' I looked around the kitchen. 'You left me a note? *Where*?'

'I slid it under your bedroom door. So you'd see it right away, as soon as you got up. So you wouldn't worry.'

I started running up the stairs, wrenching open the bedroom door, still holding the phone, still talking, still angry.

'Why a note, for God's sake, why not a text, a WhatsApp—'

'I didn't want your phone to beep and wake you up. I don't know if you have it on silent at night or not. Have you found the—?'

'Yes.' I was standing in my bedroom doorway, holding onto the door, breathing heavily. There was a crumpled piece of paper just inside. I'd obviously trodden on it in my haste to get up. My haste to see if

Poppy was all right. I opened it... and there was the scrawl of Crystal's writing, just as she'd said, telling me she was taking Poppy out for a breakfast treat and would be back in an hour or so.

'You took my daughter in your car,' I said, anger rising now to take the place of my shock. 'With no car seat—'

'I've got one. From Evie. It's still in the car, it's the right size, she was fine.'

'Right.' I felt behind me for the bed. I needed to sit down again: relief had made me weak. And then, suddenly, the rage came back.

'But even so! How could you *do* that to me?' I shouted into the phone, bursting into tears at the same time. 'A note, a stupid bit of paper that I walked over, it's just not enough – I didn't say you could take Poppy out! This is *exactly* what I said we needed to talk about! You can't take her out without my permission, you can't just do whatever you like, whenever you like, with my child, pretending she's yours, just because you haven't got your own daughter!'

There was silence for a moment, apart from the music and chatter going on in the background, in whatever café they were in – a café somewhere in town, enjoying breakfast, without me, leaving me frantic and beside myself with worry.

'OK, I'll bring her home right now,' Crystal said quietly. 'We'll be about half an hour, we're only in—'

'No. You're *not* bringing her. Tell me where you are, I'm coming to get her.' I got to my feet. I was still in my pyjamas. I didn't care. I was going – right now.

'You don't sound like you're feeling OK to drive.'

'I'm fine,' I snapped. 'Where are you?'

'Maccy D's. I knew they'd be open on New Year's Day.'

'Stay there.'

* * *

I didn't know – or care – what I must have looked like when I arrived at McDonald's, with my coat pulled on over my PJs, my hair unbrushed and my eyes probably swollen from crying. I saw Poppy straight away; she was sitting with her back to me, but Crystal looked up as I walked in, and immediately got to her feet.

'Look, I'm sorry—' she began, but I ignored her, just marched up to the table where they were sitting and, as Poppy turned to look round at me in surprise, I took her hand, pulled her to her feet and helped her into her coat.

'Hello, darling,' I said, trying my best to sound like a normal, calm, sane parent. 'I've come to take you home. Nanny's coming round at lunchtime – remember?'

Crystal was still talking, babbling something about how she hadn't meant any harm, she'd just wanted to help out and give Poppy a treat, wouldn't I just sit down for a minute, please, so that she could explain?

I didn't. I wouldn't even look at her.

'Come on, then, sweetie. Let's get you home.'

'Bye bye, Crystal,' Poppy said, looking from one of us to the other, sounding a little puzzled but not complaining.

'Bye, darling Poppy.' Crystal's voice shook. She must have known she wasn't going to be seeing her again in a hurry. If ever, the way I felt right then.

* * *

'I had a muffin,' Poppy said brightly as we walked back to the car park. 'With jam.'

'Lovely,' I managed to say.

'And hot chocolate. Ow! You hurted my hand, Mummy.'

'Sorry, sweetie.' I'd been gripping her too tightly, feeling the warmth of her little hand through her glove and vowing to myself that I'd never let her out of my sight again. I couldn't claim, of course, that this was a very sensible reaction; it wasn't in Poppy's best interests or mine, nor something I'd actually be able to carry out in reality, but my instincts had overtaken my common sense by at least 100 per cent.

'We see Nanny now?'

'Yes. She's coming for lunch.' We reached the car, I strapped her into her car seat, got into the front and sat for just a moment in silence, taking deep breaths. It was OK. I'd got Poppy back, safe and sound. And there was *never* going to be a repeat of anything like that happening, ever again.

49

CRYSTAL

I was heartbroken. It had all gone wrong – disastrously wrong, because I really didn't think Gemma was ever going to forgive me this time. It took me until the evening, turning it over constantly in my mind, before I started to understand why she'd reacted quite as badly as she had. I mean – I *had* written a note, and I'd only done that rather than texting her, to save waking her up. I'd done my best, hadn't I? I'd dressed Poppy in her warmest clothes, wrapped her in her thick winter coat, hat, and mittens, and of *course* I wouldn't have taken her in my car if I hadn't got Evie's car seat in the back. I'd driven the same car ever since Evie was with me, when she was about the age Poppy was now. I couldn't face taking the seat out of the car; it would have felt like accepting defeat, at the time, and now, even though Evie would be far too big for it of course, I couldn't bear to get rid of it. What more could I have done? – that was what I kept asking myself. But of course, it slowly dawned on me that it wasn't a question of what more I could have done, but of what I *shouldn't* have done. I shouldn't have done it at all, that was the point. My intentions had been good, but I'd done it again – got completely carried away, excited by the idea of giving Poppy a treat and giving Gemma a break at the same time. But I knew, didn't I, that Gemma was already annoyed with me about the Christmas-present outfit. I knew she wanted me to back off a bit, that she didn't really want me to take Poppy out on my own any more. How could I have thought it was a good idea to just take her daughter off like that, only leaving a note – a note Gemma didn't even see? I suppose I convinced myself that she'd be grateful. It was my own fault, and now I'd made things even worse – and just as I'd thought that her sympathy about Evie might have been softening her feelings towards me.

I was due to be back at work the next day, a Thursday, and Gemma wouldn't be back until the Monday. I knew it wouldn't be a good idea to call her, but I'd just message her, saying sorry again – just that, nothing more. I didn't think it would be helpful to send a long rambling message trying to explain myself or beg for forgiveness. If I was going to be forgiven, I'd have to wait for it.

The only thing that kept me going for the rest of that day was the knowledge that just a week later, I was going to visit Evie again. I was going *because they thought she'd be happy to see me more often.* I kept telling myself that, over and over, holding onto the bright-shining possibility of it, like a child holds tight to some special shiny shell or pebble she's found on the beach. The *magic token.* The magic that might just be able to heal my broken heart.

50

GEMMA

It wasn't until I'd got home, had a quick shower, dressed and tried to make myself look half-normal, that I thought to put the spare duvet and pillow away from the end of the sofa. I was chucking them in the cupboard, telling myself they wouldn't come out again – not for Crystal, not ever – when I realised, underneath them, she'd left behind the yellow shirt she'd worn the previous evening, plus the matching yellow scarf she'd tied her hair up with, and some underwear. I decided I'd take them back to her at work, stuffed them in a carrier bag and put it out of the way in my bedroom.

'Nanny here!' Poppy shouted; she'd been standing

on the sofa in her socks, looking out of the window for Mum's car. Then, 'Oh, Gandad here too!'

'Really?' I went to the front door and let them in. 'Hello! Dad – I didn't know you were coming back down again – Mum didn't say.'

'I haven't been back to Manchester since Christmas,' he said, smiling. 'I decided to take some time off and stay here for New Year.'

'Oh!' I looked from him to Mum, surprised she hadn't mentioned it, but Mum just smiled and said, yes, he'd actually gone with her to her friend's party the previous night.

'Did you have a nice evening?' she added. 'Or were you just on your own?'

I turned away, heading back to the kitchen.

'Crystal came round,' I said bluntly. I nodded in Poppy's direction and added half under my breath, 'I'll tell you later.'

I started getting lunch ready – I'd realised I was hungry; I hadn't had any breakfast. Mum came out to help me, giving me another look and asking me to tell her what had happened, but I just shook my head. I had to eat first; combined with the stress of the morning, I felt like the hunger was threatening to make me faint. Over lunch, Mum and Dad must have exchanged worried glances with each other at least twenty times, but fortunately Poppy was keeping us all entertained with her attempts to show off her new progress at counting to twelve. She'd already achieved one to ten by her birthday, occasionally muddling up six and seven, and had asked to go higher recently but she was now muddling seven with eleven. Mum and Dad pretended to be overcome with awe at her talent and kept encouraging her until she finally got it right.

When we'd finished eating, Dad offered to help me with the clearing up, while Mum took Poppy into the living room to play a game.

'Now then,' he said as soon as the door was closed behind us. 'Tell me what happened. You look absolutely drained.'

'I feel it,' I admitted, accepting Dad's offer to load the dishwasher while I sat down again.

'You didn't have a good evening?'

'Oh, last night was fine. It was this morning—'

I told him the whole story: how I'd woken up late, to find both Poppy and Crystal gone, her car gone, how I'd got no response when I tried to call her, and was on the point of calling the police.

'I suppose I panicked,' I admitted. 'I honestly thought the worst.'

'Well, I'm not surprised!' he exclaimed. 'Anybody would have done. What the hell did she think she was doing – taking her off like that without even asking you?'

'She'd put a note under my bedroom door but I didn't even notice it. But the point is—'

'The point is,' Dad interrupted, 'Poppy is *not her child,* and she can't be allowed to behave as if she is. No wonder you panicked. I don't trust her. I'm sorry to say it, without even having met her, but I really do wonder if she's trying to take Poppy away from you. It's all very well feeling sorry for her because she doesn't have children herself, but—'

'Well, that's the other thing. It's not even true: she does have a daughter. But she's in foster care.'

Dad's eyes widened. 'How did you find that out?'

'Oh, she told me – but only last week. She finds it hard to talk about, and she won't tell me why she's being fostered. Anyway, that's where she goes when she's away for weekends: to see her daughter. Evie.'

'So why the big secret? Why lie to you and say she didn't have any kids? And why is she still not telling you the reason the daughter's being fostered?'

'I don't know, Dad. But anyway, it's all irrelevant now. I don't feel like I even want to see her again, and I definitely don't want her hanging around Poppy any more – let alone going anywhere with her on her own.'

'Well, I can't say I'm sorry.' He sighed, and added, 'I

know you enjoyed her friendship, Gem, but frankly your mum and I have both been worried about it.'

'I know. I was getting worried myself, but when she told me about Evie, I... felt so sorry for her, I kind of relented again.'

'But enough is enough.'

'Yes.' I nodded. 'Enough is enough.'

I got up and put the kettle on while Dad finished the clearing up, and when we took the coffee through to the living room, Mum was cuddled up on the sofa with Poppy, reading her a story.

'She looks tired,' Mum commented.

'Yes. She was up early this morning.'

"Cos I went out with Crystal and I had a muffin!' Poppy squawked, suddenly coming to life. 'We went to 'Donald's!'

Mum gave me an enquiring look, and Dad touched her arm.

'I'll fill you in later,' he promised. Then he looked back at me. 'Meanwhile, *I* have some news.'

'Oh?' I looked at him a little anxiously, my mind immediately jumping to Jack – the private detective. What else had he discovered? I didn't think I could take any more shocks today.

'It's good news,' he said. 'I'll be around more, soon,

to help out whenever you need it, love. I'm moving back down south.'

'What?' I stared at him. 'How? Your job—'

'I'm working my notice. I told you, didn't I? That I'm working part-time now, from home, and that I was going to retire? Don't look at me like that!' He laughed. 'Don't you think I deserve to? I'm seventy next birthday!'

'But, Dad, this is all so sudden. I mean, it was only a couple of weeks ago when you first mentioned you might retire. I didn't think you meant immediately! I thought you loved your job. I thought you always said you'd be bored if you retired.' I paused, hesitated, then added anxiously, 'Are you *sure* it's not your health or anything like that?'

'No, of course it isn't. Look at me, I'm as strong as an ox and as fit as a fiddle.'

'But... moving back down here? What about your golf club, all the friends you've made in Manchester—'

He smiled. 'None of them are important. Not as important as what I've now realised I miss the most: my daughter, my granddaughter—'

'No, Dad.' I felt annoyed now. 'You can't do this, it isn't right. I mean, I'm grateful for what you've done for us, that goes without saying. But you can't give up everything else in your life just for me and Poppy, just because you've been worried about us. I'm not a child, I can cope, I can manage the situation with' – I paused, glancing at Poppy, who looked close to dozing off on the sofa – 'with *You Know Who*. I don't need you giving up your life to take care of me.'

'I know you don't,' he said calmly, still smiling. 'However much I want to help, I love the fact that you're independent, that you're coping so well and dealing with... problems... your own way. But you didn't let me finish. It isn't *only* for you and Poppy that I want to come back. It's for your mum.'

'Mum?' I repeated, staring from one of them to the other. 'What... what's wrong, Mum? Are *you* ill? Why do you need Dad's help?'

'For heaven's sake, Gemma, must you always think the worst?' she exclaimed. 'Stop catastrophising and let us explain.'

She looked at Dad, and they were both smiling now.

'So... what?' I said again. 'Why?'

'Can't you guess?' she said. 'We're getting back together, darling. We've been talking about it all year.'

'We've realised we should never have broken up,' Dad said, taking hold of Mum's hand and looking at her with what looked almost like adoration in his eyes.

'The divorce was a mistake. A stupid mistake. There was nothing wrong with our marriage.'

I could feel my mouth opening and closing like a fish's.

'So why *did* you break up, if there was nothing wrong in the first place?' I asked. 'I've always wondered, to be honest. I mean, you still seem to be... like good friends.'

Mum laughed. 'Yes, we are! That's the whole point. I don't know why we split, Gem. Perhaps we both thought there must have been something missing – something we couldn't even identify until we'd gone away from each other and looked for it.'

'That's exactly right,' Dad agreed. 'And I think I'm right in saying that neither of us found it.'

'Because it was just where we left it – with each other,' Mum agreed, 'and with you and Poppy.'

To be honest if they'd sat there looking at each other with that dopey look in their eyes for a single moment longer, I might have started to feel sick, but I didn't let it get that far. I jumped up, rushed to hug both of them, and before I realised it, there were tears pouring down my face – tears of happiness. So perhaps I wasn't as cynical as I'd thought!

'Mummy crying?' Poppy asked anxiously.

'No, sweetheart. I've just got something in my eyes.

No, honestly, I'm really happy,' I said, including her in the group hug.

'Good!' she said, wriggling free to pick up her book. '*I'm* happy too 'cos you said we could play another game.'

'So I did!'

I had to laugh. Now that her speech was coming on in leaps and bounds, she often had a lovely way of expressing what she wanted – or what she wanted me to do.

'All right, go and get the game you want us to play. And meanwhile,' I added to Mum and Dad as she ran off to her toy cupboard, 'I think this news needs to be celebrated with a toast of some sort.'

'I'm driving,' Mum said. 'But if you want—'

'Let's just toast each other with this coffee,' Dad suggested, 'before it gets cold.'

'Oh – I'd forgotten about the coffee,' I said, sitting down and passing them both a mug from the tray. 'OK, well, cheers! Here's to the pair of you being... reunited.' I paused and added, 'Are you talking about getting remarried?'

'Probably no point,' Mum said, grinning. 'Makes no difference, really, does it, at our age. I mean, we're hardly likely to have any more children.'

'So we might as well keep our options open in case

we decide to split up again,' Dad added with a wink, nudging Mum so she nearly spilled her coffee, and they both started giggling like a pair of teenagers.

I shook my head in amazement. Who'd have thought it? They seemed to have fallen in love with each other all over again. Could that actually happen at their age? Well, I supposed it could.

We didn't talk about Crystal any more that day. I was glad; I needed a break, to stop thinking about her and worrying about her for just one afternoon. I wanted to be happy, and enjoy my family, and pretend she didn't matter. But I knew it could only be a break. I'd have to decide, sooner or later, how to deal with this situation, once and for all, because this morning had decided it for me: Crystal had to be excised from Poppy's life, however difficult that might be.

51

CRYSTAL

I didn't see Gemma at work on the Monday or Tuesday, her first days back. She hadn't come to meet me at the normal place, by the lifts, at our usual lunch time and I decided it would probably not be in my best interests to call her extension, or go to her office. She probably needed time away from me, to calm down: I understood that, understood that I'd made yet another serious mistake, that I'd worried her, frightened her, when she'd found Poppy missing and that it was going to take time for her to forgive me.

On the Wednesday, I wondered about going to her house after work. I'd realised I'd left my yellow shirt and some knickers there – in a way, I couldn't have blamed Gemma if she'd burnt them. But perhaps I could use them as an excuse... I could just call to collect my clothes, and say I didn't expect to go in, and probably she'd relent and invite me in anyway.

But what if she didn't? What if she was still so furious with me that she just slammed the door in my face?

If it hadn't been for the fact I was going to see Evie at the weekend, I don't think I'd have managed to get through the week without going round there. As it was, I had to stop myself twice from driving over straight from work, by literally going around a roundabout twice, trying to make a decision, before turning back on myself and going home. I missed Poppy in a way I couldn't even describe. Like I'd had an arm cut off or lost the use of one of my feet. But if I'd gone to the house only to be told to stay away and never come back... well, I couldn't imagine how I'd have been able to cope with that. So I'd wait. Just for another few days, until I'd been to see Evie. That, at least, was keeping me going, for now.

52

GEMMA

We were more than halfway through January, and I hadn't seen Crystal at all, or spoken to her, or messaged her, since New Year's Day. I was still angry, every time I thought about her taking Poppy off in her car without my permission. I was too angry to even look out for her at work or wonder if she was going to our usual pub on her own. I spent my lunch breaks eating a home-made sandwich in my office, telling myself I was saving money and improving my diet. *New Year's resolution*, I told my colleagues.

The truth was that, despite my anger, I missed her. Missed her infectious smile, her outrageous outfits, her exuberance and her ability to cheer me up. But worse than that was the way Poppy missed her. Nearly every day she was asking after Crystal, and I was running out of excuses for why we weren't seeing her. It was now affecting Poppy's behaviour; she'd developed an attitude I didn't like, taking out her frustration on me and, worse, on Mum.

'Don't want Nanny, I want Crystal,' she snapped when Mum had kindly driven all the way over to pick her up one Friday morning, to save me time in making the journey myself because I had a lot of work to catch up on. She actually started crying and stamping her feet when Mum tried to take her hand to take her out to her car, and I had to intervene because poor Mum – whilst pretending to be cheerfully unconcerned by the outburst – looked shocked and sad about it.

'Come on, Pops, you know you'll have a brilliant time at Nanny's, like you always do,' I said firmly. 'How about taking your new sticker book with you? Perhaps you can finish it off together. Nanny can help you.'

'OK,' she said, running to get the book, leaving me to apologise, saying I hoped Poppy would settle down.

'Oh, don't worry, she's cheered up already. She'll be fine.' She dropped her voice and added, 'You're doing the right thing, cutting that woman out of your life.'

'I haven't exactly cut her out,' I said, flinching at the harshness of the term. 'I'm just not... actively seeking her out. Not at the moment, anyway.'

'Best to leave it that way, in my opinion. Poppy will forget all about her before long.'

Would she really, I wondered? And... would I?

* * *

Dad was working his final month up in Manchester, before moving back down to Devon permanently.

'So he's moving back in with you?' I asked Mum that Sunday, while Poppy was engrossed in a children's film. 'Into this house?'

'Of course!' She stared at me. 'Why wouldn't he? We've been sleeping together whenever he's stayed here, since we agreed to—'

'OK, OK,' I laughed. 'I didn't ask for details! I just wondered... how that's going to work, financially. Not that it's any of my business, I just wouldn't want you to be disadvantaged in any way... if it didn't work out again.'

'Look, the house still belongs to both of us. We paid the mortgage off years ago, luckily, and when we divorced, Dad decided the best arrangement would be to keep the house in joint names unless either of us ever needed their share of its value. We've always talked everything through together; even while we were apart, there was no animosity between us. Your dad only wanted that little studio flat for himself in Manchester – he was never sure how long he'd stay there anyway—'

'It's beginning to make me wonder whether either of you was ever very sure about splitting up in the first place.'

She shrugged. 'Maybe we weren't. Perhaps it was just something we needed to get out of our systems. We should have just had a trial separation, instead of getting a divorce, but at the time...' She hesitated and then went on, 'We both thought we might meet someone else; we were open to that possibility. But, well, as it turned out, the grass wasn't greener, at all. The grass, such as it was, was decidedly unappealing! It's been a wake-up call, if nothing else. At least we appreciate each other more now.'

I gave her a hug, holding onto her for longer than I normally would.

'I'm so pleased for you both, Mum.' It was hard to stop myself from crying. 'I... would have loved to spend almost my whole life with someone I loved, like you and Dad have.'

'There's still time for you to meet that person,' she said, consoling me. Her own voice sounded trembly with emotion. 'You're still young, and beautiful, and—'

'And I've gone off men for life,' I added a little bitterly.

'Never say never, sweetheart.'

* * *

That evening, after Poppy was in bed, I sat on my sofa without the TV on, feeling sorry for myself, feeling lonely, wondering what all the other lonely people in the world were doing right at that moment, and trying not to think specifically about Crystal.

I need to get in touch with some of my old friends. It was no good continually telling myself that but doing nothing about it. All right, so several of them now had two or three children, to say nothing of partners or husbands, but even if they were too busy to get together, there was nothing stopping us being in touch on social media, was there? I picked up my phone and went into one of the WhatsApp groups I'd neglected ever since Poppy was born. It was still active, with two or three of the other girls regularly exchanging baby pictures, pics of their dogs or cats, their dinners, their children's birthday cakes... I'd turned notifications off some time ago, as it had all seemed a bit pointless and boring compared with the joy and intensity of my real life back then. But now, well, surely it was better than sitting on my own, feeling left out and alone?

> Hi all. It's been a long time, how are you all? You might have heard, I've been on my own with Poppy since early last year. She's three now and doing fine, and I'm… kind of surviving. Would love to hear from you all some time.

I wasn't under any illusion that they'd all rush to my side now, after I'd failed to keep up the friendships myself. But at least I'd given it a try, made a start. I sat for a while, scrolling through Instagram, before giving up and going onto Google to look for a recipe for a pie I'd made once before, using up leftovers, and which Poppy had really enjoyed. From there I googled the weather for the week ahead, going on to look up the website of a new client who'd approached me, and then idly scrolling, as you do.

I don't know what made me finally look for it. I think perhaps when we scroll through site after site like that without engaging our brains, eventually some kind of instinct takes over and we automatically bring up something that's been playing on our minds. I'd looked for Crystal often enough, and after she'd told me she'd closed down all her social media years earlier, I never bothered to look again. But that evening, scrolling from site to site in my bored, subdued, somewhat depressed state of mind, something made me search, for the first time, for her real name. It helped that her surname is pretty unusual – and to my surprise, within minutes, a feature from a local Devon news site, four years earlier, popped up:

LOCAL WOMAN ARRESTED ON SUSPICION OF CHILD ABANDONMENT

Suzanne Fernsby, 33, was arrested yesterday, after police were called to an incident at an address in Upper Street, Claydon Leigh, where a two-year-old girl had been left alone. The child was considered to be at risk and has been taken into temporary foster care. Ms Fernsby was held in police custody overnight before being discharged into the care of the mental health authority. Police say there was no danger to anyone else in the vicinity. A neighbour who had alerted the police after hearing the child screaming in the empty property, said, 'She seemed a nice woman but I didn't really know her. I'm a bit shaken up.

Things like this don't normally happen around here.'

I logged off, my hands shaking. It must have been a coincidence, I told myself. There must have been more than one Suzanne Fernsby. But I knew, in my heart of hearts, that there wasn't; not in Upper Street – where Crystal still lived – not in Claydon Leigh, not any-where in the whole of the county. It was her. She'd been accused of abandoning her daughter – that was why Evie was taken into care.

For a full ten minutes I sat, staring at the screen, unable to move, shivers running down my spine, feeling like I was about to vomit. I'd let this woman take Poppy out for walks, to the park, to the shops – I'd trusted her with my precious daughter, without know-ing, without her ever telling me, what she'd done to her own child.

Every instinct was telling me to call her – imme-diately – to tell her what I'd found out, to scream at her, to tell her to stay away from me, to tell her that if she ever came anywhere near me or Poppy again I'd report her to the police. I had my finger hovering over her name on my phone but I was horribly afraid that as soon as I started speaking to her, I'd burst into tears – and I didn't want to. I needed to be in control,

I needed to be cold and ruthless when I cut her out of my life, so that nothing she could say would deter me from my purpose, but at that moment I was still too shocked, too emotionally fraught. It wasn't just Poppy that Crystal had befriended, after all – she'd come into my life just when I needed a friend; she'd rescued me from despair and heartache and now everything I'd believed about her was in ruins. I couldn't even begin to talk to her until I could come to some kind of acceptance – to actually *grieve* the death of what I'd thought of as our special friendship.

I went to bed, but barely slept at all, and in the morning the heat of my shock and fury had begun to give way to the icy determination I needed, to cut all ties with my *ex* best friend. I decided the best thing would be to take her by surprise, rather than giving her any chance to think up excuses – not that anything could possibly excuse what she'd done. I put the carrier bag with the clothes she'd left behind at New Year in the car, took Poppy to nursery as usual and had a quiet word with the nursery manager, asking to collect her later than normal as I had an urgent 'meeting' at the end of the day. Then I drove to work and kept my head down, hoping above all that this wouldn't be the day that Crystal finally decided to come to my office to beg me to go out to lunch with her again, or the day I bumped into her in a corridor and couldn't avoid her.

I left work a little late, deliberately, to give Crystal time to get home – and then I drove straight to her flat. For a few minutes I had to sit in my car, taking deep breaths to try to calm myself down. I didn't want this to be an emotional confrontation. It just needed to be... a permanent excision.

I could hear the excitement in Crystal's voice when she answered the buzzer.

'Gemma!' she said. 'How lovely – come up, I'll get the kettle on.'

But when she opened the door to her flat and saw the look on my face, her smile dropped.

'What is it? Are you still angry with me? Oh, Gem, I can't tell you how sorry I am. Come in, at least, and let's talk.'

I nodded and followed her inside. I didn't want a confrontation on her doorstep.

'Look, I've given us some space, haven't I?' she went on as soon as we were inside. 'I've done some thinking – I know I've been too—'

I was holding up my hand. 'Stop. It's no good, Crystal. I've... come to tell you, I've found out what happened, and frankly, the fact that you didn't even tell me about it...'

I watched the blood drain from her face. She felt behind her for the sofa and sat down, heavily.

'You know? How... how did you find out?'

There was no point pretending. 'Googled your real name. There was an old news article. Child abandonment! How could you keep that from me, when I was giving you free rein with *my child*?'

'Oh!' she said, looking up at me, wide-eyed. 'You've found out about *that*?'

I stared back at her. 'What did you think I meant?'

'Um...'

For a moment, we both just looked at each other. Her face went from white, to red, and she staggered to her feet again.

'I think... obviously... we do need to talk again,' she said slowly. 'Do you mind if I make us both a cup of tea first? I... think I need it. And you might do, too, when I explain. I will explain,' she added quietly. 'I know I have to, now. I have to tell you everything.'

53

CRYSTAL

I'd already been wondering if the time had come to tell Gemma everything. I'd begun to think that she was never going to forgive me for my faux pas, taking Poppy out on New Year's Day – she'd kept her distance for weeks and although I was missing her and Poppy so much that it hurt, I knew I had to wait until she was ready to give me another chance – but was that ever going to happen? I guessed her parents were probably telling her to drop me. I supposed I could understand it; they'd only ever seen, or heard, the worst about me, and that was partly my fault too.

Despite all this, I'd been so happy. The extra trip to see Evie had gone so well that the social worker was actually beginning to talk about the possibility of her coming to see me at my own place soon. Of course, the foster mum would come with her, but it was such a massive step forwards and everyone was sounding so positive about it. Evie had actually let me give her a quick hug, she'd smiled, called me *Mummy* again and during the entire visit hadn't run out of the room or started crying. Whatever had happened to promote this change – the social worker suggested it was simply a case of Evie growing up a bit and beginning to understand the situation better – I had clung to the memory of that day and the hope for the next visit. It had, at least, lessened the pain of the separation from Gemma and Poppy, just a little.

But now this. She'd found out about the so-called *child abandonment*. I'd thought, immediately, that it was the other thing... and because of my reaction, she now knew there was something else I'd been hiding. Now, I could see that the only possible way forward was to tell her about that, too. If I didn't, there was never going to be any coming back from this: it was obvious that she'd come to see me that afternoon with one clear purpose – to break up with me, permanently. To ban me from seeing Poppy, ever again. I had to try to explain why I'd lied to her, and all I could do was hope she'd understand.

But it was going to be the most difficult conversation of my life.

54

GEMMA

I was fuming, pacing Crystal's living room, listening to her clinking mugs and stirring tea, as if it was more important to have a bloody cup of tea than to have this conversation. I stood at her fireplace, waiting, counting the minutes, wanting this all to be over so I could go back to collect Poppy from nursery and put Crystal and all the lies or excuses she was going to come up with, out of my mind, hopefully forever. But then I saw it again – the photo of Poppy – she'd put it back on her fireplace.

Again, I picked it up and stared at it, and I knew immediately that I'd been right the first time: it *had* been taken here, in this flat. She'd been sitting on this rug. Poppy had been here –

Crystal had brought her to her own flat without telling me. I should have known I was right by the guilty way she'd reacted when I saw the photo the first time, but as usual, I'd made excuses for her, convinced myself it was me that was wrong. Well, that was over; it was never going to happen again.

I turned to look at her as she carried the mugs of tea in, and to my amazement, as I held up the photo, challenging her to explain it to me, she simply sighed, nodded, sat down as if she was exhausted, and said she was going to explain.

'But first,' she went on, in a shaky voice, 'I need to tell you about the so-called child abandonment.'

'So-called?' I retorted. 'The article stated quite clearly that you were arrested—'

'But never charged. Did you notice that? I was never charged, Gemma, because I wasn't guilty. But I *did* have a breakdown. I was hurtling towards one anyway. Everything in my life was unbearable at the time, and the accusation, the very idea that I'd ever have left my daughter alone in the flat – that and not being able to prove my innocence – sent me completely over the edge.'

I wanted to say I was sorry to hear it, but I couldn't. I just wanted the rest of her explanation.

'So how come Evie was found on her own, then? Where were you?'

'With my dying mother.'

I blinked, swallowed, fought against the instinct to sympathise.

'Evie's *father* was supposed to be looking after her,' she went on, and the way she pronounced word *father* told me everything I needed to know regarding how she felt about him.

'So why wasn't he arrested, rather than you?'

'He was, after I'd given my side of the story. But of course, he denied ever agreeing to stay with her. And he had an alibi. His brother lied to the police, saying he'd been with him, that it had been a special occasion and he'd always agreed to spend the evening with him so it just wasn't possible – he said – that he'd ever have promised to stay with Evie that night.' She closed her eyes and sighed. 'But he *had* done. He was at home; he was there when I left to go to sit with my mum. I'd never have gone and left her otherwise. Never!'

There were tears in her eyes now. Against my will, I found myself believing her.

'So was he – your ex – was he convicted, or—'

'No, of course not, he was too believable. His brother stood by him. So in the end, neither of us were convicted. There were no witnesses and no way they could prove whether either of us were lying or not. But they couldn't trust either of us, either. And by then I was in hospital, having a breakdown. So—'

'So that's why Evie was taken into foster care.'

'Yes.' She closed her eyes for a moment. 'It was only supposed to be a temporary solution. Social services were going to monitor me when I came out of hospital, keep a check on me to make sure I was a fit mother – the shame of that would have been bad enough without everything else. But then my mum died. She'd been ill for almost a year and I'd been trying to care for her as well as looking after Evie, but because of being in hospital, I couldn't be with her when she died, and... well, everything in my head just escalated. I ended up staying in hospital for a lot longer than planned. And they weren't sure, when I came out, whether I'd be able to cope with having Evie back, even under supervision. To be honest, I probably would have struggled, at first.' Crystal sighed. 'But the nearest registered foster carer they'd been able to find, with a vacancy, was in the Isle of Wight. Donna's lovely, she's always done her best to help, telling Evie all about me, telling her that I loved her but couldn't look after her when I was ill. But... over the months and years that she's lived there, despite me visiting her as often as possible, I've become a stranger to her. I'd get so upset when I saw her cowering from me, hiding her face, that she just got more and more frightened. The social workers suggested reducing the visits to once a month, as we were both getting so upset. I started to think I'd never get her back.'

'But now?' Despite my determination to get to the bottom of everything Crystal hadn't told me, I would have had to be heartless not to be moved by her account of how she'd virtually lost her daughter.

She smiled. 'Now, I have so much more hope. Evie suddenly seems to have turned a corner; she was so different with me when I went on the extra visit this month. I really am daring to hope she'll eventually come back home. I know it can't be rushed, but, well, the social worker's keen now for us to move things forward while Evie seems so willing. Donna's bringing her to visit me next week, and if that's a success, we'll gradually do it more regularly, and eventually they'll let me have an overnight stay, with Evie on her own.'

'I'm really pleased for you,' I said. But then I paused, frowning to myself. Was I allowing her to distract me, to gain my sympathy with all this talk about her daughter? 'I still don't really understand, though,' I went on. 'Didn't your ex fight to keep custody of Evie? Surely he'd have wanted—'

'Huh!' she said. 'No, he didn't. He showed his true

colours. He didn't want her at all. He had other interests, by then.'

I swallowed, struggling to take this in. I couldn't
help but feel another pang of sympathy, remembering
how we originally bonded because this, presumably,
was the ex who walked out on Crystal, just as Jack had
walked out on me. I really wanted to move the conversation on, to demand answers to the question of the
framed photograph I was still holding – but I sensed
we were leading up to it and that I needed to let
Crystal tell her story at her own pace.

'So... he didn't even want his own daughter,' I
summed up, 'and meanwhile he completely got away
with leaving her – a two-year-old child – at home at
night on her own, and going out on the razz with his
brother? That's obscene.'

'He wasn't with his brother that night. That was a
lie, and his brother lied, too, to protect him.' There was
a silence; she looked up at me, and there was something in her eyes, something that told me her next
words were going to be shocking. 'He was with you,
Gemma.'

'What?' I stared at her. It was so preposterous, I
actually started to laugh. Had she completely lost the
plot now?

'What the hell are you talking about? With *me*? I

don't even know your ex, I can't even remember what you said his name was!'

'I told you his name was Simon. But I lied.' She looked down, closing her eyes for a moment as if she needed strength to go on. 'And you did know him. His name was Jack.'

I felt like I'd been smacked in the face; like all my breath had been sucked from my lungs. I couldn't talk, couldn't even gasp.

'I'm sorry. Are you OK?' Crystal asked, sounding anxious. 'I knew it would be a shock. I didn't want to tell you – I've tried not to tell you, but I knew it would probably come out eventually and, well, to be honest, you need to know. To understand.'

'Jack?' I managed to say. It came out as a squeak of pain. 'You don't mean... *my* Jack? How? What? I don't understand. Are you saying—'

'I'm saying, we were both betrayed by the same guy. The same Jack has fucked up both our lives.'

'Why didn't you *tell* me? For God's sake, Crystal, all this time, all these months I've trusted you, I've confided in you, told you everything, and you've kept this from me? You were with Jack, before I met him? You had his child – oh my God, *Evie* is his child, his daughter?' I shook my head, trying to take it all in. 'So, what, he started seeing me while he was still with you? I didn't know, I swear he didn't tell me, not about you, not about Evie or the... the allegations of leaving her on her own. I never knew he was still in a relationship – I'd never have—'

'I know, I know that, I knew it as soon as I met you.' She'd moved to sit next to me now and had her arm around me. We were both crying. It was awful – horrible, unimaginable. I didn't want to believe it, and yet... I knew, I knew instinctively that it was true. 'It wasn't your fault,' she went on. 'It was him – everything that's happened is his fault. He left me to move in with you, just when I needed him most of all, when I was at my lowest possible ebb. I'd just come out of the psychiatric hospital, my daughter was in foster care, my mum was gone, my brother was refusing to see me or even speak to me because he'd heard what had happened and he believed Jack's lies, believed I'd left my own child, his niece, on her own. And Jack just turned his back on me, packed his bags and... left.'

'Moved in with me,' I said, shakily. 'Oh my God. If I'd known, if I'd had the slightest inkling—'

'Of course you'd have run a mile. I wish you had, for your sake, for Poppy's sake.'

I wiped my eyes, blew my nose. Anger was beginning to take over from the shock.

'Did you know?' I asked. 'When you found me

bawling in the loos at work that day, did you know it was me, that I was the one Jack had left you for?'

'No, I didn't. I just wanted to help. I could see you'd been through something similar to my own experience. I genuinely just wanted to give you some support.'

'It feels... so unreal.' I stared at her, still trying to get my head around it. I'd forgotten, somewhere in the last few minutes, that I'd gone there, to Crystal's flat, because I was furious with her and never wanted to see her again. Suddenly we were just two women who'd been treated like crap by the same guy. 'Such a coincidence.'

'Not really. He was a manager at our company, after all, wasn't he? He got me my job there when I first met him. Then he left, of course, after he started seeing you.'

'Yes, of course – that was when he started his new job – I'd only just started seeing him. He'd chatted me up at somebody's leaving party.'

'While I was at home with our little girl.' She managed a smile. 'I've never blamed you; I knew what he was like, by then. I guessed he'd have kept his new girlfriend in the dark about me, about our daughter. He's a liar and a coward.'

I nodded. I could hardly argue with that. 'So when did you realise... who I was?'

'I did wonder, when you told me his name. But I knew for sure as soon as I saw a photo of Poppy.' She got up and picked up the framed photo from where I'd let it fall onto the sofa next to me. There were tears in her eyes again as she held it up to me. 'The likeness is absolutely incredible.'

'What do you mean?' I started – but then, instantly, I understood. I took a deep breath. 'This isn't Poppy, is it?'

'It's Evie. She was about two and a half in this picture – about the same age as Poppy was when I first met you. It was taken just before everything went wrong.' She looked at me, her voice shaking as she continued, 'It's the last picture I took of her here, in her home.'

'Oh, Crystal.' I pulled her back down beside me and hugged her. 'I wish you'd told me all this – why on earth didn't you?'

'I thought you'd run a mile. That you'd think I was... stalking you, or something. Planning to get revenge. Or worse, that you'd think I was trying to steal Poppy, because she's so... so like Evie. That I'd try to steal your daughter because mine had been taken from me.'

I dropped my head. 'But I *have* thought that! Can't you see, all this secrecy has actually been what's made me so unsure of you, so suspicious.'

'But I didn't think you'd trust me once you knew I'd been suspected of abandoning my child – of having my own daughter taken into care. I know how it sounds – I knew perfectly well what people thought about me at the time. That's why I came off social media – I was being bombarded with hateful messages.'

'That must have been awful for you. But the fact is, I didn't trust you because of *not* knowing about all this!' I said. 'I couldn't understand, I knew there must be something you weren't telling me, but now – now I know—'

'We can still be friends?' Her voice was so hopeful, I just wanted to cry again. I felt like I needed a week at home, on my own, just to absorb everything, to calm down and to make sense of it all. 'We can go back and start again? We're... almost like sisters, in a way, aren't we? That's what I felt, from the outset, like we've got this connection—'

'A despicable, lying connection called Jack.' I looked at her suddenly, another thought just occurring to me. 'Do you get any child support from him?'

She shook her head. 'Before I met you, my priority

was still trying to get him to admit that it was him who'd left Evie on her own, to clear my name and take some responsibility. He was supposed to be paying child maintenance to the foster carer, but he was trying to dodge that. Eventually even his brother started telling him he ought to have a conscience – I suspect, now, that this would have been after you'd had Poppy. I think even for Ryan, him going on to have another child, without doing anything to support his first one, was more than he could stand by him for.'

'Ryan. The same brother who messaged me from Australia to warn me Jack was with someone else – but who's still, apparently, ended up going on the run with him and the rest of their lousy family.'

'Yes. I suppose I shouldn't have been surprised to hear Jack had gone to Australia. I knew Ryan had already gone by then, to join their parents, and I guessed Jack would follow – to get away from everything that was hanging over him. He'd do anything to avoid his responsibilities. He knew there was a court case coming up, he'd have had to pay years of back-payments in maintenance—'

'But there was never any mention, never anything that made me suspect he was running away from anything – surely I'd have known if he was trying to avoid a court case, paying maintenance, anything like that –

he never said, he never acted as if he was going away because he was in some kind of trouble.' I shook my head, bewildered. 'It was all about starting an exciting new life. I was supposed to be going out to Australia to join him!'

She looked at me, with something like pity in her eyes. 'That's just what he told you.'

I nodded, feeling the last shreds of my own innocence falling away. Jack didn't go to make a new start for us, at all. He was running away – from Crystal, from Evie, and from me and Poppy too. Even from my parents, who he'd surely have guessed would have skinned him alive rather than let him hurt me or their granddaughter. But Jack didn't care about any of us, in the end.

'I'm even more pleased now, that he's been found,' I said. 'I'll ask my dad to get his private detective on the case for you – for Evie – as well as for me.'

'I don't suppose your dad will want to do that.' She sighed. 'I know it's my own fault – I've got off to a bad start with them, but your parents don't like me, do they?'

'They will. When I explain.' I looked at my watch and jumped to my feet. 'I've got to go. I've asked the nursery to keep Poppy for an extra hour and it's already been nearly that.'

'Are you OK to drive?' she asked anxiously. 'I know this has all been a horrible shock. I'm so sorry, you're right, I should have told you about it all, much sooner, but there never seemed to be a right time.'

'I'm all right.' I'd have to be. I had to behave normally for my daughter. 'And... I understand. At least, I think I will, when I've had time to absorb it all.'

I looked at the picture of Evie again, shaking my head. The likeness really was incredible.

'They've both taken after Jack,' I said, and the regret in my voice was so obvious that Crystal actually laughed. 'The same beautiful red hair, the same eyes—'

'Well, about the only good thing about him is that he's a good-looking bastard.' She paused, then added softly, 'And I suppose you realise: our daughters are half-sisters.'

'Half-sisters – yes, of course,' I mused. 'What does that make us, I wonder?'

She gave a little snort of laughter. 'A pair of idiots?'

And despite everything, ridiculously – I found myself laughing back.

55

CRYSTAL

The relief, after I'd told Gemma the whole story, was instant. I felt exhausted, as if I'd been operated on, surgically, and had half of the contents of my brain removed. It had been difficult to answer, when she'd asked why I hadn't told her before. Although it was true that I'd always been afraid she wouldn't trust me if she knew the truth, I think if I was completely honest, that was only half of the reason. Perhaps there was a tiny element, too, of not wanting her to know who I was until *I* was as sure as I could be, of *her*. Both of us having daughters by the same father was a bond we hadn't chosen, but one that I sensed could be important to us both, as well as to our children as they grew up. As soon as Gemma saw what I'd seen – that Evie

and Poppy weren't just half-sisters but almost carbon
copies of each other – she wouldn't be able to help
feeling the same peculiar, instinctive tug of attraction... like two magnetic surfaces, pulling towards each
other... that I'd felt for Poppy, the moment I first
looked at her photo.

Whether we liked it or not, our daughters were
linked in an amazing, special way, and through them –
so were we. Even though Gemma had been angry
enough with me – with good cause – to storm over to
my place that afternoon, obviously intending to tell
me she never wanted me anywhere near Poppy again –
what I'd had to tell her had changed the whole picture, inevitably, and I hoped, perhaps permanently.

I loved Poppy, yes, but I do admit I'd got carried
away sometimes, pretending to myself that she was
Evie – it was hard not to, the likeness was so indis-
putable. It was wrong, it was hurtful to Gemma and I
should have known better. If anyone had behaved like
that with Evie, I'd have been outraged. If Gemma was
going to give me another chance based purely on the
fact that she felt she should because of our *connection* –
the dubious privilege of both having had a child with a
cowardly louse called Jack – then it felt a little as if my
behaviour was being forgiven for the wrong reasons. I
now had a duty, I knew, to prove to Gemma all over

again that she could trust me with her daughter – and I wouldn't expect that trust to be easily regained.

But already, I knew I was going to find it easier, now, to take a step back and love Poppy in a more appropriate way; like the kind 'auntie' I really was, instead of like a slightly deranged wannabe mother. Because I *was* going to be a proper mum in my own right again, soon – Donna had told me she was sure of it now, so was Sarah, our social worker, and I'd finally found the confidence to feel sure of it myself too. Evie was going to come home. We wouldn't rush it, but we didn't need to; all I needed was the confidence that she could start to love me again, and I could, finally, start to be a real mum to my own child, all over again. Without the father who'd let us both down in such a spectacular and unforgiveable way.

56

GEMMA

Half-sisters. I pondered on this, trying to settle my fevered brain as I drove back to the nursery to collect my darling Poppy. One of my regrets, once I'd realised my relationship with Jack was definitely over, had been that Poppy would never have a brother or a sister. But she did, now – a half-sister so like her in looks that, if it weren't for the three years' age difference, they could have been twins. How would she react, when – if everything went the way Crystal hoped, and Evie came back to live with her – I told Poppy she had a big sister? Would they be friends? Would the like-ness extend to their personalities?

I wondered, too, whether Evie would like having a

little sister. Perhaps it might help her to adapt to being back with her mum, starting a new life, at a new school – all of which would be hard for her, of course. I felt a sudden new burst of sympathy for Crystal – for everything she'd been through, all the trauma she'd now told me about, and on top of everything else, being separated from her beloved daughter for four whole years. Thank God it looked as if things were now improving. I hoped with all my heart that Evie would soon be back permanently – perhaps even in a matter of months.

The afternoon certainly hadn't gone the way I'd anticipated. I'd imagined saying goodbye, relinquishing forever the friendship that had meant so much to me just six months earlier. Instead, I'd come away with a whole new perception of everything. A whole new version of my *own* story, as well as Crystal's. It was going to take time to come to terms with what Jack had done, the reality now making him even more despicable in my eyes than I'd already realised. On top of all this was the fact that he'd now gone on to father another child somewhere in Australia. That little boy was also a half-brother to Poppy and to Evie. Would they ever meet? I doubted it. But when Jack was finally forced to pay up for all of his responsibilities, I wondered whether his current relationship would also be

cast off like unwanted baggage. Poor woman, poor little boy.

It was going to take time, too, for Mum and Dad to
accept Crystal. She knew she'd made that difficult, and
I could already imagine my parents' scepticism when I
told them the latest revelations. But they'd come
round. They were decent, loving people and all they
cared about was protecting me and Poppy. They'd understand, they'd even sympathise, once they'd got over
the shock.

But even though I was still reeling from everything
I'd been told, I somehow found myself smiling as I
went to collect Poppy and helped her into the car for
the short drive home from the nursery.

'Did you have a nice time today?' I asked her as I
pulled away.

'Yes. But I'm very tired. Did you have a nice time at
your meeting, Mummy?'

'I did, sweetheart. It was... very interesting. And I'm
quite tired now, too.'

'Shall we snuggle on the sofa when we get home,
and watch some *Peppa Pig*?'

I laughed. 'Do you know what, Poppy? That
sounds like the nicest idea I've heard for a long, long
time.'

Jack could easily have ruined my life as well as

Crystal's, and he could have blighted my daughter's life, the way he'd blighted Evie's. But I wasn't going to let him – because I was going to make a good life for us both, and be happy. And if I could, I'd help Crystal do the same, too. That probably wasn't going to be easy – I knew it might be hard to completely believe in her again, after all the mistakes she'd made. I understood some of the things, now, that had raised alarm bells before. She'd never taken Poppy to her own flat; that photo was of Evie. She'd never even taken her to her own part of town. Crystal had explained now that the woman on the bus who said *hello again* to Poppy, must have remembered seeing Crystal with Evie, years earlier and was too muddled to think about the age difference. The 'mother and daughter' outfit was bought for Evie, who never got to wear it when it would have fitted her – that broke my heart, but Crystal should have known it was a terrible error of judgement to give it to Poppy. Yes, for sure, she'd been too over the top with Poppy; I'd have to be sure she was going to calm that down in future – it had stopped her from thinking rationally about what she was doing. But I had a feeling we were going to put a lot of effort into making our friendship work now. And perhaps, in time, we could start to feel like a little family of our own.

But however much I pondered and wondered

about the future – whether things would work out with Crystal, whether Evie would become part of our lives, whether I'd reunite with some of my previous friends and whether I'd eventually get enough money from Jack to actually make a difference to my life – I knew that none of this really mattered, as long as Poppy was happy. She might not have her daddy any more, but she had me, she had her grandparents – soon to be together again – and her friends at nursery, who were gradually becoming more important to her as she grew up. But her little world centred on me, and mine on her. Being the centre of somebody's world was a privilege I'd never take lightly.

We were going to be OK. I'd make sure of it, no matter what. Jack would never know what he'd missed, and frankly I didn't care. I'd promised Poppy I loved her more than all the daddies in the world could ever love her, and I was never going to forget that promise. Poppy and I were moving on. Together.

ACKNOWLEDGEMENTS

I'd like to thank my lovely editor Emily Yau, and everyone else at Boldwood Books who works so hard to make every book a success, including, but not limited to, Nia Beynon, Claire Fenby, and Niamh Wallace. Also thanks to copy-editor Candida Bradford for her invaluable input, and of course, to my literary agent Megan Carroll for her support and for taking good care of all the things I would find far too difficult. Thank you all!

ABOUT THE AUTHOR

Sheila Norton is the author of contemporary, feel-good fiction set in Devon. In 2022 she won the RNA's Best Christmas Novel and now writes emotional women's fiction for Boldwood Books. When not working on her writing, Sheila loves exploring the contrasting countrysides of Essex and Devon.

Sign up to Sheila Norton's mailing list here for news, competitions and updates on future books.

Visit Sheila Norton's Website: www.sheilanorton.com

Follow Sheila Norton on social media:

X x.com/NortonSheilaann
f facebook.com/SheilaNortonAuthor

ALSO BY SHEILA NORTON

A Good Enough Mother

Not Your Child

Boldwood

Boldwood Books is an award-winning fiction publishing company seeking out the best stories from around the world.

Find out more at www.boldwoodbooks.com

Join our reader community for brilliant books, competitions and offers!

Follow us
@BoldwoodBooks
@TheBoldBookClub

Sign up to our weekly deals newsletter

https://bit.ly/BoldwoodBNewsletter